the vampire queen

BRANDI ELLEDGE

WHEEL OF CROWNS
BOOK THREE

The characters and events portrayed in this book are products of the author's imagination and are used fictitiously. Any similarity to real persons, living or dead, is coincidental and not intended by the author.

Printed by Aelurus Publishing, April 2019

Cover design by Molly Phipps

ISBN 13: 978-1-912775-11-8

www.aeluruspublishing.com

This one is for Cole—
You are destined for greatness. I knew it from the
moment I laid eyes upon you. I am proud to be on this
journey with you. Now, go amaze me some more.

acknowledgements

First off, thank you to my readers for taking the time to read Vampire Queen. I hope that you enjoyed this story as much as I have. I had so much fun writing about Tandi and her shenanigans and without all of you Tandi's story wouldn't be heard. So many thanks.

Thanks to my family... Matt—a loving husband, my sweet kiddos who are my biggest accomplishment, a mom that is the epitome of a 'ride or die' chick, an amazing dad that... just kidding dad (I told you! You get no shout out until book five), and two wonderful aunts that are not just a part of the fan section they are starting the 'wave' while holding banners and looking good while doing it. I'm thankful to God for giving me these crazy loons. Honestly, I would be lost without my village.

To the fantastic team at Aelurus: my publisher, Jeff, who works tirelessly to get this series where it needs to be. I will forever be grateful for all that you do. Thank you for everything. Rebecca Jaycox, for never going easy on me. Bring the heat, babe! Katherine, for proofreading. Molly, for this cover and the previous one. Thank you all for making this series the best it can be.

chapter one

lenching my fists, I took several breaths, trying to assess the situation. Where the hell was I? Four walls were covered with floral wallpaper. Whose room was I in? Then the last twenty-four hours hit me like a tsunami. Several different images flooded me at once. There was a meeting that I had no business attending because I was different than the others who were there. I was human. Everyone else was some sort of supernatural. I shouldn't have been there. I remember a crazy psychic. Keys. My best friend crying. Vampire blood. My death. Oh, shit.

Hours ago I was a vibrant, young teenager, and most importantly I was alive. Then I died just to be brought back to life. Well, not really, I was technically called the Undead now. My stomach clenched at the thought. I remembered how I died. My hands shook as they felt my throat and chest. Ghouls had attacked me: those hideous creatures were the ones responsible for my death. The holes were gone, and my skin felt flawless. The events after that were a little foggy.

Don't panic. Don't panic.

Looking around, I took note of my surroundings and let out a small groan. Everything was slowly starting to come back to me. The bedroom I was in was massive with an old, creepy vibe. I loved antiques as much as any true Southerner did, but this… this was overkill. The drapes looked like they belonged to an antebellum mansion from the eighteen hundreds, and the canopy hanging over me in clouds of blue and gold had less of a princess feeling and more of an Abraham Lincoln feeling. The old furniture screamed expensive. I propped myself up in the bed, feeling dizzy, when I heard a knock on the door.

My voice was hoarse as I said, "Who is it?"

"Stephan. May I enter?"

He didn't wait for a reply. The door swung open, and I immediately recognized the gorgeous man who strolled in. He was nice to look at, but there was something just below the surface that reminded me of a cobra, waiting to strike. Stephan was the one who saved my life or gave me a second chance at life—however you wanted to look at it. Some psychic chick foresaw my death, and Stephan, a friend of a friend—who at the time was little more than a stranger—told me I had two choices. I could either take his blood and come back as something entirely different, or I could die and cease to exist. I didn't have to weigh my options too long. The psychic ended up being right. I had been attacked later that night, and the only thing that had brought me back was Stephan's blood in my system. I glanced down at my trembling hands. But now I was different. I survived the most horrific night of my life, but for what? I had no clue what the future held, and the thought left me on the edge of a nervous breakdown.

Stephan sat down at the edge of the bed as his eyes gave me a once over, and everywhere they touched I almost felt the burn.

"How are you feeling?" he asked.

"I've been better." I didn't know what the protocol was for this kind of situation. Did I thank him for not letting me die? Technically, I did die. Or maybe that was the wrong way to look at it.

Before the silence could get any more awkward, he said, "Tandi, I know that when you were a small child you probably didn't envision yourself as a vampire, and I know the transition will be hard on you, but I'm here to guide you through it. Think of me as your mentor."

I knew things were going to be different for me now, but I thought I would adjust better at home. I appreciated being on this side of the ground, but I was ready to check out of wherever the hell I currently was.

"Do you remember us leaving your best friend's house?"

The last twenty-four hours were blurry. "Maybe a little." That was an overstatement. "Where am I?"

A look of sympathy crossed over his face. "Far from home."

"How far?" I tucked my trembling hands into the covers to hide them. "Are we still in Louisiana?"

My heart dropped as he shook his head. "You will be staying here with me for a while. This is my home in Athens, Georgia."

What did he mean for a while? A day? A week? A month?

"Speaking of time… I have four months left of high school, and I'm sure my best friend is worried sick about me. When do you think I can go back home?"

"Do you remember that upon your arising you tried to harm your friend?"

My hand shook as it touched my parted lips. I had? What would she think of me? Did she hate me?

Stephan gave me a small smile. "You girls are thick as thieves. It would take more than a little neck biting to end your friendship. In fact, Charlie has called me several times asking about how you're feeling and then she threatened to stake me if I didn't take great care of you."

I laughed. That did sound like my ride or die bestie. As soon as I got myself together I would give her a call. Through my eyelashes I studied the strikingly handsome man—who looked like he was maybe twenty, but who knew his real age with him being a vampire and all. He seemed— uncomfortable.

"Will I be able to go home soon? I have to finish school and—"

He shifted on the bed. "Tandi, I regret to tell you that you will have to finish your school year with online courses." At my gasp, he continued, "I took the liberty while you were recouping to send an official letter to your school letting them know you have been selected for a rare opportunity to be an exchange student with a very wealthy family in Germany. I have some online class information. This will be how you graduate, if you choose to do so."

Choose to do so? WTH?

I clenched the exquisite quilt in my fists. I had to remain calm. This was all fixable. I could be home in my bed by tomorrow.

He was still talking, but I had tuned him out until he said, "I also had a friend go to your parents' house and convince them they already knew about the exchange program. When my friend left their residence, your parents were happy that you were able to take this opportunity."

I felt numb. "So, you had someone Jedi mind trick my parents, and I can't graduate with my classmates. No spring break. No prom. No graduation parties."

I just died, and yet I was thinking of sparkly dresses and celebrations. One would think that I had lost my ever-loving mind, but in actuality I had lost my life. I was desperately trying to hang on to any part of it.

Truth was I wouldn't miss my parents, and I was sure they were just fine without me. My family consisted of very pretentious people, and I thought that as long as they believed I was in an exchange program in Germany learning the ways of a different culture, they were content. Don't get me wrong. They had no intention of me educating myself, so that I could become an empowered woman of today. They just wanted me to be around the right people, rubbing elbows with the upper crust, so that I could find myself a suitable match, join a country club, and give them at least two grandkids.

But Louisiana hosted more than just my parents. It was where my best friend was. Within the last couple of months, she had found out that she was a witch, and she was going to need me just like I was going to need her.

"You have a new life now," he was saying. "I am truly sorry, Tandi. But becoming a vampire is a hard transition, and those vampires who don't have help along the way usually don't make it."

"But I would have help!"

"Are you talking about your friend, Charlie, who just learned that she is a witch?" At my silence, he said, "Tandi, you need help from your own kind. Whether you like it or not, you will be staying here until the world is ready for you. And what happens the next time you lose control and try to take a bite out of your friend?"

Could I control myself? And was I willing to take a chance on my best friend?

"To be honest with you that night you showed great restraint. For being newly turned things could have been a lot worse."

Swallowing the lump in my throat, I decided to change the subject. "What do you mean when you say if vampires don't have help, then they don't make it?"

His sigh was heavy. "For the first couple of days, you will not be able to hold yourself back when you're hungry. A lot of vampires go half-crazed if they don't have a strong enough sire to help them with their blood lust. In fact these first couple of months are critical in learning how to control the urge you will have when you hear a pulse beating. Not to mention the fact that you have to learn how to get your… supply."

I cringed at what he was implying. The weight of what it truly meant to be a vampire was starting to hit me.

"Tandi, if I were to take you back to your hometown, it wouldn't be days until you killed someone by accident, but hours, possibly minutes, before the urge controlled you. You are here to control the urge, not the other way around. The vampires with no guidance go berserk without proper training, and are snuffed out by other vampires in the area. It's our way of making sure that what we are is kept a secret."

"I would never intentionally hurt anyone." But I had already tried to hurt someone. Someone that I love.

He gave me a look. "Tandi, I came in here because I could feel your hunger from the other room—"

A strong pain I didn't recognize hit me so hard I screamed. Before I could stop myself, I flew at him, half straddling him to get as close as I could to his neck before my new fangs ripped at his smooth throat. My body tingled with a desire not for Stephan, but for his blood. With every swallow of blood, I felt out of this world. Higher than a kite. After a few minutes, my wits came back to me, and I scrambled off of him, looking at the damage I had done. His beautiful neck looked like a chew toy, and his pristine white shirt was now smattered with blood. I heard a dripping sound and when I realized it was his blood running from my chin, I scrambled back on the bed.

I was completely shocked. "What have I done?"

He scooped me up with such gentleness and rocked me in his lap. "Shh. Tandi, this is what I was explaining to you. This... this hunger is not your fault, and this will get easier. I'm actually stupefied it took you almost a week longer than most baby vamps before the hunger overcame you."

I had been asleep for a week? How was that even possible? I remembered the ghouls attacking me yesterday. I watched as his neck was slowly closing up, and embarrassment washed over me in waves. "I am so sorry that I hurt you."

"I'm the Prince of the Vampires. You couldn't hurt me if you tried. Besides, I came in here knowing that you needed to feed. Usually, newbies shred more flesh than you did. I'm truly impressed with your restraint."

While he rocked me, I cried until his shirt was soaked with not only his blood, but my tears, too. Even my tears were different. They now had a tinge of pink to them, which made me cry harder. After my hiccups stopped, he laid me gently down on the bed, brushing the hair away from my face. I felt something in my chest tighten like a string that was being pulled taut. His eyes met mine and widened in shock. He backed away from the bed, bumping into a chair before reaching for the door.

Gone was the sweet, charming man that had comforted me mere minutes before, and in his place was someone cold and distant. "I have to go, but tomorrow we train, so get some rest."

My eyes were too heavy with sleep to give too much thought as to what just happened. Yawning, I turned on my side and watched him exit my new bedroom. Everything was changing, but it was up to me how I handled those changes. Before I let sleep overcome me, I had already decided I was going to be a fabulous vampire. I would conquer the hell out of vampirism.

chapter two

One week later…

Oh, my gawd! I sucked at being a vampire. Digging my nails into the bark of the tree I currently hid behind, I clenched my eyes shut and mentally let out a string of curses. Why did it have to be a fawn? Why not a mean looking buck that pawed the ground in aggression at any unfamiliar scent? One that wouldn't mind running me over, so that somewhere in the back of my mind I could claim it was self-defense.

As I peered around the tree, I cut another glance at the spotted animal looking like it had recently just learned to stand. I weighed my options. Technically, the raw hunger wouldn't overpower me for at least another six hours. I could go back to the beautiful, but slightly outdated, manor house that I refused to call home and pretend like I didn't see any game. Maybe Greta, the housekeeper, would feel sorry for me and give me a pint or two of Stephan's supply she kept in the refrigerator. If Stephan could drink out of a bag, why couldn't I?

My decision made, I turned to head out of the forest when I felt a now familiar tight pull in my chest. The link between my creator and me thrummed with energy, which meant he was close. As soon as I cleared the forest, I saw him leaning up against a tree, his hands hidden in the pockets of his jeans, and his black shirt pulled taut over his ridiculously toned torso. Through his thin cotton shirt, I could see the potential beneath. His shaggy brown hair in need of a trim was the same color as his eyes—the same color of the fawn that I couldn't kill, which probably explained the lethal look on his face.

Wanting to get this confrontation over with as quickly as possible so I could go watch The Real Housewives of New Jersey, I said, "What's up, Stephan? You decide to come outside and catch a breath of fresh air?"

"No, Tandi. I came out here to see how well you progressed on your hunting skills." His eyes narrowed at my empty hands. "Disappointing as usual."

Being from the South, we were raised to never show our temper. Thankfully, I was blessed with a naturally sweet disposition, so I let that comment fly by me as I continued to the house, ignoring him. That was me. A real class act.

Stephan did that trick I still hadn't mastered and flashed right in front of me, blocking my path. "I have sired lots of vampires in my time, but you, Tandi, are by far the worst."

"Listen here, jerk face, no one asked you to make me a vampire, and I sat in those woods for hours. All I found is one freakin' deer." I jabbed my index figure into his rock-solid chest. "And it was a baby! I'm not going to kill a sweet, innocent baby just because you insist that I hone my hunting skills." As my eyes glared so hard they twitched, I realized I might have lied about my temper. Lying to oneself was never a good thing, but in my defense, this asshat brought out the absolute worst in me. Every day this past week had been torture. It was as if I couldn't do anything to please this man. Power leaked from every pore he had, and I knew that I should be terrified, but I was too tired from this constant dance we did with one another. He would give me a task and when I failed at it, he would either show how disappointed he was with his snide remarks or give me the cold shoulder.

He grabbed the bridge of his nose, as he mumbled something sounding pretty close to a Catholic prayer. "Tandi, the reason why you only found one animal on my property that consists of more than three hundred acres…" He looked at his watch, "In five hours, is because you wouldn't keep that mouth shut for long enough. You kept scaring all the wildlife off with your horrendous singing of everything pop. At this very moment, there are probably squirrels heading to the main road in hopes of finding a passing car, so they can commit suicide after your rendition of everything Justin Timberlake."

In twenty seconds, my head was going to start rotating while pea soup spewed from my mouth, because I was about to go all Exorcist on his hot behind. Counting back slowly from ten, I made it to nine and a half before saying, "So, Stephan, if I started singing every Lady Gaga song I know, and trust me, buddy, I know them all, would you go join the squirrels? Because I can be accommodating when I want to be. Besides, my singing isn't that bad."

He scoffed. "There for a while, I had horrible thoughts of doing bodily harm to Bruno Mars for encouraging you to listen to his songs. It's amazing how you are consistently singing and humming, considering how awful you are at it. The worst part is you don't just try to sing; you try to perform."

Refusing to let him get under my skin, I said, "But I'm a terrific dancer, and I need music for that—"

He held up a hand. "Say no more. I will buy you a fantastic iPod if that will help keep the screeching down to a minimum."

I nodded, knowing better than to turn down a free gift, even if I had no intentions of quieting my beautiful singing voice. I mean, I didn't expect birds to be landing on my arm in an open field while seven small-statured men worked around me, but my voice couldn't possibly be that bad. Then again, I was tone deaf, but that wasn't my problem.

His light brown eyes narrowed. "Do you understand that I'm trying to train you, so you are not completely helpless, Tandi? There is a war that is imminent—"

I threw a hand up, cutting him off. "Just stop."

I was so tired of hearing about this stupid war. A war no humans were allowed to know about and yadda, yadda, yadda. It was the same ol' same ol'. Bad guys versus good guys. They were all fighting over some stupid keys that opened up portals to this world. The good guys didn't want to let the bad guys have the keys because they would make earth their playhouse, where they would pilfer and cause undoable havoc, and earth would be destroyed. Was it important that they not get their grubby hands on those keys? Hell, yes. Was it important that the good guys find the remaining keys before Team Craptasic did? Duh. But for one hour of the dang day, I didn't want to think about a war that would eventually come to our doorstep. And I sure as Hades didn't see how eating Bambi was going to help me prepare.

"Because, Tandi, Greta is not always going to be around to hand you a pint of blood when you're feeling hungry. You have to be able to survive on your own."

Shoving him, I shouted, "I've told you to stay out of my head!" Since this arrogant piss-ant had made me, he had proven that not only could he pick up on my emotions, but he could hear my thoughts as well. Which was a little embarrassing, considering how often I thought how good his butt looks.

"And I've told you that I have better things to do than spy on your trivial thoughts, but when you broadcast them as loudly as you do, it's hard not to hear what is being shoved in my brain. If you would practice mentally throwing up your walls, then you wouldn't have to ever worry about me hearing what outfit you are going to wear that day."

Before I could shove the arrogant ass in the chest again, he moved and appeared behind me, whispering, "Not allowing me into your thoughts by blocking me is parlor tricks; ones that you should be able to do by now. Stay in your room and work on building your shield with your mind, and until you've made headway, there will be no food for you."

I glared at his retreating back. Without a shadow of a doubt, I knew he was disgusted with me. You don't get to be Prince of the freaking Vampires by donating to the Girl Scouts of America, but by being a totally ruthless, conniving, barbarous bastard, and that was a triple check for him. He was annoyed with me, but I found it hard to believe he would let me starve to death if I didn't at least improve a smidge. As I kicked a pebble, I wondered why the deer couldn't have been an opossum. No one likes opossums. I could have so gone all badass and drained an opossum. There I went, lying to myself again. I swear I could hear Bambi out in the woods laughing and sputtering, "Sucker."

I practiced putting up my mental shields for hours until sweat dripped down the back of my neck, and my head felt like it was about to explode. I was proud of myself for my improvement, not only because of the dinner I was about to devour, but because now I was one step closer to having Stephan out of my head. A girl needed her privacy.

After taking a quick shower, I slid my pink baby doll dress over my head because a girl needed pink, too. I guessed I should thank Stephan for all the clothes he had put in my closet. Being born a fashionista, clothes were one of my weaknesses, and he did such a wonderful job picking out my entire wardrobe. Had to give the Devil his due. Perhaps I would thank Stephan after he allowed me to eat. Ha! Allowed. I couldn't believe he had resorted to withholding food from me to get me to train. He would be better off giving me an incentive like more clothes.

Humph. Maybe I would thank him with a high five to his pretty boy face.

I did a little spin in front of my dressing mirror, smiling at my reflection. Who would have thought that being turned into a vampire would make you this dang hot? I mean, there was always the potential there, but if I was really honest, there were a few things that I was self-conscious about. All right, maybe more than just a few things with my weight making the top of that list. However, being made into a vampire ripped right through that self-pity list.

My green eyes were still the color of jade but brighter, and I swear my eyelashes had grown and thickened as soon as I was brought over to be part of the Children of the Night club. My lashes were the only thick things left on my body. I was no longer chubby. That in and of itself deserved a fist pump. It was hard to remain depressed when you looked in the mirror and got all excited over the fact that you had freakin' cheekbones. They were defined and everything.

Being a vampire had its pros and cons just like anything else. I was alive, and unless I stood too close to a bonfire, suddenly found myself without a head, or ventured out into the sun, I was immortal. Major plus. But I did miss the sun. I also missed my small hometown and everything that was familiar to me, from the Cyprus trees to the smell of cooked crawfish. I missed being human, but I was extremely appreciative that Stephan gave me a second chance. I wasn't pushing up daisies, and that meant that one day I would get to feel the cool moss under my feet again. I just wished for two things: that my time here in Georgia was limited, and that Stephan wouldn't treat me like an incompetent, worthless being. Maybe the pros would keep coming.

Sometimes, I would catch him gazing at me as if he was trying to memorize everything about me. A hungry look. Like he was a chocolate addict, and I was the last Reese's cup on earth. Those looks always made me a little warm. When he realized I had caught him staring at me, he would usually say something about my uselessness before storming off. I could never get a good read on him, and his mood swings were starting to tear at my sanity, which made me miss the smell of the bayou even more. Louisiana was my calm.

I shook myself from my depressing thoughts. They would get me nowhere. Checking out my reflection one more time, I forced a smile. Another pro of being a vampire was my long, blonde hair was no longer coarse but hung to my waist in silky, shiny waves. It was a shame that I didn't have a good curling iron and hairspray. In the South, one teased their hair within an inch of its life. The bigger the hair, the closer to God and all that. The things I could accomplish with a can of Aqua Net.

My best friend, Charlie, was transitioning into her new life as well. She had a bit of a shock when she learned that she and her brother were part of the supernatural world. She was a fantastic witch in my biased opinion while Wes, her brother, was death reincarnate. The grim reaper. With our new hectic schedules, I'd only been able to talk to her a few times since I'd been here, but she had expressed how concerned she was with my sanity. Other than me trying to take a bite of her on first arising I didn't know why she's all worried that I wouldn't be coping with being a fanger. I mean, obviously, I had a setback with the whole fawn thing in the woods. But if I had known that the best boot camp in the world couldn't touch on what being a vampire could do for your body, I would have run around the streets years ago, screaming, "Free blood, come getcha a bite," to any pale face I could find. That perhaps was a flat out lie, but whatever. It helped to cope with the unfixable. I'd noticed that there were only a few downsides so far to being undead. The whole drinking blood out of a bag for dinner was totally gross, not to mention the fact that I was having a hard time being what was construed as a "normal" vampire. My eating habits were inconsistent, and it seemed as if I could go longer than most new vampires before eating. This should be another tally on the pro side, but Stephan ruined that with his confused looks, which were a step up from the disdainful looks I usually received because my hunting skills weren't up to par.

Maybe I'm being selfish and that's why I've been lying to myself. I really do understand why Stephan whisked me away from my family and my B.F.F. to take me to another podunk town, so that he could train me. No matter how much I thought I could control the hunger when it actually hit, I couldn't. When it was chow time, I went a little cray-cray. And the thought of hurting my best friend, Charlie—who was more like a sister to me than anything—left me feeling sick on the inside.

The sad truth was I couldn't go home. Not yet. I was stuck here with Mr. Mood Swings. The end game was to learn from Stephan how to not turn into a raving lunatic when it was feeding time. And possibly learn how to source for food, if marrying the owner of a blood bank was not an option. Once I mastered those tiny skills, I could go back home. I would be home before I knew it—I was determined.

chapter three

Two weeks later…

"Yo, Stephan, buddy, how much longer do you think I'm going to be stuck here in Georgia? Not that I don't like the state or anything, but if we're being fair, how would I know what it even looks like since I have to stay on your property? Also, I heard from Greta that you can stroll out into the sun because of that handy dandy metal cuff you wear. Why won't you give me one of those?" Honestly, the man was selfish. "If I am to stay here longer, I wish you would take into consideration that I haven't seen another person other than you and Greta in more than three weeks. That is so not good for my social welfare."

Stephan closed the book he was reading and sat up on the antique couch he was lounging on. He closed his eyes briefly. It was possible he could be tired, or he could have been praying for patience. Either way, as we say in the South, "It didn't comfort me none." I tapped my teal green nails on the wet bar, waiting for him to answer me. I swear the man was slower than molasses.

His eyes, the color of Tennessee whiskey, met mine as he ground out, "And I've told you several times, Tandi, once you have mastered all the skills it takes to survive, and I know for a fact that you won't draw attention to yourself and let humans know what you are, or worse, lead them back to me, then I will gladly let you go. In fact I will be so happy to see you leave, I will throw you a going away party. The whole room will be decorated in pink, and there will be enormous amounts of tacky glitter everywhere. Your life will be complete."

Rude much? My eyes narrowed. This man was so damn good looking it almost hurt to glance at him, but manners? Sheesh. His hotness didn't make up for his butthole-ness. I blamed it on his mother. She should have raised him better. Why just the other day, he let the back door slam in my face, and when I told him a gentleman not only held the door open for a lady but let her enter first, he dared to ask, "There is a lady nearby?" Humph. Bastard.

The fire roaring behind him cast a warm glow on his striking features. I rubbed my chest as I felt that familiar pull again. Never in my life had I ever seen a more perfect male specimen, and yet he had to go and ruin it with his grouchy attitude. I must have been frowning because he asked, "Tandi, are you truly that unhappy here?"

Feeling bad for how ungracious I'd been, I went to sit beside him on the couch. I pulled my knees up underneath me. "I'm a brat and I'm sorry."

He raised one eyebrow, an exasperated expression on his face that said that might have been the understatement of the year.

"But you haven't been no Georgia Peach yourself, mister. Let's just say this is an adjustment period, and I might be struggling a tad with being a vampire."

He threw an arm over the back of the couch and leaned back with a smile tugging at the corners of his mouth. "A tad, Tandi? You are the prissiest vampire I have ever met. In fact, it's like you have put a lid on every vampire instinct that you possess. Greta said yesterday she caught a rabbit for you and was going to see if you could break its neck and feed off it. But when she went to answer the phone, she came back to an empty pot, and you were sitting there pretty as you please, swinging your legs on a barstool in total innocence. When she asked you where the rabbit went, you said it escaped. It's funny how smart rabbits are nowadays. He knocked off his lid, crawled out of the huge pot, and somehow managed to open the door to the great outdoors."

"First of all, it was a bunny, not a rabbit, and it was snowy white and cuddly. And secondly, that is why magicians use bunnies because they are known for their trickery."

"You know I can tell when you're lying, right?"

Dang. Must be another one of those "I'm your master" thingies. Then again, maybe he was lying about knowing about my lying. In that case, it was best to deny.

"How the heck should I know how the bunny escaped? All I know is that it wasn't in the pot where crazy Greta said she left it. The woman is coo-coo, if you ask me. Maybe she has dementia. That would explain a lot."

He smiled. He actually smiled.

My heart tightened a little. "Back to your original question before you got sidetracked, like you usually do—"

"You have that effect on people, Tandi."

"See? There you go again." He wasn't smiling, but I could tell he was trying his hardest not to. "I do miss my best friend. We have been together since kindergarten, and she is the honey to my comb."

He ran a hand through his shaggy hair. "When you become a vampire, everything is different, and you have had a lot of things changed for you. I know that you feel like you are missing out on things—"

"Um, hello, I'm missing the last part of my senior year. Like prom and graduation. Pretty big deal."

"Prom? Let me guess. You had a hot pink dress with feathers or sequins already picked out."

No, it was black and flattering, considering I used to weigh the same amount as a small submarine. If I had worn a pink dress with feathers, I would have looked like a flamingo that had swallowed an alligator. My weight was a constant disappointment for my mother. She wanted me to be a size two debutante. But I refused to go down that twisted road. At least not while I was enjoying this easy banter between us. "You know it, buster, and I would have totally rocked it."

Holy hell. Another grin. "I'm sure you would have."

Pretending as if I'd never noticed before, I said, "Why, Stephan, you have dimples. Who would have ever noticed that with all the scowling you've been doing?"

His eyebrows came together as he gave me a disgruntled look. "We're not talking about me. We were talking about your transitioning and your family, and speaking of family, I have a sister who is bored out of her mind, blowing through my credit cards while shopping in Paris for the latest trends. I have asked her to come here for an extended stay. I thought that you might enjoy the company."

He said the last part almost as a question. "Stephan, I think that is a wonderful idea. When will she be here?"

"Tomorrow night, if that is okay?"

"Of course, it is. This is your house, and just because you're stuck with me until I can figure out how to work this whole vamp thing, doesn't mean that you have to ask me for permission when it comes to inviting your sister to your home. And no offense, but I'm kind of excited to have another female around here other than Greta. Don't get me wrong; Greta is my homegirl, and she treats me better than my own mother ever did, but the downside to that is Greta treats me like her daughter. Last night we were sitting on the couch watching an MMA fight. By the way, all that blood made my fangs grow in more ways than one, and she said if I made one more sexual innuendo, that she was going to send me to my room."

Stephan's eyes narrowed. "Well, I have to admit, I'm with Greta on that one."

"Listen, we are talking about Greta being a motherly prude, not about me being all hot and bothered over an eight-pack. Even though you look twenty-ish, I'm sure you've probably been here since the dinosaurs roamed, so why is it so shocking to you that a young girl… what do you old people call it, swoons over a hot guy?"

"Tandi, we won't be having this conversation." He grimaced like he was in pain. "In fact, I think it's my cue to leave."

It was the longest discussion we'd had without snide remarks to each other, and I was reluctant to let the almost pleasant conversation go. I grabbed his arm to stop him from standing. "Remember, I'm a lonely girl in need of friends, so you deserting me right now when I'm wide awake will force me to go through every drawer in your desk. Just sayin'."

Stephan looked around his study before his eyes settled back on me. "Just so we understand each other, if you touch any of my things in this room, I will cut your fingers off."

And we're back to his ostentatious, overbearing, and ill-tempered ways. Must be Monday.

I shrugged. "It's cool. They'll grow back."

"Tandi, you could try the patience of a saint. Is this where we play twenty questions, and I dodge and refuse to answer at least half of them?"

"What a good idea. Ladies first…" I paused to see if he would contradict me. After no smartass comments or defamation of my character came my way, I cleared my throat. "Hmm, let's see. What does one ask the Prince of Vampires? How about why are you the Prince and not the King?"

"Leave it to you to go straight to status ranking." His eyes were playful as he said, "Because I'm not the original vampire but the second that was made."

My eyes widened. I was made by not just a high-ranking vamp but by a primordial. I was half joking about my prehistorical comment, but it looked like I hit the nail on the head. "The second ever made? So, you are Dracula's baby?"

"Yes, and Akeldama would skin you alive if she heard you calling her Dracula."

"Okay, so the woman that made you can't take a joke and has a strange name. Interesting. Why you? What made you be the first she turned?"

"A stranger name than Tandi?" At my glare, he smiled. "Her name is very fitting, considering it means 'Field of Blood.'" A shiver ran through my body as he looked off into the distance, no longer seeing me beside him. "Anyone that is unlucky enough to make an enemy of her or catch her on a bad day is incinerated on the spot... if they are fortunate. The unfortunate ones are played with sometimes for years before she turns them to ash. She made me because she wanted me. Wanted me for an eternity."

A shiver ran down my spine. The woman that made him sounded like she was pure evil. We sat in silence for a few minutes, and when the fog lifted on whatever memories he was holding onto, I put a hand on his arm. I felt him tense, but he didn't fling my hand off.

"Well, she sounds like a real peach." He looked at my hand then my face, but the light didn't quite return to his eyes. "Are you all right?"

"Of course, I'm fine, and that was your fourth question, little one."

"That's cheating! Asking how you're feeling should not be counted." I honestly wasn't too mad because I was secretly busy preening on the inside over the "little" comment. I had never been called small in my life.

A half smile returned to his beautiful face. "You asked. I answered. I will give you a total of five tonight, and then you can ask five more questions when your hunting skills get better, and you actually come back with something." At my disgruntled look, he laughed. "I might not ever have to answer another question while you are under my roof."

"But remember I can now keep you out of my head."

"This is true, and you do it better than most. If only your hunting skills were as good."

"I would hate to be perfect in every aspect, then you would have nothing to complain about." I still had one more question, but I didn't want to ask anything about Akeldama, if for no other reason than I hated seeing him go into that dark place. It was almost like I could feel his turmoil. Which brought me to my last question.

"Sometimes, I can feel your emotions…" He shifted uneasily and for the first time looked uncomfortable, so I rushed on. "Not all the time, but just little glimpses here and there. It seems to happen only when I'm in close proximity to you. Is this normal? Can all of the vampires that you've created read your emotions?"

His answer was blunt. "No." There was no explanation, so I raised my eyebrows, hoping that he would feel the need to elaborate. After a brief staring contest, I gave up.

He stood up abruptly, stopping me from demanding to know more. His stony mask was back in place, and I had a feeling it had to do with my last question. "So, tomorrow morning my sister will arrive." At my incredulous look, he said, "She is an ancient vampire, and she has a daylight cuff. She can move freely in the sunlight; therefore, allowing her to come in on any flight that she chooses. I will be away on business for two days, and then on my return I expect you to have made great strides in your hunting skills."

"Yes, boss." Apparently, only the cool kids got a cool metal cuff. "I will be here anxiously awaiting your return, just so that I can show you my mad hunting skills. I think I will be so good at it that vampires across the nation, generation after generation, will tell stories to their children about the huntress/goddess of the night that could bring down a single deer quick as lightning." His eyebrows raised in question. "An adult buck that has had a full life."

Tilting his head back, he roared with laughter, making my jaw drop. Smiles were one thing, but laughter? Who would've thought he was capable? He started for the door.

"Wait a second. You said you would answer five more questions for me if I got better at hunting, and now you're saying that you won't even be here?"

"Trust me, I have time."

"How rude." I would so show him.

"Good night, Tandi."

"Good night, Prince of Vampires."

I felt happiness from him and… confusion. It was as if he realized I was reading his emotions because a change came over him, and his face no longer showed any hint of warmth. Talk about your above average bi-polar vampire.

Good thing he was hot, or he would be totally intolerable. I needed a plan to get back to my life, and it would seem the only way I was going to leave this state was to become a better vampire. The first step was hunting, so I would hunt... something. I wondered if I could find a chicken farm close by. Chickens were ugly with their cockatoo hair and gnarly feet, and everyone loved the taste of chicken, especially if it was fried. But I wouldn't be eating the chicken, I would be sucking its blood. A shudder ran through me. Eww, gross. Something was fundamentally wrong with me. I must be the only vampire in the world that had minimal cravings but still couldn't stomach the thought of drinking blood.

In my bones, I could feel the sun wanting to rise as I let out a very unladylike yawn. It was a little depressing that I would never feel the sun on my face again. I could feel him watching me from the sofa as I climbed the steps, and I thought to myself maybe, just maybe, I could convince Stephan's sister to get me a metal cuff.

chapter four

woke as soon as the sun went down, feeling more than a little hungry. My feet hit the floor, and the boards creaked under my weight. Stephan's beautiful house was an enormous luxury cabin that looked more like a ski lodge resort. He was a fan of antiques, so everything in the house was extremely old, including the reclaimed barn wood that he used for the floor. The whole house smelled of pine and cedar, and I had to admit it was a comforting smell.

Throwing on some clothes, I ran down the steps hoping to find Greta waiting with a blood bag in her hand. The woman always spoiled me with the blood slightly warmed, just how I preferred it. If I had to have it, it might as well be warm. She was always giving me affectionate smiles and patting my head, making me feel loved. Growing up with my parents, love and laughter were two things that I didn't get much of.

It was a shame that Greta didn't have kids. She would have been a terrific mom. One time I had asked her if she

was a vampire and she laughed. Later, I found out that she was a human consort, enabling her to live longer than most humans, but she was still very much human. Lucky goose.

Coming into the kitchen, I was disappointed to find no Greta. I went to the refrigerator, pulling out a bag before dumping it into a mug to be heated in the microwave. Dang it, the woman had spoiled me.

Someone cleared their throat behind me, making me jump. Whirling around, the first thing I saw was a beautiful girl about my age standing in front of me. She had chin-length honey brown hair that complemented her brown eyes and a crooked half smile on her face. I wasn't tall by any means, but the girl in front of me made my five feet, five-inch frame looked Amazon-ish. If she reached five feet, I would be shocked. Hope she didn't like roller-coaster rides.

I smiled in question at the dainty girl. "Hi, I'm Tandi. You must be Stephan's sister?"

She extended a hand and I didn't hesitate to shake it. "I am his favorite sister, and I'm not just saying that because I am his only sister." At my laugh, she said, "I have heard a lot about you. My name is Daniella but my friends call me Dani, and I have a feeling that we will become fast friends." Her voice was quiet and had a sexy edge to it.

"And I promise not to hold it against you that you are his sister. After all, we don't get to choose our family."

"That right there is why we will be friends." Hopping onto the barstool, she swung her tiny legs that were miles from touching the ground. "Stephan has never asked me for help a day in his life, so when I got his phone call yesterday, I immediately packed a bag and took a private jet." Of course, they had a private jet! I had already figured out that Stephan must be as rich as Bill Gates to have a pad like the one he had. "He says that you need a friend, but I feel that it might be more than that." She gave me a once over. "You are stunningly beautiful, but he has been with many beautiful women before—"

I held up a hand, shaking my head. "Let me stop you right there. I promise that Stephan doesn't like me like that. In fact I think he can barely tolerate me at all." She cocked her head to the side, as if disagreeing. "I think the reason why he has asked you to come is because I'm not a… well, I'm not a normal vampire."

One defined eyebrow arched as her brown eyes, which were a shade darker than her brother's, twinkled with amusement. "How can any of us truly be normal? But what makes you think that you are so different than the rest of us?"

Could vampires blush? Because I felt blood rush to my face. Turning to the microwave that dinged, I pulled out my hot mug, warming my hands that nowadays always seemed cold. One of the numerous things that remind me I was a vampire now. "Um, for starters, this is the only way I can eat."

Dani stifled a laugh. "Out of a mug?"

"That's one way of looking at it." Taking a sip, I sighed as the first wave of hunger started to ebb. "You see I can't hunt. It's not that I don't want to; it's just that the thought of taking a life leaves me sickened. Don't get me wrong,

I could kill, but the baby bunnies in the woods aren't psychopaths trying to gut me."

"And pray tell, Tandi, where do you think that blood came from that you're chugging down now?"

I put the empty mug on the counter. "I know it came from some poor animal, but here's the thing. When I was human, I could eat a tenderloin, even though I knew it came from a cow because I wasn't the one going out into the pasture, looking into its big brown eyes, and whispering, 'Baby, you're about to be a medium-well.' That's just not cool."

"Um—"

"I know it probably doesn't make sense to you, but I am struggling with the whole hunting thing."

Dani's smile dropped, and a look of understanding came onto her pretty face. "I do get you, Tandi. Maybe not with the hunting aspect, but we all have our struggles, and each of us that has been turned has to deal with them. You do know why Stephan insists that you learn to hunt, right?" At my nod, she said, "Good. Now, enough about my brother. Let's go attempt to hunt in the woods before we spend the rest of the night doing girly things like painting our nails, doing facials, and talking about how hot Shemar Moore is on SWAT."

I gave her a questioning look. "Who is—"

Interrupting me with a fierce expression and a wave of her delicate hand, she said, "If you are about to tell me that you do not know whom I'm referring to, then this relationship will end before it begins."

I had no clue who the heck she was talking about, but it was obviously a make or break for her. "No, of course, I so know… um him. He is hot?"

Her eyes narrowed. "Damn straight." She stood up and winked at me. "Let's go out in the woods, so you can show me what we're working with."

First impressions were a big deal. With that being said, I was nervous, and the anxiety overcame me in waves. I felt like I needed to offer her an explanation. "Dani, I think you should know right off that I'm the reason there are participation trophies."

"Well, we will just have to change that. My philosophy is that second place is first loser, and who the hell can remember third place? I don't fail at anything, and that includes training you. After I am done with you, you will be a stealth killing machine."

Already defeated, I followed her outside into the gloomy night, wishing that I didn't have to embarrass myself in front of my new friend.

For some reason, I truly wanted to impress Dani. Greta insisted on coming with us. I had a feeling it wasn't because she was a nature lover, but more that she thought I was about to make a fool out of myself, and she didn't want to miss out on the action. I would show her! I walked about a hundred yards in front of Dani and Greta. There was a distinct smell coming from a tree cavity up ahead, and I planned on taking whatever was in there by surprise. I didn't have to kill it: I just needed to show Stephan's sister that I was able of hunting, cornering, and capturing an animal if I had to.

I made sure to avoid most sticks littering the ground as I approached the tree, quiet as a mouse. Step one: find the animal. Check. I dropped to my knees in front of the small hole at the base of the tree. Step two: corner the animal. Check. This was a lot easier than I thought. Now, for the capture part. I would reach in the hole, grab the animal, then wave it around like a captured flag before I stuffed it right back into its little hole.

I thrust my hand into the hole and pulled back a… baby raccoon. It was about the size of my palm and completely helpless. The precious thing couldn't even see yet. I was so enamored by the small creature in my hand that I didn't see the mama raccoon flying at me. Her claws slashed my face while she screeched like an owl.

"Ouch. Cut it out, will you?" I tried to throw the mama off of me while not dropping her baby. I went to put the baby back in the hole, so the mama could see I meant it no harm, but she became even more aggressive. "I don't want your other babies! For Pete's sake, I'm trying to give this one back." She flew at my head again, and I tried to scramble away from the attack but she had ambition. She landed on top of my head. I crawled on my knees and thrust the baby back into the hole. "I'm sorry. I'm sorry. You've got to let go now." I started screaming all kinds of names and curse words all but begging for her to let me go.

With one last hiss and swipe of her claws, she jumped from my head and raced back to her den. I sat there for a second, trying to decipher what just happened. Standing up, I dusted my knees off and tried to slick my hair back. Dani and Greta stood there with their mouths open. Greta had her phone pointed at me, and I had a sick feeling that she just videoed that whole debacle.

"So, that escalated pretty quickly, huh?" I asked.

Trying to save what little dignity I had left, I started off towards the house with them hot on my trail. I pretended I couldn't hear their laughter and reenactment of the performance I'd just given them.

"Wow. I failed miserably," Dani said, shaking her head with amusement instead of disgust as we made it back to the house. "Hmm. Guess there is a first time for everything."

I dropped down on the couch next to her like a bag of potatoes, feeling like a reject. It was quite possible that I was the worst vampire ever made.

Greta sat on the other side of me, sandwiching me between the both of them.

Sourly, I said, "Well, isn't this comfortable."

Greta leaned across me to hold the phone, so Dani could see the images on the screen. Laughing hysterically, she said, "This picture is the one where the raccoon started chasing Tandi out of the hole." She swiped her hand on the phone to scroll to another picture. "And this one is right after she shrieked and fell into the mud trying to scramble away from the… what did she call it?"

"Horrid beast," I quietly said.

Both of them started rocking with laughter so hard I felt like I was on one of those cheap honeymoon beds that vibrated. My self-confidence sunk lower.

I didn't have to sit around while they made fun of my horrible hunting skills. I stood up to make my haughty departure only to have Dani put a finger in the loop of my shorts, bringing me right back down on the couch.

"Tandi, we are not making fun of you. Right, Greta?"

I looked over at Greta who was drying her eyes with the bottom of her T-shirt. "I kind of was." At my look, she amended, "It's just that in all of my years working for Stephan, I have never seen anything like this."

"Wow, way to make me feel great about myself." Resting my head back against the cushions, I said, "Maybe that is why Stephan is so mean to me. Maybe he knows that there is something wrong with me and since he turned me, he takes it as a personal insult." I caught the look Greta sent Dani and my heart stuttered. Oh lord, I was right. Greta grabbed my hand while Dani claimed the other one. Oh, no, here came the pity.

"I am not sure exactly what my brother is thinking, Tandi, but there is nothing wrong with you," Dani said. "Many of us lose some of our humanity, if not all of it, when we are first turned, and it takes us years to find some sort of balance. The fact that you have a warm heart and a beautiful conscience says a lot about whom you were before you were turned. If anything, be proud of your light. Besides, you never fail at anything if you try, regardless of the outcome."

Greta nodded. "It's true, but even if you are an abomination to Stephan, that doesn't mean that you're not wonderful. I was never able to have children, but if I could have, I would have been proud to have a daughter like you."

Squeezing both of their hands, I gave a shaky nod at their encouraging words. Part of me knew maybe they were just trying to make me feel better, but it worked. So what if I was different than every other vampire? So what if I was a disappointment to Stephan? I had an eternity to get the hang of this whole being a vampire thing, so it didn't matter if I was a slow learner. While the hare took a nap, the dang turtle won the race.

"All right ladies, I was promised some nail polish and some SWAT, and if this guy isn't as hot as Dani claims, then I get to pick out the next movie. And I promise it'll be a musical."

Greta shook her head. "Of course, a rescuer of bunnies and a Bambi lover would like musicals."

"Blah, blah, blah. I hear nothing at this point."

Within a flash, Dani had retrieved a container of nothing but nail polish and was sitting back next to me. When I grew up, I was so going to be that fast. No, I would be faster, unstoppable like a pink glitter bullet. I looked at all the different colors and decided to be spontaneous as I grabbed the red.

"That's Stephan's favorite color."

Making eye contact with Dani, I dropped the nail polish back into the bucket before fishing out a pale pink. It was tried and true and most importantly wasn't the devil's favorite color. Dani giggled before picking out a pretty blue, and Greta, of course, picked a clear polish. We sat around swapping stories while painting each other's nails. Dani made up some kind of homemade facial that smelled to high heaven as she smeared it on our faces. I glanced over to Greta, who wore a white hair band to keep her short, gray curls away from her face that was currently smeared with a chalky, thick green paste. She reminded me of E.T., if he would have been on crack and had hair. I laughed so hard that Dani smacked me, telling me to be still or I would ruin the mask. I gave her an eye roll.

"Um, hello, vampires don't get pimples, or wrinkles for that matter."

She narrowed her brown eyes through the ridiculous mask. "When you are centuries old and you have seen as much as me, doing girly things like this is sometimes the only thing that keeps you going. Being immortal can be exhausting."

I patted her knee with reassurance, like I understood the pressure of being as old as the stars, when I actually couldn't relate to her. I'd only been a vampire for a hot minute. "Sure thing, buttercup, so let's keep this slumber party going. Put us on some SWAT."

Two hours later, I realized that there would be no musicals tonight. It was almost comical how Greta was leaning in toward the television. Sometime through the night, Dani had started making cocktails. She told me they would have no effect on us, but it was fun pretending we were normal teenage girls. So, as I sat pretending that Mr. Moore's figure had started to get blurry on the screen, I realized it could have been worse. We could have been watching the Divergent series. Theo James, who played Four, could have been a dead ringer for Stephan, and that was all I needed to be thinking about right now. Behind the sun-proof curtains, I could feel the darkness slipping away as my eyes grew heavy. My last thought before the sun came up was Stephan hated me because the Prince of Vampires had made a defect.

chapter five

Someone shook my shoulders. Hard. I tried to swat the hands away, but they just laughed. Prying one eye open, I saw Dani looking like an amused fairy as she sat there on my bed. She must've carried me to my room sometime this morning. Her little hands were still shaking me awake as she gave me a beaming smile.

"Oh. My. Gosh. What do you want, Tinkerbell?"

She knelt beside my pillow and started bouncing on my bed like a kid at Christmas, anxiously awaiting the rise of their sleepy parents, so they could race downstairs and tear into all the pretty packages. "The sun is down, and yet you still sleep. Get up." Before I could pull the covers up over my head, she crooned, "I talked Greta into taking us with her when she goes to town tonight."

I bolted out of bed. "Really?"

"Yes." She giggled. "She said if we hurry, we can catch a few shops on Main Street before they close."

No need to tell me twice. I threw on the clothes that were scattered on the floor before either one of them

could change their mind. "I haven't been out in public in almost a month."

"I know. Greta is going to make sure you are well fed, and we won't stay in town long." I was about to ask if Stephan had giving us permission when she said, "And we will have to keep this between us girls, because Stephan would flip if he knew you went out of the house without him."

I held up three fingers. "Scout's honor."

Greta insisted I drink two cups of blood before we left. I was so excited to get out of the house that my enthusiasm was overflowing onto Dani. We chatted all the way to the black Lincoln Navigator and then all the way into town. Greta kept smiling fondly at us from the rearview mirror. I told Dani how I was taking online classes and how Greta was helping me with geometry, which was a class that was invented by the devil. Even though I would still get my diploma, I hated how I couldn't walk across that stage with everyone else. She reached out and squeezed my hand, as I rattled on about all the things I was missing out on.

As Greta parked in front of a store on Main Street, Dani said, "Hey, there is no reason why we can't go ahead and get you a gown. I mean, obviously, you won't be able to go to prom, but there are always masquerades that the undead go to. Stephan hasn't been to a ball in decades, but I know that between the two of us, we could twist his arm into taking us."

My spirits lifted. "Really? You would do that for me?"

"Oh, honey, don't doubt for a second that I don't have selfish intent. I would never turn down an opportunity to wear something pretty."

Maybe this friendship would last forever with that kind of attitude. "You are my kind of girl. We might as well go all out and get us a couple of tiaras, too. I mean, we are showing up with the Prince of Vampires, so we should be legit. Side note, if he is a prince, does that make you a princess?"

"Afraid not. I would've had to either been born from the queen or have been the first made by her."

"We can have kids?"

"It's extremely rare, but yes."

"I thought that we were basically corpses."

"Well, that is a horrible way of looking at it, though extremely accurate." Dani scoffed. "The original vampire along with her offspring can have children, but for the rest of us, there is only a small window for us to have children. A female vampire can get impregnated as long as they conceive within six months of their turning. My window of opportunity is way past expired."

She didn't seem to be bummed about that so I let the subject go. Arm in arm, we strolled down the street while Greta clucked behind us, but I could tell she was happy we were happy.

"Girls, you know Miranda's Bridal Shop is just a couple of blocks over," Greta said.

We halted right there on the sidewalk and smiled at each other. Greta laughed as we turned around and started following her to the shop. I was sure the girls back home were already picking out their dresses for prom with it being just around the corner. Trying on a few dresses would take some of the sting out of not getting to go to prom. Or at least I hoped it would. Plus, Charlie wouldn't be at prom—not with her being the new Queen of Witches—so I wouldn't have wanted to go anyway.

An hour later, we both had twirled and modeled so many gowns for Greta that she was feigning a headache and complaining she wished she would have brought her knitting with her. I finally settled on a red dress that hugged every curve I owned and had made both women gasp in admiration. It was fairly modest in the front but the back… Well, it was so low it showed the two newly acquired dimples I had on my lower back. Dani ended up walking out of the shop with a midnight blue dress that flowed around her thighs, making her look even more like a fairy princess.

All three of us wore a smile until a tingling sensation formed on the back of my neck, leaving me with a cold feeling in my stomach. I glanced over at Dani who was frozen in place, and I knew that she felt it, too.

Greta took one look at our faces. "What? What is it, girls?"

The cute little fairy princess was gone, and in her place was a lethal weapon. Dani grabbed my arm. "In the car, now!"

Neither I, nor Greta argued with the command, instead we ran as fast as we could towards our vehicle. We all jumped in the car as Greta's shaking hands fumbled with the keys before finally getting the engine started. I could hear her heart pounding from where I sat. I didn't say a word as Dani sat tense and half crouched on the seat next to me, constantly glancing out every window of the SUV. When we hit the highway, she relaxed a smidge. We were so close to Stephan's estate, and as soon as we got there, I was going to light her butt up with twenty questions.

I felt the danger before I saw it, but it was too late. At an intersection, a Hummer T-boned us so hard our Navigator flipped. There were multiple screams as our vehicle rolled before coming to a screeching halt.

Six vampires dressed in all black stepped out of the Hummer. From where

I was in the upside-down SUV, I could see at least two quickly approaching our car. A pair of black biker boots crunched the broken glass next to where Dani lay so tiny beside me, looking like a broken doll. I felt tears well up as I saw blood dripping down her pale face. Her eyes were closed and she wasn't moving. I snarled as the vampire reached in to grab her when all of a sudden, the broken doll pulled a lethal looking blade out of her knee-high boots, flew out of the vehicle, twisted in the air, and brought her blade down in an arc. The vampire's head hit the ground long before his body. It wasn't until she took the second vampire down that I snapped out of it and started crawling on the ceiling of the car towards an unconscious Greta.

Her pulse was barely there, but she was still hanging on. Crouched on my knees, I stuck two fingers in her mouth, prying her teeth apart. I bit into my wrist with little finesse and held my arm up to her lips as I let my blood trickle into her mouth. Thanks to my fast healing, I had to tear into my flesh twice to make sure she got enough of my blood. There was a possibility that she only needed a little, but I hadn't been the best pupil, and I wasn't going to chance it.

After I was satisfied that she had consumed enough, I unbuckled her seatbelt and put my hands under her arms. I dragged her out of the navigator. I had to get her away from the other vampires. I hesitated as I saw my little friend taking down the third vampire like she was killing a fly. I screamed as the fourth one came up behind her, but she must have already sensed him because at the last second, she dodged his blow. In a blink of an eye, she came up behind him and started slicing pieces off of him left and right. She was toying with him. I should be shocked by the violence, but all I felt was rage that these vampires had attacked us.

Frantically, I looked around until I found a bush twenty feet away. I could drag Greta there and hide her before going back to help Dani, even though Dani looked like she was taking care of business all by herself and enjoying it. My eyes darted around, searching for the two remaining vampires. Right before I reached the bushes, a hand struck out quick as a rattlesnake and grabbed me by the throat, lifting me up until my feet no longer touched the ground. Even though he shook me so hard my teeth rattled, I didn't start panicking until the other vampire fell on top of Greta. I had to get away—I had to help Greta. My hands flew out, making contact with the leering vampire's face.

The vampire laughed at my feeble attempts to free myself. His oily black hair hung in strings around his face. "Aww, what do we have here?" One of my feet finally made contact with his thigh. "Oh, that wasn't very nice, was it? You must be the one. We could have so much fun, beautiful, if time weren't of the essence."

I didn't have a chance to react before his teeth bit the flesh right above my breast, mauling my skin as he put one hand on my back to hold me still. He was chewing his way slowly up to my neck, and I could feel the blood leaving my body as I cast one more glance to Greta, lying on the ground and unmoving as a vampire feasted on her. My last thought before darkness took me was, Please, Greta, don't die.

chapter six

My head throbbed, and no matter how hard I tried, I couldn't pry my eyes open. It was as if my body was floating away. In the distance, I could hear voices shouting my name and then shouting at each other, but I couldn't be bothered listening to them. I was just too tired.

"You have broken an order, Daniella, by taking her off the property, and I will punish you for this."

"Brother, she was suffocating here. Anyone could see how miserable she was."

"It's better than her being dead!"

"As soon as I got her back here, I forced my blood into her, but she's not healing."

A growling sound came before something smashed into the wall. "That is because her head is almost completely detached, Dani."

I felt the mattress dip with weight before someone started murmuring sweet words of encouragement in my ear, begging me to live. Funny, I didn't know I was dying.

I was just tired, and sleep was calling my name, but the person next to me wouldn't let it claim me. They gently forced my mouth open, pressing a hand against the deep wound on my neck.

Something warm tingled all the way down my throat. The person gently cradling me whispered, "Heal."

After several minutes, sleep drifted farther away as pain sliced through me. My throat was on fire and as I began to thrash on the bed, someone else came over and held me down, forcing me to endure this horrible, never-ending pain.

It could have been minutes or hours, but finally most of the pain ebbed. I was still unable to move or even open my eyes, and I was mad at the ones who brought me this pain when all I wanted to do was sleep.

"She'll survive, but no thanks to you, Dani."

The quiet voice that was farther away from me said, "I'm so very sorry." I heard the door open but instead of leaving, the voice asked one more question. "You weren't supposed to return until tomorrow. How did you know we were in trouble, Stephan?"

There for a second, I thought the conversation was over. Then a bitter voice said, "Because I felt her panic."

"You… you felt it? Do you mean to tell me that—"

A snarl rumbled. "It is none of your business, Dani."

The other voice neared. "Of course, it's my business. She is my friend. How many times have you fed her your blood?"

The voice growled, "Twice."

A gasp. "Twice?" A high screech followed. "You knew, and yet you gave her your blood twice? You walk a very thin line, brother."

A deathly calm settled over the room. "And you almost killed her. Get out of my sight before I do something I will regret."

"Before I go, you should know that I overheard one vampire talking to Tandi, and he said that she must be the one. Someone caught wind of why you were gone and wanted to teach you a lesson. You know what this means. Imagine the distance they would go for her if they knew—"

"Out!"

A door slammed closed, and the voices quieted down. There was no noise other than the sweet words that were mumbled into my ear, as I was gently rocked. Finally, I was allowed to let sleep claim me. Hallelujah.

When I woke, I knew something was terribly wrong. I had remembered everything from the ambush that had taken place last night, and yet I was still alive. When that vampire dug his teeth into every muscle and tendon in my neck, I knew I would not live another day. I shouldn't have survived that but I did. So why this sick feeling in my stomach? Not bothering to change out of my lacy nightgown someone had put on me, I ran down the stairs, taking them two at a time. I was exhausted by the time I reached the kitchen. Note to self: Learn that flashing thing that Stephan could do. Cardio was so not my friend. Just another strike against me. Vampires shouldn't get exhausted but yet here I am. Panting for air.

When I saw the grim faces of Stephan and Dani looking back at me, I knew. Oh lord, I knew. I shook my head as Stephan offered me a warm mug. Slowly stepping away from the both of them, I shouted, "No. No!"

My knees hit the unforgiving marble tile as I pulled on my hair, curling into a little ball. Strong arms came around me, holding me tight while I wailed. Then I remembered my safety net. Hope flooded me.

"Stephan! I fed her my blood. She'll be okay, right? We just need to wait, and she'll be fine and—"

"I'm so sorry, Tandi. I know how close you and Greta had become, and for what it's worth, I loved her, too. It's a loss that we all are going to feel for a long time."

"But I fed her and—"

"Sweetheart, she is not coming back. I'm sorry but she is gone."

No. I couldn't believe that she was gone. I refused to believe it. Tears streamed down my face, as I was picked up and carried back up the stairs. Sleep. My sweet escape came for me, and this time I would be damned if I allowed anyone to keep me from it.

A week had gone by, and I hadn't got out of bed. Every day there was a mug brought in and sat on my end table close enough for me to reach. Finally, something in me snapped. They took the only person away from me that had looked at me like I was their beloved daughter. I felt treasured and loved, and those vampires just stole her from me. They would pay. If it were the last thing I ever did, I would make them pay.

Dressing in black, I pulled my blonde hair back in a ponytail. Heading down the stairs, I found Stephan and Dani waiting for me in the kitchen. It was the first place I always went upon awakening, and they must have known this. I wondered how many times this past week they headed to the kitchen at sunset, hoping that I would stumble down ready to face the world. I needed that time to grieve, but now I needed something totally different. I needed revenge.

Before either of them could talk, I demanded answers. "I want to know who sent those vampires."

Stephan said, "Tandi—"

"Don't you Tandi me. You wanted a hunter. Well, here I am, but I'm not going into those woods to find squirrels; I have a different kind of prey in mind, and if you stand in my way, I will go around you, maker or not."

"I would like to see you try, little one," Stephan said, in an eerily quiet voice.

Dani shot a nervous glance at Stephan before looking at me. "That's what we're trying to figure out right now. The vampires that attacked us that night are dead, so unfortunately we can't get information from them." Her eyes shone brightly with unshed tears. "Tandi, I am so sorry for taking you into town. I will never forgive myself."

As hard as I tried, I could not be mad at her. "Don't be sorry, Dani, unless you plan on stopping me from finding who sent those vampires, and in that case, our friendship is over," I said with enough menace in my voice to let her know the fun, happy-go-lucky Tandi was gone. This

Tandi meant business. "The one who ripped into me said something. I'm having a hard time remembering exactly what, but I want to say that he might have been looking for me. Do you think that's a possibility?"

Stephan's nonchalant shrug didn't match his demeanor. "When you are Prince of the Vampires, you make enemies. I'm not entirely sure why they attacked with Dani in the car, but they underestimated her by a landslide."

Dani gave a bitter smile. "Damn straight."

Maybe I didn't have a built-in lie detector, but I knew he wasn't entirely telling me the truth. I also knew a stone wall when I saw one. My arms crossed over my chest as I changed tactics. "Did you save me?"

Stephan looked like he hadn't slept in a week. He was still handsome, but there was a haggard air about him. "Yes, with my blood. It is very potent and as your sire, I can command you to do things, and you have to obey."

"You commanded me to heal?"

"More or less."

"I appreciate that you were saving my life, but just so that we are on the same page, unless I'm dying, don't you command me to do anything against my will."

"I understand that you are upset but know you are my charge and I your master. I do not need permission from you, even when it concerns you."

Stephan's cell phone rang, cutting off my next biting words.

"Ah, Ariana, so nice of you to call." Then he stood there, barely moving, without saying a word. Whoever was on the other line was giving him no other option but to listen. After a long stretch of silence, he said, "Reading my future now, too? It seems as if you are everyone's soothsayer nowadays. Isn't that violating some sort of supernatural law? Because this could be considered a conflict of interest between multiple different parties." The laughter left his voice as he listened to whatever the speaker was saying. "Why would I do that, Ariana?" His eyes met mine briefly and narrowed. "Consider it done."

After he disconnected the call, my eyebrows raised in question. "Well?"

"That was… I hate to use the word friend, so I'll say an ally of mine."

"A soothsayer who obviously can predict the future from what? Her intuition and magic?"

"Yes."

My fists clenched. "Well, where the hell was she yesterday?"

Giving me a pitying look, Dani said, "Maybe she needed this Tandi instead of the girl who wears pink."

My glare was for Stephan and Stephan alone. There was no justifying Greta's death.

"She told me that it's my turn to find one of the keys. Again, I hate to use the word friends, so my allies Jamison and C.G. have found their keys, and now it's my turn."

"I know a little about the keys, but tell me more. I want to know everything." At his pointed look, I said, "I'm listening this time."

Dani found busy work in the kitchen while Stephan sat on a stool. "There are two groups of supernaturals. The Lux and the Degenerates. The Lux are basically the good guys who have made a home here on earth without causing danger to anyone. While the Degenerates want to come here to rule it. In order to do this, most humans would not only find out about supernaturals, but would die at the hands of one. Over the centuries, the keys have been stolen from the Lux guardians and have found their way into the hands of the Degenerates."

"How did this happen? And if the Degenerates have the keys, why is the world not already destroyed?"

"The keys were stolen because the Lux safeguarding them were not strong enough. A long time ago, there was a battle between the two factions, and the Degenerates who weren't killed were dragged back through the portals to live their lives in a different plane that was supposed to be sealed off. But there were a few who escaped, and they went into hiding. They laid low for a while until they came up with a plan to get their hands on the keys. They haven't destroyed earth because they enjoy it here too much. Crime rates are up, but the earth keeps spinning. However, the more Degenerates that cross over, the more dangerous it is for humans, and the less chance we have of keeping the supernatural community hidden."

"When the Degenerates stole the keys they did what? Opened up the portals to earth?"

His light brown eyes flickered with rage. "Some portals were opened but not all. That's why it's important that the remaining keys are found quickly."

"Remaining?"

"Two have been retrieved back by the Lux. I am to go after the third under the soothsayer's orders. The two werewolves who possess them now will guard the keys with their lives. Even death himself couldn't pry the keys out of their hands… Well, he probably could, but considering his sister is mated to one, I highly doubt he would."

"So, the soothsayer called to tell you to retrieve the third key, but will you?"

He gave me a sad look. "You can't fight destiny."

I thought of Greta. "Maybe. Maybe you're right. But that doesn't mean you have to just give up hope either."

He reached out and grabbed one of my hands. I gave a pull to escape his grasp, but he wouldn't let go. "Tandi, you are to have a part in finding a key. The soothsayer said that the one who killed Greta is also the one who has the key. She told me that you are the piece that I will need to lead me to the key."

"Anything else I should know?"

Dani whipped her head around and leveled a look at Stephan. He gave her a warning stare in return that didn't leave me feeling reassured.

"No, only that she said you were going to get a chance to wear that fancy dress. Apparently, we are going to be invited to a ball, and it is imperative that we attend."

"How do you know that she is telling you the truth?"

His phone rang and Dani laughed. I crossed my arms while Stephan had a polite conversation with whoever was on the other line. After several minutes, he hung up and gave me a smirk. "There is ball tomorrow night at a governor's mansion in Georgia not too far from here. I told Pierre that the three of us would be in attendance."

"What is this ball for?"

"The governor usually has a party every year to get support from the vampire community. Considering that he is one himself, it's a very clandestine event where no

63

humans will be in attendance," Stephan said. "Usually, I decline the invitation, but it seems that fate has other intentions."

"I would like to train tonight."

His eyebrows furrowed "Train?"

"Yes, I want to learn how to fight. We will start now and not stop until daylight."

"We?"

Now, it was my turn to smirk. "Yes, we. What's wrong, Prince? You scared that you won't be able to teach me how to fight? It would say a lot about you if I were a complete failure in every aspect, wouldn't it?"

Dani laughed. "Better watch out, brother. This kitten has claws."

I didn't wait for him to answer me, as I headed out into the forest like a woman on a mission. As I made it to the open pasture, Stephan flashed in front of me and started my training. Apparently, he had mastered different forms of martial arts in his downtime, which made him the perfect teacher. The first thing he taught me was to hit someone where it would cause the most damage. Because his hands were constantly on my body, I made sure to have my walls up, so he wouldn't know exactly what his touch did to me. He didn't say a word unless it was to correct me in my fighting positions. After hours of conditioning me, my muscles screamed in agony, but I ignored them all. His lips curled up in a sexy smile as I blocked his punch. I could tell I was impressing him with how fast I was learning. This Tandi had a reason to learn quickly. Thirty minutes before sunrise, Stephan took me to where Greta was buried and then left me alone, so I could have some privacy as I wept over her grave. Placing a hand on the fresh dirt, I smiled through the tears. Karma was a bitch, and I was going to let her enjoy ripping hearts from the vampires who had ended Greta's life.

chapter seven

s soon as the sun went down, I jumped in a bubble bath and while I soaked, I thought of what tonight might reveal. Would I learn who sent those vampires who took my Greta's life? The selfish part of me didn't care about Stephan's mission of finding the key or the soothsayer's prediction. If she wanted me to help her, then she should have called a day earlier to warn us of the danger we were about to be in. When my water had turned cold and my skin was the equivalent of the backside of an eighty-year-old, I got out of the large tub. There was a knock on my door as I was putting on a silky robe.

"Come in."

Stephan opened the door, and the way his eyes devoured my body, I knew the things Greta had said about him being a lady's man were completely true. I felt hot and tingly as his gaze roamed over me. I waited for his eyes to travel back up to my face. "Can I help you with something, Stephan?"

His eyes dropped to a box he held. "I have a present for you."

Usually, his voice was gruff, but tonight it was soft. He probably was going easy on me because he knew I was still grieving and three seconds from snapping. As he handed me the golden wrapped box, I asked, "What for?"

"I think that you deserve it. This is what I was away on business collecting."

"And here I was thinking you left because you needed a break from the defective vampire you created."

"Do you want the present or not?"

I tore into the wrapping paper and opened the box. Rubies were encrusted in a dark metal cuff. I realized I hadn't said a word when he nervously asked, "Do you not like it?"

"What's not to like? It's beautiful."

"As long as you wear it, you can—"

"Feel the sun on my face again," I finished for him. I didn't realize how much I missed the sun until I felt tears trailing down my face.

"Right now, your body is on a different schedule. As soon as you adjust to being a vampire and are able to stay up when the sun rises, I'll take you out for a morning stroll."

He stepped closer to me, wiping the tears from my face. "Tandi…"

"Save me from your 'it's going to be all right' speech, and let's find the bastards that did this to Greta."

He took the box from me and slid the ruby cuff on my wrist. "Sounds like a plan."

"Thank you for this," I said. He still hadn't let go of my hand, so I looked up at him and saw that his eyes were on my mouth. My stomach fluttered with anticipation.

There was a loud knock before Dani strolled into my room with her garment bag slung over her arm. "Hey, guys. Whoa, am I interrupting something?" She glanced at my hand and let out a yelp. "Is that what I think it is?" At my nod, she said, "Oh, my gosh, do you know how hard it is to get a metal cuff? Oh, wow."

I turned to thank Stephan again, but he had already disappeared from my room. Dani grabbed my hand and was inspecting the cuff with its rubies, like she was contemplating its worth.

"You come to get ready with me?"

"If that's okay?"

"Absolutely. I can do an amazing smoky eye if you want me to do your make-up."

She threw her bag on my bed. "Yes. And I'll curl that gorgeous hair of yours. I can't wait to see Stephan's face when every male there is tripping over his feet to introduce himself to you."

I wanted to hear her answer, so I asked, "Do you think Stephan would care?"

"Good question," she said.

I waited to see if she would add anything but when she didn't, I said, "Hopefully, no one there will know that I'm a little different."

"My brother was trained by the Queen to value the strongest vampires and have little tolerance for the weak, so tonight you are going to show no fear."

"I can do that."

"Yes, you can. Plus, you are gorgeous and have a body that creepy, middle-aged white men write poems about." At my chuckle, she pointed a finger at me. "Seriously, as soon as you enter that ball tonight, you are going to be causing sexual frustration and damn it, you better own it."

She was looking at me so seriously I had no other choice but to agree. "I don't know what to expect from tonight."

"None of us do. We will just wing it."

As I went into my closet to bring out my dress, I felt a lump in my throat when I remembered how Greta's eyes had lit up when I had modeled it for her. That's what sealed the deal. As I struggled to fight back my emotions, I said, "Winging it. That is a horrible plan, but since we don't have a better one, we will wing the hell out of tonight."

Two hours later, we headed down the long, spiral staircase. Stephan stood at the bottom with his hands in his pockets, watching me like a lion watches its prey. There was such hunger in his eyes that mine widened, and I nervously licked my painted lips. I came to a stop directly in front of him, waiting for him to say something, anything, but he just stared until Dani cleared her throat from behind me. That weird feeling in my stomach returned.

He was the first to break eye contact as he looked over my shoulder at his sister. "Dani, you look lovely."

She squinted at him like he was stupid. "Of course, I do, and isn't Tandi here absolutely breathtaking?"

His eyes drifted back to me before he gave a curt nod. Two seconds ago, he looked at me like he was undressing me with his eyes, and now he was dismissive.

Dani insisted we all take pictures. It was her way of trying to make up for the things that I was currently missing like prom, all while trying to bring some normalcy back into my life. Even the lordly Stephan was forced into standing beside me while Dani clicked away. There was at least a foot in between us, and he stood so still that Dani put the camera down and gave him a look, which he returned, and the silent communication between the siblings went on for at least a minute. I wanted to say, "Hey, I don't want to take pictures with the asshat anyways." My mental shields must have been down because his head swiveled toward me, his eyes narrowing. Dani started clicking away again. I was completely shocked when he put his arms around me and pulled me tight against him, until I felt a wall of muscle behind me. I made sure my mental shields were up before I thought about how amazing he felt.

Dani barked, "Act like you're enjoying it people. It's a party, not a vasectomy."

"Well, it could be both if Stephan asked me nicely," I said.

I felt his chest rumbling through our embrace. I tilted my head back to glance up at him to make sure it was laughter, and he wasn't just convulsing. He stared down at me with a genuine smile, making my heart constrict.

"Is this the part where I dip you for visual effect?" Before I could scowl at him, he was bending me towards the ground, the ends of my hair grazing the floor. Dani

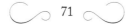

laughed, bless her sweetheart. She knew she couldn't fill the void in my heart left by Greta, but she was trying to make up for me missing prom, and it made me love her even more.

After many silly photos that made my heart smile, we all gathered our things and hopped into one of the many black cars Stephan owned. We had driven south, leaving the beautiful mountains of northern Georgia behind. None of us spoke on the way, whether it was because of tension, anxiety, or our moods didn't welcome chatty banter, I couldn't say. Regardless, I was content on being out of the house and going to my very first party for the Undead, even if the night turned to total crap. At least I felt like I was doing something to find out who was involved in Greta's death. Giving a side glance at Stephan, I studied his profile. There was no doubt about it: the man was heart-stopping handsome. He was always so well put together, and tonight was no exception. I knew that it was some sort of ruse to downplay the lethalness barely hidden under the surface, waiting to be unleashed.

chapter eight

When we arrived, the first thing I noticed was how breathtaking the property was. The mansion was beautiful with its big columns out front of the white, plantation-style house. There were several mossy green trees lining the walkway to the inviting porch that was made for sipping juleps. It was picture perfect. As we entered the large foyer, I had to smile at the irony. This huge mansion with its Southern vibe held many different friendly faces and was the epitome of hospitality, and yet every person currently studying me with such acute interest wasn't wondering which Baptist church I attended, but rather what my darkest desires were. I could tell by the way some of the men were licking their lips while scanning my body.

Releasing a small shudder at the thought, Stephan grabbed my elbow and whispered, "Remember, most of us can smell fear, so right now I need that overbearing, feisty, temperamental Tandi at the forefront."

I automatically lifted my chin up and whispered back, "I do not have a bad temperament. I am meek and sweet." Glancing down at where his fingers were still gripping my arm, I said through clenched teeth, "And if you don't unhand me this very second, I will show you how I can make you pee blood with my free hand."

His eyes twinkled as he released me, but not before his fingers gently brushed the inside of my arm. "Good girl. Now, let's head towards the ballroom and mingle. Stay beside me the whole time."

Dani swiped three flutes of champagne from a tray as a waiter was passing by. I immediately drank the one she handed me in record-breaking time and snagged Stephan's glass before she could pass it to him, downing his in one gulp. Dani hid her glass behind her back. "Sorry, sister. I don't share my men or my bubbly and not necessarily in that order."

Stephan was staring at me, his brows raised. I shrugged. "The thought of dancing with dead people makes me nervous, and another thing while we're on the topic. None of them are going to be looking at me like I'm tonight's dessert because I'm like one of the club now, right?"

"First of all, alcohol has no effect on you, so the champagne was meant to be savored and secondly, Tandi, you do realize that you are now 'Undead' as well, don't you? And I can assure you, no one will be sinking their fangs into you."

I rolled my eyes because flipping him the bird in front of a ton of vampires was off the table. As he ushered me into the middle of the ballroom and Dani followed closely behind us, I found myself in awe of the grandeur around me. The ballroom was half a football field in length, and everything was marble from the floors to the walls to the massive columns running from ceiling to floor. Enormous chandeliers hung from the ceilings, casting a warm orange glow over everyone in the beautiful room. The Governor was great at his job or was skimming from the top, either way his mansion was beyond amazing.

Dani gave Stephan a knowing nod that could have meant a million different things and sashayed off towards the beverage table offering many different types of blood, even the rarest form, Rh-null. Stephan whisked me from vampire to vampire, introducing me while he announced the full vampire's name along with what area they were from, like I would remember any of this tomorrow. I had no interest in remembering every vampire here along with their territory, but thanks to my Southern roots, I just smiled and waved.

While Stephan and some vampire from Michigan chatted about vampire politics, I chatted with a newbie like myself. Apparently, the old dude from Michigan had recently turned him, and he loved his new life. He was maybe five-foot-six with dark hair cut close to his scalp and dark eyes. Like myself, he got turned at a young age. My guesstimate was he was around eighteen.

"I'm Spencer," he said as he held out a hand.

I shook his small hand in mine. "Tandi."

"That's a different name."

"So I've been told."

"Oh, I didn't mean that in a rude way."

I gave him a smile to show him that I took no offense. "It's okay. It is a strange name. So, you're new to this too?"

"Yes, last week actually. We arrived in Georgia last night, and my sire took me to hunt in the woods. It was exhilarating."

I gave a little nod. "Thrilling."

"Exactly!" He acted as if we were sharing some kind of secret as he leaned in close. "Everything seems to be better. My senses… from seeing, hearing, tasting, to touching. You know."

I had no clue. "Totally. It's pretty amazing."

Stephan was done talking to the vamp from Michigan and signaled for me to follow him.

"It was nice to meet you," I said, as I was half dragged away.

"You, too, Tandi."

If anything, I felt more like an epic failure after talking to the other newbie. Being a vampire should come with a manual. I took a look around at the vampires that were strewn throughout the ballroom. They were all different shapes, sizes, and ages but they had one thing in common. They were elegant predators that reeked of confidence. Top of the food chain. I gave a little sigh. Not everybody could be a shark. Somebody had to be the seal.

I was trying not to pout over being a seal as Stephan continued to make the rounds of introducing me. Every female presented to me either gave me the stank eye or ignored me entirely, all while flirting with Stephan. It took everything I had not to scream. I had eyes. I could see what the appeal was. Stephan was the most gorgeous man I'd ever laid eyes on, but if they were cooped up with him on top of a mountain, they wouldn't be batting their eyelashes or making so many sexual innuendos.

Stephan's lip twitched as he leaned down close enough that I could feel his lips on my ear, causing me to stifle a shudder. "Your shields are down." At my incredulous look, he laughed. "Don't worry. I'm the only one that picked up on your insults. Only some of the very old and dangerous can read your thoughts, but to be on the safe side, don't let it down again tonight."

At my nod, he shuffled me along to another group.

"So, you think I'm the most gorgeous man ever?"

Oh, the insufferable jerk would never let me live this down. I snorted. "Yeah, but don't get all carried away. My hometown has more alligators than humans, and I've never traveled anywhere, so I'm kind of limited in my judgment. Since I've been blessed with immortality, I'm sure you won't hold the title long, buddy."

Mission accomplished. His frown caused me to give myself a mental pat on the back. The man had to be conceited, and the truth was he had every right to be. I could probably live several centuries and never find a male as beautifully made as the one by my side, but that didn't mean he should know that.

Rousing me out of my thoughts, a feminine voice said, "Well, hello, Stephan what do we have here?"

Turning to the voice, I was stunned into silence by the woman gliding towards us, wearing a crown. And me being speechless was a hard feat to accomplish. She was so tall, at least five feet ten, and every inch of her ivory skin was as smooth as glass. Her long, red hair flowed behind her as she came towards us, and her slightly tilted green eyes narrowed in speculation at me, then Stephan, before bright red lips sneered. A gaudy silver crown sat upon her head. It was too large for her slender face and it had several points jutting out at every angle. Blood red jewels were encrusted in the center and on the points of the crown. With her being queen one would've thought she could have afforded a better crown. My eyes dropped from God-awful crown to study her face. She was beautiful, but there was something about her that made me want to run and hide. It was her eyes. They were void of any kind of emotion just like a true shark.

I looked up at Stephan, waiting for him to make the same introductions he had all night, but they didn't come. I felt my palms start to sweat as I felt emotions rolling off of Stephan. He looked pissed as he stood statue still, jaw clenched, and eyes narrowed. I tuned in on his hatred. He looked around at the ballroom, and for a brief moment, I thought he wasn't going to answer. Finally, he said, "Akeldama. It's been a while."

My saliva dried at the thought of being in front of Dracula herself, especially since whatever relationship Stephan had with her was obviously not a good one.

She tilted her head to the side like a cat studying a mouse. "Aww, Stephan, are you still sore with me? It's been so long since I last saw you; surely, even you wouldn't hold a grudge for that long— especially over something so silly."

His facial features were relaxed, and he looked as cool as a cucumber, but for whatever reason, I knew he was anything but calm. He was livid.

"Only you would think something like slavery and blackmail is silly."

She threw her head back and laughed, causing me to raise my eyebrows because I wasn't expecting that kind of reaction. If Stephan were treating me like he was her, I would roll into a little ball and pray for forgiveness, but apparently, she wasn't scared over his bitterness of their history.

"Stephan, really, you must let that go, love." My hackles rose at the affectionate term. Her eyes alighted on me with curiosity. "Are you going to introduce me to your little pet, or shall I have to find out about her from the gossip mongers?"

"I believe you will find yourself disappointed, Akeldama. Seeing as she is brand new, there is not much to talk about."

Her eyes skimmed over my body, and she let out a gasp. "So, it is true? You did seek out Alberto to have a cuff made."

Stephan gave a casual shrug. "Why is it any of your business?"

Her hair started lifting like someone had set a fan in front of her. Power rolled off her in waves, and I prayed that my fear didn't scent the air.

Her delicate nose scrunched up. "Interesting. I hope she's not weak—that would be a travesty. I have no tolerance for weak things. That is the one thing both you and I can agree on."

Stephan's face remained a pillar of stone. "You touch her, and this place will get messy very quickly."

"Aww, love, how quickly you forget." She pointed at her enormous ugly crown sitting upon her head. "You can't touch me."

"No, but what about the twelve bodyguards that you have posted right now that don't think I see them? They are no match for me. You know how hard it is to create new, loyal vampires." His smile never reached his eyes. "Besides, Akeldama, you're wearing white, and you of all people should know that white is a bitch to get blood stains out of."

She drifted a step forward to get closer to Stephan, and I began to panic. There was no doubt in my mind that Stephan was lethal, but could he go against the original vampire and live to tell about it? And what did she mean by he couldn't touch her because of her crown? I was too new to all of this to understand the politics, and I didn't want my maker dying on me before I even learned how to hunt successfully. Not to mention the thought of Stephan dying did something funny to my insides.

What seemed like minutes dripped by slower than molasses as Stephan stood like a cobra eyeing his prey, looking for the right moment to strike. While Akeldama's all too familiar gaze was scandalous as she stripped him bare with her eyes. Slut.

"Hi, I'm Tandi." Not wanting to give up any more information than that, I smiled politely. "And we have to make the rounds before I turn into a pumpkin, so if you will excuse us?"

At her surprised look, I grabbed Stephan's hand and dragged him through the throngs of people, hoping to put a distance between us and the original.

80

When we were far enough away from the crowd, he jerked me to a stop. Laughter filled his face. "Do you know what you just did?"

My head whipped around to stare at him. "The question is what are you doing?'

"It's another one of my powers. I can directly speak to your mind, and try not to let the whole room know. I would like to keep this one a secret." I tapped my high-heeled shoe on the marble, letting my impatience shine through. There was a whole lot I wanted to say, but apparently right now wasn't the best time.

"You just insulted the queen of all vampires."

"And how do you figure that?" I whispered.

"When she has a conversation with anyone from her line, you have to wait until she dismisses you, or it's considered treason, and I have seen her rip vampires' hearts out for less."

If I weren't already a bloodsucker, my face would have paled. "Congratulations. Way to be an outstanding teacher, Stephan. That is probably something you should have mentioned before we came here tonight. In fact, that probably should have been taught before squirrel hunting."

His brown eyes twinkled. "First of all, I haven't seen her in more than fifty years, and I didn't know that the Queen would be here tonight, or I would have probably told that soothsayer that she can kiss my ass and find someone else to track down that missing key. Secondly, I'm glad you gave us an excuse to leave the conversation because she was looking to unsettle me, and she knew that I couldn't touch her because of her crown. Her crown alone holds powers that are unfathomable. And last but not least, you are not part of her line, so she has no jurisdiction over you."

My brow lifted at that one. "I'm assuming I'm under you?"

"No, lass. If you were under me, the last thing you would be doing is asking questions."

Was it possible for vampires to blush? Dear Lord.

Deflecting and sidestepping was apparently the name of the game. "You know what I meant."

"Yes, you are a part of my line."

"How did you branch off? Was business just better going solo?"

He leaned in until his lips were touching my ear, and I was barely able to suppress a shiver. I had to strain to hear his quiet words. "Here is another vampire 101. Even though we cannot be seen by anyone from this little alcove, they all can still hear if they choose to. In fact several are not too far off, gossiping about you right now. You would know this if you would just focus."

Whispering back, I said, "And why exactly are we here, Stephan?"

Again, he spoke to my mind. "You know why we're here. To find who played a hand in Greta's death and to find one of the keys that will save the world."

I stood on my tiptoes and whispered in his ear, "Couldn't you have asked the soothsayer for some more direction? I mean, obviously, we can't just stand here waiting for someone to come to us and say, 'Hey I'm the bad guy, and I feel horrible about trying to destroy the world, so let me atone for my sins by showing you where

I hid the… you know.' She should have at least told you what to be on the lookout for."

"You don't know Arianna. She is a woman that is as old as time and has a very distinct way in how she meddles in others' lives. She never tells you so much that it will alter you off the path that she has chosen for you to take."

It was getting increasingly hot in this alcove with us taking turns whispering in each other's ears. I took a step back, putting some much-needed space between us. "I have some questions about the…" I mouthed the words, "crown."

"Not here. We will talk of it later."

Changing the subject like he clearly wanted me to do, I said, "We should have a name like 'League of Heroic Vamps' and maybe a mascot."

He grabbed my hand and walked us back to the dance floor. "Heroes are overrated."

Maybe he was right, but I wouldn't mind a cape. I looked around in disbelief. All these vampires in a ballroom, and yet not a one was dancing. There wasn't even any music. I ran a hand over my hip, feeling the way the dress molded to my body. Seriously, it was such a shame that there wasn't any dancing, considering this was the first time my body wasn't sucked into a pair of Spanx.

Laughter rumbled back to me as Stephan cast a look over his shoulder. "Shields, Tandi. Put up your shields."

"Hey, bud, the one good thing about being a vampire is the weight loss. You can't blame a girl who wants to dance after going from double digits to single digits. Besides, this girl can dance." The random thought of the day entered my brain. "Question. Does becoming a vampire make everyone lose weight?"

He gave me a strange look. "No, usually you stay the same weight."

"Then how do you explain my huge weight loss?" I whispered.

"I'm not sure I can explain it. Becoming one of the undead doesn't drastically change your appearance: it only enhances it."

At my "ain't believing that crap" look, he sighed. "Tandi, you were already beautiful; you just didn't see it. If you don't believe what I'm saying, take a look around. You will find just as many average looking vampires as you would humans. There are few rare beauties here tonight, and you are one of those."

I didn't get a chance to respond as he came to a stop in the middle of the floor, where he reached out and grabbed a waiter by the arm, who trembled, slightly terrified of the attention that Stephan was giving him. He leaned in close, whispering something I couldn't decipher even with my new hearing. Maybe my vampire hearing sucked just as bad as my hunting skills. I watched as the waiter nodded so fast he looked like a bobblehead before hurrying off, trying not to spill a drop of the champagne he was carrying. Major skills.

Stephan turned me into his arms. He lightly grabbed my waist just as the music started pouring out of the speakers, which were sporadically positioned everywhere in the massive ballroom.

"Stephan, if you wanted to dance with me, you should have just asked."

He laughed and pulled me tighter, as I cast a quick glance around the room, studying all the vampires currently scrutinizing us. I guessed we were making a spectacle out of ourselves. But if the soothsayer was correct, then we needed to be here, so maybe us getting everyone's attention would jump start this mission of finding Greta's killer and Stephan's key. Letting the music flow through me, I swayed to the rhythm as Stephan pulled me so close our bodies melded together. Sliding my hands down to his chest, I made sure my damn shields were up and locked into place before admiring the hard contours of his body. The first song ended and faded into a second. There was something so dangerous about Stephan, but dancing in his arms, I had never felt safer. For the first time in my life, I just enjoyed the moment because if Greta's death had showed me anything, it was that none of us were promised a tomorrow.

chapter nine

On the third song, a man approached us. He was an inch taller than Stephan but less muscular. Where Stephan had a soccer player's build, this man looked more like a runner. His light blond hair was styled in such a carefree manner it made him look like a surfer. Electric blue eyes met Stephan's as he clapped Stephan on the back. "Hey, old friend. Mind if I cut in?"

I think the man knew Stephan was about to object because he said loud enough for everyone to hear, "Thanks ol' chap. I'll return her to you in a few."

Stephan gave me a questioning look and I nodded. He reluctantly released me to the man who flashed me a brilliant smile. I watched Stephan's retreating back, knowing he wasn't going too far, and if I needed him, he would be within shouting distance.

Giving my full attention to the man in front of me, I said, "And you are?"

There were more and more couples on the dance floor now, and as he took my hand in his, he laughed. "Blunt. I like it. I am Dakin. General of the First League."

I was pretty sure I didn't need to say anything because my facial expression probably spoke volumes. "I'm sure you probably don't know this, but I'm newly turned, and that means nothing to me."

He smiled, and I was disappointed to notice that this attractive man didn't have dimples like Stephan. "Oh, I know you're new. I would have remembered someone so beautiful."

I knew I should have at least smiled at the charming creature in front of me, but my feet were killing me, and he was laying it on a bit thick.

After a brief silence, he said, "General of the First League just means I am the original's first hand."

Knowing he was part of Akeldama's group was not charming at all. "Interesting. Well, I'm Tandi, Honorary President of the Southern Belles." Rolling my eyes, I added, "Or at least I was until this whole undead thing put a crimp in my style. I'm sure the society girls have probably already appointed someone new to lead them by now."

"I have a hard time believing that anyone could replace you."

He seemed genuine when he said it, which made me even more nervous. He had to have an angle. I just needed to be patient and figure it out. Unfortunately, patience had never been my strong suit.

"So, Dakin, we could go through the next couple of dances with you giving me compliments and me smiling, or we could just cut to the chase. You tell me what's the objective. Don't get me wrong, I love flattery, but these heels are high, and my feet are starting to hurt, so can we just be real for a sec?"

He tilted his head back, and a musical sound rumbled from his chest causing several vampires to look our way. "You are a true gem. Most vampires, especially newly turned ones, tend to lose their humanity and most of their personality, but you… There is just something so different and rare about you." I made a pointed look at my tired feet. "Okay, okay. If you must know, Akeldama insisted that I come over to find out about Stephan's new pet, but I must admit that she didn't have to force me too hard."

"Why would the all-powerful Akeldama want to know anything about me?" I searched the crowd to see if I could find where the beautiful redhead had slithered off to.

"She has been in love with Stephan for a very long time." At my frown, he smiled. "You must see the way Stephan looks at you. You, Gem, are a threat."

I glanced up into his blue eyes to see if he was teasing. "I think you are mistaken, and you can tell Akeldama the same. There is no threat where I am concerned."

He grinned down at me. "Whatever you say, Gem."

Every time we made another loop around the ballroom, I caught sight of a glaring Stephan. One thing was for sure; he wasn't happy. As we waltzed by him, I tried to give him a reassuring smile, but at the same moment, the space between Dakin and me decreased to a mere inch. And it seemed to make Stephan even more pissed.

Dakin chuckled. "Yes, Gem, you are right. Akeldama has nothing to worry about."

Frustrated, I sighed. "She doesn't when it comes to me. Now, Stephan might not dig her the way she fancies him, but it won't be because of me."

Dakin raised an eyebrow. "Then why did he bring you here tonight?"

"He brought me here because… I needed to get out of the house." I gazed up into his eyes to gauge his reaction. "I was very close to a woman named Greta. She was Stephan's housekeeper, and she was recently attacked by rogue vampires, and it cost her her life."

I considered myself to be an outstanding judge of character. I'd always been able to tell the shady bitches from the non, and the look on his face was confusion.

"Stephan was recently attacked?"

"Well, no, but Dani, Greta, and myself were."

"Same thing, Gem. Every vampire knows that if you mess with someone close to a vamp, you might as well be messing with the vamp himself. Why didn't he bring Greta back?"

"Um, because she's dead?"

"If it's the same housekeeper I'm thinking of, she's been in his employ for many years. She had to have been a human servant. They need their master's blood every month in order to prolong their life, so your friend more than likely died with his blood in her."

"Well, she obviously didn't have his blood in her because she's dead. However, she did die with my blood in her, but apparently mine wasn't strong enough to bring her back."

Dakin looked more confused. "If she died with enough vamp blood in her, no matter how potent it was or wasn't, she would have come back as a vamp unless someone made sure that she couldn't."

My vision blurred, and I noticed we had stopped dancing.

Out of the corner of my eye, I could see Stephan swiftly moving through the crowd toward us with a lethal look on his face. Dakin dropped his arms from around my waist and placed his hands on my cheeks, pulling me in close to him. For a second, I thought he was going to kiss me. He laughed at my startled expression before he whispered in my ear, "Relax, Gem, one thing before I go. Don't let Akeldama or anyone else see how much compassion you have. They will take it as a sign of weakness."

Stephan came up to my side with his hands in his pockets. In a room full of possible enemies, I wanted to keep up the appearance that we were united, so I refused to make eye contact with him because I was beyond pissed.

Dakin gave him a knowing smile before tilting his head towards me. "I have taken a liking to your protégé. She is quite refreshing."

Stephan's jaw clenched. "Well, maybe you should take a liking from a farther distance."

Dakin gave me a saucy grin and winked. "But she is so much better up close. Wouldn't you say?"

Still not acknowledging Stephan's presence, I said to Dakin, "My feet are killing me, and I'm in the mood for Netflix—"

"Why, Gem, are you inviting me back to your place for movie night?"

Dakin's eyes twinkled, even as Stephan let out something close to a growl.

I tried to keep the smile pinned to my face, but it was pointless. "What I was going to say is I would like to go home…" I frowned. "Well, the place I currently reside at—my temporary sanctuary I guess you could call it. But before I head out, I was wondering if I could ask you something?"

"You can ask anything, Gem, though I might not be able to answer."

"Fair enough. You wouldn't know who could have been responsible for my friend's death, do you?" His face shuttered. I knew he might not have known about the wreck, but he had a clue who was behind it.

For the first time, I looked over at Stephan, whose eyebrows were raised. His voice taunted me in my head. "Subtlety is obviously not your strong point either."

I shrugged and tried again. "So, Dakin, do you know who murdered my friend?"

The good-natured socialite was gone, and in its place stood a warrior ready for battle. Usually, my Spidey senses would be going off, but my feet really did hurt. I wanted to get in the car, so I could ask Stephan if what Dakin had said about Greta was true. It had to be a lie. But if it wasn't, I had two options. Move out and pray that I didn't kill anyone by accident, so I would never have to speak to him again, or murder him in his sleep. Vengeance wouldn't return Greta, but as Stephan always liked to point out, I didn't have many good points. And forgiveness wasn't one of them either. Grudge holding, calculating, tenacious, biatch? Why, yes. Check, check, and check.

Dakin brought me back from my plotting. "I'm not sure I know what you speak of, Gem."

"Sooner or later, we will find out who was behind the attack on one of mine," Stephan said. "And I will show no mercy."

"I wouldn't blame you." Dakin searched the ballroom nervously, and I knew that he was looking for Akeldama. "I like you, Gem, but this is something that I cannot help you with."

Before he walked off, I snagged his arm, making Stephan growl again. He sounded more like a werewolf than he did a vampire. "I like you, too, Dakin, but I have got to tell you when it comes to my friends, there is nothing that I wouldn't do for them. There is only black and white. No gray. I will avenge her death. You are either with me or against me."

Dakin looked almost sad for a moment. "I totally understand, Tandi." Then he walked away.

I had a feeling that the use of my real name showed me where we stood. If Akeldama were behind this, which I was positive that she was, then he would back her. He was obviously on a different side than I was, and something about that made me very sad.

Stephan had collected Dani, and we all walked back to the vehicle. Once we were inside, I knew Stephan knew precisely what I was about to ask. His hands clenched the steering wheel so hard I was surprised it didn't come off. Dani was uncharacteristically quiet.

"Is it true?" I asked.

"Tandi, there are some things that—"

"Answer the question. Why is Greta not here with us right now? Did you somehow stop her transitioning into a vampire? Yes or no, Stephan?"

"Oh, shit," Dani exhaled.

I whirled in my seat to peer at her in the back. "You knew that he could have brought her back, too?"

She didn't even have the courage to answer; instead, she dropped her gaze to the floorboard.

"Tandi, I couldn't let her come back as a vampire," Stephan said quietly.

"You are telling me that what Dakin said was incorrect. And he was also misinformed when he said that you were occasionally giving Greta some of your blood, so there is no way that she died with your blood in her system. Or better yet, even though I'm a weak vampire, my blood alone should have brought her back. But he was lying, so you could not bring her back as one of us?"

"No, that is not what I am saying—"

"So, what are you saying?"

"Damn it, Tandi. I am trying to tell you, but you won't listen. Yes, Greta did take my blood because it prolonged her life, and yes, she was a human servant. She wasn't immortal, but she could live for a very long time. Did she have enough of my blood in her to come back as a vampire? I'm not sure. Did she have enough of your blood in her to come back as a vampire? Yes, she did."

I could barely control my anger. "What did you do to ensure that she didn't rise?"

"Tandi, she did not want to be brought back as a vampire."

"What about what I want?" I shrieked. "I need her! And you could have brought her back, but instead you let her die. The rogue vampires killed her, but you sealed her fate by not bringing her back."

His palm hit the steering wheel. "What about what Greta wanted, hmm? Over the course of the years, I have tried to sway her to become a vampire, to become immortal, and she vehemently refused. It is not want she wanted, Tandi. You can't possibly be so selfish as to ignore her wishes to appease your own."

I knew I was being unreasonable, but I was in pain, and it felt good to lash out, even if it was undeserving. With venom in my voice, I sneered. "What did you do, Stephan? Put a stake in her heart to make sure that she didn't rise back up as a vampire?"

His jaw clenched so hard, I heard his teeth crunch. "I had her cremated, which was also her request upon her death. Her grave holds her ashes."

My insides twisted with so many different emotions. Greta was more of a mom to me than my own mother, and I missed her so bad it hurt. I wanted another one of her long hugs, but she would never be able to give me that again, and it was all because of the man sitting next to me. I knew somewhere in the back of my head that I was being unfair, but I was in too much pain to think about what would have been right or wrong for Greta or if I was being selfish. Dani hadn't said one word, and it was just as well. At this point, I considered her an accomplice after the fact, and I was just as pissed at her. No one talked for the rest of the trip home. Before I exited the car, Stephan tried to grab my hand, but I quickly evaded him.

"Don't. Touch. Me," I snarled. "I will find out who sent the rogue vampires, and I will help you find the key, but I need some space."

I got out of the car, slamming the door so hard I expected the glass to break, and was more than a little disappointed when it didn't. I stormed up to my room and locked the door before falling on my bed, where I wished for things that couldn't be and cried myself to an unrestful sleep.

chapter ten

The next night there was a knock on my door. I refused to open it, so Dani talked through it.

"Listen, I know that you are just as upset with me, because some part of you thinks I betrayed you, too, and for that, I am very sorry. Please believe me when I tell you that if we had brought Greta back as a vampire, she would have hated us for that. She would have never forgiven us. My brother is nothing short of an honorable man. He has his faults, but he would have never gone against Greta's wishes, no matter how badly he wanted to." I heard her sigh and then the sound of a thump, like maybe she had laid her head against my door. "Try and remember that he loved her like a mother, too. He is hurting just as badly, even though he might not show it like you."

I heard her soft footsteps as she walked away from the door. She was right. Stephan did the right thing in honoring Greta's wishes, and I was acting like a selfish brat. Just because he had the opportunity to bring Greta back didn't mean he should have. Especially if those weren't her wishes. My lines between right and wrong were blurrier than Stephan's. Embarrassment flooded me when I thought of how childish I acted. I needed to apologize. Stephan was obviously grieving for Greta, too; he didn't need me blaming him for honoring Greta's wishes.

I jumped in the shower, threw on some clothes, put my hair in a messy bun, and ran down the stairs to Stephan's study where I knew he would be because I could feel him.

Without knocking on the door, I walked right in. He was sitting behind his massive, dark desk. The whole room was made for him with its masculine hues of dark brown and forest green. He looked up from a ledger of some sort that he was writing in. His gaze slid over me from head to toe like he was assessing the damage.

When his eyes met mine, I said, "I understand what you had to do, and why you did it. I did not agree wholeheartedly because of my selfishness, but that is between my maker and me, and I'm not talking about you. I would have brought Greta back, even if that meant she would have hated me for the rest of my days, and I would have been wrong."

He gave me a sad smile. "As many conversations that Greta and I have had on the topic, I just couldn't do it to her. Especially with how strongly she felt about the subject. I just couldn't."

I swallowed the lump rising in my throat and nodded. "I wish you would have told me the truth."

There were two leather chairs in front of the colossal desk, but I opted to sit in neither. Instead, I walked around and sat on the corner of his desk. He swiveled in his chair, his knees almost brushing my legs, and waited for me to say what was on my mind.

"I know that there are other things that you are keeping from me, Stephan, and I ask that you tell me about those things now before someone like Dakin does. He blindsided me, and I don't like that feeling."

His jaw clenched at the name, but then he leaned back in his chair and studied me. "You're right, little one. There are things that I have withheld from you like Greta." When I began to interject, he held up a hand. "But the reasoning behind that is you're not ready to hear everything I have to say. You have just become a new vampire, and you are still struggling to adjust to this new lifestyle, not to mention you were uprooted from the only home you have ever known. I didn't want to add unnecessary worries."

"Well, I think I can handle knowing everything—"

Stephan put a hand up. "Maybe you can and maybe you can't, but some things I might need more time to figure out."

"Um. That's weird. I mean, if it's about me, why can't you just tell me? For starters, I assumed that I magically lost all of the weight that I had on me as a human because I turned into a vampire, but when we went to the party last night, I saw that there were vampires of all different sizes. I realized that my theory was shot to hell with multiple bullet wounds. I can go abnormally long without feeding. I don't seem to be a vampire, but yet I have fangs. Why am I so different?"

Stephan sighed. "Tandi, I have some very important things to take care of today." He shuffled some papers

on his desk and refused to make eye contact with me, signifying that the conversation was over.

I cleared my throat. "I have some questions that I feel will make me a better vampire, and I would like for you to answer them."

"As I've said, I have other things to focus on today. Shut the door behind you on the way out."

"You are an ass," I said. "Just thought you should know."

His brown eyes narrowed. "Are you done with your little tantrum?"

"What? You claim that you need me to be a better vampire, and yet there are so many unresolved questions that could possibly help me to be better or at least understand why I am not. Stating a fact is not a tantrum, buddy." Tantrum? He thought me asking questions that I had every right to know the answers to was throwing a tantrum. He had been the one to act like I was an anomaly. By him being so secretive, I'd been made to feel that I was something so different than the norm that I was nothing but a failure. I came here to extend an olive branch, and he couldn't meet me halfway. Bless his precious heart. I would show him a tantrum.

I walked over to the door where a priceless vase was standing on a pillar. "Just so you know, buddy, this," I said, picking up the vase, "is throwing a tantrum." I let the vase slip through my fingers and watched his jaw clench when it shattered into a million pieces.

"Do you have any idea how much that was worth?"

"No, but I know how much it's worth now." I did a little finger wave then spun around on my heel. "Good talk, Stephan."

In a flash, he was before me, gripping me by my arms. The anger radiating off of him made me stop the nasty retort on the edge of my tongue.

"Anyone else, Tandi, anyone else, and I would have made them pick up those pieces with their teeth."

"I would have just spit the mouthful of ceramic in your face."

He rested his forehead against mine, and his nostrils flared like he was breathing in my scent. Wasn't expecting that. I also wasn't expecting the tightening in my stomach. "I know you would have, and that is another thing that I admire you for." What was that scent? He smelled like heaven. He was a drug and being this close to him was intoxicating. I was having a hard time thinking straight. "I know you have questions and I need time. Can you give me that? You deserve the answers to your questions, and I'm working on giving them to you. I just need a little more time. Please be patient."

I nodded and he released me. As his arms dropped from me I felt a surge of sadness. Oh no, this couldn't be good. I was severely attracted to the Prince of Vampires.

Pasting on a fake smile, I joked, "Just remember, patience isn't one of my strong suits."

"I will see you later tonight. Maybe by then, I will have some answers for you."

I left him in his study, and as I walked my way back up the steps, I thought that maybe I wouldn't like the answers he found. But wasn't it better to know? What if there was something truly defective about me? I couldn't fit into the human world anymore, but would I also be ostracized from all vampires as well, to live a life of solitude. Stephan would have to wipe his hands clean of me in order to not be alienated either. I would be all by myself in this new life.

If this was something that was out of my control, then worrying about it would bring me nothing but more trouble. I took off my cuff and left it on the bedside table. A long bath, painting my toenails, and watching reality shows would fix anything. Well, almost anything.

chapter eleven

The sun cast its warm rays on my face, and I had almost forgotten how good vitamin D felt. Wait. Why was I in the sun and not frying into a pile of ash? I sat up from the Adirondack chair I was reclining in and removed the sunglasses I wore to have a better look around. There was nothing but miles and miles of white, sandy beach. The ocean's waves were gently rolling, and it was so clear that I could see all of the ocean floor and its inhabitants. I stood up to get a closer look at my surroundings and noticed I wore an unflattering, blue-striped one piece with a ruffle skirt. It was hideous. Yeah, this would not do. Right in front of my eyes, my bathing suit turned into a cute black bikini. What. The. Hell. Obviously, I was dreaming, but I didn't remember falling asleep in the tub.

I heard a strong voice behind me. "Hello."

Quickly turning around, I saw a sixty-ish looking man standing behind an empty tiki hut bar. He had shiny gray hair hanging down to his shoulders, and it was the

same length as his silvery beard. His beautiful blue eyes sparkled with humor and amusement. Considering the ugly Hawaiian shirt he was wearing, I was glad to see he was able to be a good sport about anything.

"You have part fae in you," the man said in an accent that I couldn't quite place.

"Um, are you talking to me?"

He picked up a glass and started to clean it with a linen napkin. He repeated what I said a few times until he produced the perfect southern accent. Was this old geezer trying to mimic me?

He smiled at me. "You see anyone else on this beach? Of course, I'm talking to you. You looked confused, so I am clarifyin'. You have part fae in you. That is why you can travel between the planes."

I must have gotten into some bad blood because I was tripping.

Nodding to an empty bar stool, he said, "Come, take a seat, and I'll explain some things."

Slowly moving towards him, I said, "And you are?"

"Your grandfather. Actually, there are a lot of greats in there, but who's counting? All that matters is we share the same blood."

This was crazy. "Of course, we do."

"No, you're not dreaming, but you'll figure that out when you get back."

"So for right now, I just need to roll with it?"

He cocked his head to the side. "Roll with it? Yes, I like that."

I was pretty sure he was talking about my lingo, not that I was confident of anything anymore. "So, you are my granddaddy?"

He smiled, and it looked as if the heavens were casting down rays. I almost had to put my shades back on. "Granddaddy. I like that even better, but with this drawl, it will take forever to say. Why don't you call me Pops?"

"You would think my subconscious would have picked someone older, especially if you were a… however many greats you are."

"Oh, but you don't get to choose how I look, even if you had requested this meeting. I am who I am, and that will never change. My appearance is accurate and since I'm fae, I don't age normally. This is actually my setting," he said, gesturing to our surroundings. "I have been knocking on your door literally for some time, but you have just now relaxed enough to answer, and since I asked for the meeting, I chose the background." He smirked. "Obviously, you didn't like the bathing suit I picked out for you. Guess it was a little too grandfatherly."

I looked down at my bathing suit. It was the one that I had salivated over in the new issue of Vogue.

"So, you are saying that if I didn't like something, I could change it… while I'm here. Wherever here is?"

"Yes. Unless it's my physical appearance and like I said, what you see is what you get with this old timer."

While concentrating on my surroundings, I imagined a different scenery. Before my eyes the white sand changed to a pink hue. I had once seen these pink sand beaches on a brochure advertising a coastline on Komodo Island in Indonesia.

"See? You are a natural, kid. Must take after me."

I slumped down on the barstool, studying his features. This was me, rolling with it. "You are fae, and you have wanted to talk with me because?"

He looked sad for a moment before putting the whiskey glass down. "Because my line has been so diluted with the intermingling of humans, I haven't been able to talk to any of my children's children. It's pretty depressing being able to watch your family go through success and heartache, but never being able to reach out to them."

"But you can talk to me?"

"Yes, dear granddaughter, I surely can. Thanks to the vampire blood in you. It has strengthened the fae in you, and that is the answer to the question you asked your young vampire."

He thought Stephan was young? I didn't even want to know how old he was.

"My question?"

"Granted your fae blood was very diluted, but since it's still there, you would have lost the extra fat that you carried once you came into adulthood. Which was just a couple of months away, correct?"

"Um, yeah. My birthday is soon. What does it mean that I have fae in my bloodline, other than I can, um, travel to here?"

He tugged on his beard. "How about if you visit your Pops every once and a while, I'll teach you all about the fae?"

I was pretty sure that none of this was real anyway so why not. "Sure. I'll visit every night."

His eyes got round as saucers. "I would love that, but I wouldn't recommend it. Your vamp would go insane."

"He's not my vamp, and why would he care?"

"When you come to a fae plane, the time operates differently than it does in the real world."

I shrugged, because hey, this was me rolling with it again. "Of course, it does. What can you teach me while I'm here?"

"I could state the basics, such as fae are known for their ethereal appearance because they come from fallen angels, or I could answer some of the questions that are burning inside of you."

"All of the above, please." His bushy eyebrows rose. "Would you like a drumroll?"

"You get your attitude from my late wife. She was so feisty. All right, we will start with the easy stuff. A long time ago, some angels were cast out of heaven for their wrongdoings. They found themselves not able to fit in with those on earth, but no longer welcome in heaven. Most grew lonely and started intermingling with the humans in a romantic sense. Of course, the relationships were doomed from the beginning because the fallen angels never age, so they had to watch their loved ones, including their children, grow old and wither. The fallen angels' children were a new breed called fae."

"So, fae are mortals?"

"Yes and no. If they live on earth, yes. If their blood is not too diluted by human blood, then they can live their lives in the fae plane where they will become immortal," Pops said. "Now, on to more juicy stuff. You, my granddaughter, are the only one of your kind."

"Maybe you should be a little bit more specific."

"Your body is made up of three different beings."

"Three?" I yelled. "What the heck? Vampire, fae, and what else? If you say troll, so help me, I will imagine a bridge and then go jump off of it."

Pops chuckled. "No, Tandi there is no troll in your body, but what I'm about to tell you is worse. Just remember you have been demanding answers from that vampire of yours."

"Again, he does not belong to me." I crossed my legs, swinging the top one. "Spit it out, Pops."

"Ghoul."

It took me a moment to find my voice. "Ghoul? As in the things that killed me? I have a part of them in my genetic make-up?"

"No. It's complicated."

"Well, then un-complicate it for me."

"This is all kind of an anomaly. No one has ever died from being attacked by ghouls with vampire blood in their system. Not to mention the fact that you carry fae blood as well."

I thought of the ghouls that attacked me. They were hideous beings made up of rotten flesh that seemed to give them a more zombie appearance than anything. My voice shook as I asked, "Will I turn into a ghoul?"

"No, you will not end up looking like a ghoul, but you do carry their poison in your blood. That's why that rogue vampire died when he bit you."

I thought back to the night the vampires attacked us. I had assumed that Dani killed all the vampires. Maybe that is what the secretive looks between brother and sister were all about. "My blood is poisonous to all vampires?"

"To all creatures, I would imagine. But again, this is uncharted territory, and I can't be positive. There are so many unknowns."

"You said that whatever fae blood I have in me is very minimal, so other than playing a part in my appearance, is there anything else I should know about?"

"Oh, but your fae blood will continue to get stronger and stronger if I am not mistaken. Over the years, I've seen humans with small traces of fae in them be turned by a vampire only to have the fae in them grow. That means that you will hopefully be able to wield some of the powers that most low fae can wield, and if we are fortunate, then you might have some similar powers of the high fae."

"My parents came from old money and were all about wielding the power that came from it over the lesser folk's heads. If they knew this, they would be ecstatic to learn they might become more powerful. Not that they would use their power for good, because I can promise you they wouldn't unless it paid. But I'm not like them. I just want to be a normal vampire, so I can try and fit in a little better."

I could sense his indecision a moment before he produced an intricate, hand-held gold mirror in his hands. "Tandi, look into this mirror, and tell me what you see?"

"Um… is this a trick question?" I asked, as I gazed into the mirror.

"You're as gorgeous as any fae I've ever laid eyes upon. Your hair is the color of wheat in the sunshine, and your eyes are as green as fresh cut grass. Your face is perfectly symmetrical."

My eyes met his across the bar. "Thanks?"

"Your parents, describe them to me."

"Well, Dad worked for a—"

"No. I want to know what they look like."

I scrunched my forehead in thought. "Well, my dad is an ordinary man. Average height, receding brown hair, and brown eyes that are always behind a pair of glasses, which constantly slip on his nose. He's slightly pudgy. My mom is pretty short and has similar coloring. Except her brown eyes are darker, and her hair is lighter, thanks to all the highlights she puts in it."

Pops nodded. "Would you say that there is anything that stands out about them in a crowd?"

"Their money set them apart. The fancy way they dressed, their mannerisms, and the fact that they always thought they were better than everyone else because they could trace their ancestors all the way back to the Mayflower. But I guess if you took away their money and their lineage, then, no, there is nothing about their looks that would make someone stop and take notice of them." I laid the mirror down on the bar with a thunk. "What exactly are you trying to get at, Pops?"

"How could two people like that have someone that looks like you?"

"Are you saying they aren't my real parents?"

"Of course, those aren't your real parents. No offense to you, but those people you call parents are a disgrace to parents everywhere. This might come as a shocker, but be thankful that you don't carry their blood. Your real parents died in a car crash when you were three weeks old."

Neither one of us said anything for several minutes while I tried to wrap my brain around what he had just said. The ones who raised me had lied to me all of these years. I waited for the feeling of rage to come, but instead I felt ashamed. Ashamed that I felt a loss from never meeting my real parents and was relieved the people who raised me shared none of my blood. They had always treated me more like a trophy than a daughter. The gardener taught me how to ride a bike, the cook taught me how to bake cookies, and one of my nannies gave me the birds and the bees speech.

When Stephan had convinced my parents that I needed to study abroad, I knew they were happy for me to go and weren't upset that they didn't get the chance to say goodbye. I wondered what it would have been like if my true parents would have lived. Would I have still become part of the supernatural community? Would I have ended up right here sitting in front of Pops?

After I had worked out the different emotions going through me, I glanced up into Pops' concerned eyes. "Thank you for telling me."

Realizing that I wasn't going to have a meltdown, he gave me a smile. His green eyes that were the same shade as mine twinkled back at me. "When you are immortal, time is irrelevant, but I'm sure that your young vampire is going mad looking for you."

My eyes drifted to the pink sand and the crystal-clear waters before settling back on Pops. "I've been gone for a hot minute, and besides that, I've learned more in these

past few minutes than I have the entire time I've been with Stephan. He's infuriating, and I suck at being a vampire."

Pops dared to chuckle at my self-pity. "This is all just theory, but I believe that you are getting worse at becoming a vampire because you are trying too hard. Let all three counterparts work naturally together and in your favor. You see by this point, a vampire should be a well-built, killing machine acting on instinct alone. When a vampire sees a source of food, they should get hunger pains just by hearing its heartbeat. The adrenaline should be pumping through their veins just from the excitement of the chase, but you, my dear, well, you just see a cute animal."

Wincing, I asked, "So, you saw the whole deer debacle, or are we talking about the stupid bunny?"

He laughed. "I might have bared witness to the baby fawn. Unfortunately, I missed the bunny scene, but it sounds like it would have been interesting to watch."

"Yep. I'm a total failure."

"I think that you are looking at it wrong. You see when vampires are newly turned, it takes them a very long time— sometimes decades—before they can curb their appetite before killing anything weaker than them. The only thing that you have managed to kill, and unintentionally might I add, was a vampire that was by far stronger than you. I believe what is suppressing your need to kill, ironically, is your fae blood, which seems to be growing stronger. It's not the fact that you are not killing anything that makes your fae blood strengthen, because you are still drinking blood, even if it comes out of a bag." I could tell he was holding back laughter. "It's as if all three different types of blood currently coursing through your veins are working together to make you a different type of being. You shouldn't exist, and yet you do."

"So, now that I'm more of a Rubik's Cube instead of a huge disappointment, Stephan will lay off of me a bit? Well, that is if I can convince him of all this. If I tell him I met my fae great something or another grandfather in a different plane, and he told me why I'm not the perfect vampire, he might have my blood drained and have me mummified."

His bushy brows furrowed. "Since he already knows all of this, I don't see why he would doubt you about meeting me."

"What do you mean, he already knows? That man has done nothing but be condescending and made me feel like I am lower than low just because I'm not the perfect vampire, and you're telling me that he knows why I'm not performing at top speed."

"That is not why he has been standoffish, and as far as the rest," Pops said, shrugging, "while you've been gone, he's made some discoveries. Try not to be too upset with him."

My jaw dropped. He acted like I had been gone for days when I knew good and well that I just asked Stephan thirty minutes ago if he had any answers. "Try not to be too upset? I'm past that and am currently residing in the 'I'm about to stake someone' zone."

"Just playing fae advocate here, but I'm sure there is a great reason for him not wanting to tell you. If you would just ask him, then—"

"Listen, Pops, I appreciate the grandfatherly advice, but I think I'm going stick with staking him. It sounds more therapeutic."

He leaned his elbows on the bar and released a long sigh. "I thought you would say that." He laid a hand on one of mine. "I have given you a lot to think about, and I have immensely enjoyed getting to see your fiery spirit in person. Promise me that you will come see me again?"

I turned my hand under his so our palms touched. "I have enjoyed myself, too, and if I don't wake up in a cold bath and realize that I have a very vivid imagination, then I promise that we will do this again. Besides, I sure do miss the sun."

He squeezed my hand with a smile. "I'm going to say a word to send you back, and all you have to do is say the word in your mind or out loud anytime you want to come for a visit."

At my nod, he said, "Teia."

My eyes closed as the sensation of falling into blackness swept over me. I'd never met Alice, but I was positive that this was the way it felt when she fell down that dang rabbit hole. The more I fought it, the more I became nauseated, so I gave up and just relaxed.

chapter twelve

atin sheets and the canopy from hell could only mean one thing. Total bummer. I liked the old man. After a quick stretch, I swung my legs off the bed to realize two things: I had excellent taste in fashion, and it hadn't been a dream. I twirled part of the string from the bikini around on my finger. Hmm. So not only did I have a Pops that had been watching over me, but I had some answers to my questions. Which meant that I had every reason not to trust Stephan. He knew so many things and to withhold the answers from me was callous. We had a saying in the South, 'That dog don't hunt,' and it was about time I let him know that this girl don't play.

Not bothering to change, I stomped my way down the stairs, knowing precisely where he was. I could sense his emotions pouring off of him in waves. Misery. Well, if he thought he was miserable before our soon-to-be encounter, he had another think coming.

I threw his study door open. "Honey, I'm home."

I don't know what shocked me more: the broken glass that was all over the floor, the massive overturned desk, or the red rim around Stephan's eyes. He looked like caveman meets Tom Hanks from Cast Away.

"Did someone break in and destroy your study and decide that, that wasn't good enough, so they stole your hygiene products, too? Good lord, you look awful."

His head swung to mine, and he slowly stood from the chair, which was the only thing that wasn't destroyed or flipped upside down. He took in every inch of me. "Where have you been?"

I crossed my arms over my bikini-clad body. "Don't you dare shout at me, Stephan. I have been visiting with my great-great well, lots of greats grandfather, and do you know what we discussed?"

"I don't give a damn what you talked about. You were off gallivanting around with your grandfather? Do you realize how long you have been gone? Wait." In a flash he was in front of my gripping my arms and in a quiet voice that was scarier than a shout, asked, "What do you mean, your grandfather?"

A smug smile came across my face. "First of all, I was gone a hot minute, not 'gallivanting,' and secondly, I mean my real grandfather; you know the one that is fae, and he had some pretty interesting things to say. Some things that apparently you knew, but because of whatever hidden agenda you have, you decided not to share with the class. I thought you kept me in the dark because I totally suck at being a vampire, but now I wonder if it's because you knew how different I am."

Jerking me by my arms, he dipped his head, resting his forehead on mine. "I'm not sure what you are accusing me of this time. I found out about your fae heritage the first week of your disappearance."

He let go of me and I stumbled. "What are you talking about?"

He went about the room, kicking what was left of his study out of his way as he made a trail to the overturned desk. With his vampire strength, he picked up the solid chunk of wood with one hand like it was nothing, and settled it back in its original place. "What else did you and Gallen talk about?"

Oh, so he was just going to ignore my questions. At least we were back on familiar ground. Two could play this game. "This and that. It doesn't surprise me that you know his name. I didn't even think to ask his real name. But then again you seem to know a lot. Secrets don't make friends; they make hormonal, teenage girls premeditate murder."

He rolled his chair to his desk and sat down in the disheveled room that was once the most organized O.C.D. lover's paradise. "It doesn't matter at this point what you two talked about. We have more pressing matters. Akeldama has requested all vampires' presence for her daughter's wedding. She has given everyone ample time to gather, and if we don't go, it will be looked upon as an intentional insult. So pack a bag quickly, and we will leave tonight."

"Ample time? This isn't ample time, buddy. And for the record, I am still going to help you find this missing key, and I will find Greta's killer. But know I do not trust you for one second."

He rubbed a hand over his face, looking thoroughly and utterly exhausted. "Duly noted." As soon as I walked out of his study, he said, "Oh, and Tandi, you weren't gone for a 'hot minute,' you were gone for two months. I have used every resource and traded in every favor owed to me searching for you. That is where Dani is right now, looking for you. You left without a trace. All your belongings were still here, including your cuff, and your bath water was still warm. The wards I had around the house weren't triggered, and there were no foreign scents coming from your room. You literally disappeared. You dream walking and having a mini-vacation with Gallen never crossed my mind, even after I found out about your fae heritage."

My jaw dropped as I took in the weight of his words. Was I the reason for the state of his study and the half-crazed look on his face? I started to walk back in the room, but with a flick of his wrist, he slammed the door shut in my face. It wasn't until I was packed and ready to go that I realized Stephan was telekinetic.

The car ride to the Queen's infamous Georgia castle was intense to say the least. Stephan had cleaned himself up, and I felt horrible that I was the reason for his demise. All these months, I'd felt like a total failure and come to find out, there was a reason I wasn't a fantastic vampire. Because I wasn't a vampire. Well, not wholly. I wanted to ask what he thought of me now that he knew

I was different, but I wasn't sure he would tell me. My peripheral vision revealed that he was still gripping the steering wheel. I was surprised it hadn't popped off the dashboard and landed in his lap yet. Maybe if I started a conversation, it would alleviate some of the tension, lighten the mood, or at least cure some of my boredom.

"Why are we leaving today? I saw the invite, and it says we need to be there by tomorrow." In my best English accent, I said, "Dinner will be promptly served at six."

Crickets. That's what I got, crickets. I was studying his profile, and his facial features didn't change. I'd be danged if I was going to be ignored.

My arms crossed and I sighed. "Look, I'm sorry. I didn't ask to have a chit-chat with my... with Pops; I didn't even know that he existed. Apparently, he had been summoning me, and I denied the call." Even though I wasn't entirely sure how I did that. Maybe it was the pure relaxation in the bathtub. Stephan remained silent. "And at one point, he did mention that fae time was different than normal time, but I assumed he meant like central versus eastern. Not a month for every half hour. Also, I would just like to point out that I wasn't a hundred percent sure I wasn't dreaming."

After a couple of minutes, he said, "Fine. Apology accepted."

"That's it? Apology accepted? Where the hell is my apology?"

He scoffed. "What in the world do I need to apologize for Tandi?"

"You have got to be shitting me, right?" Holding up my hand, I started ticking off the reasons on my fingers.

"Let's see, you knew that I was struggling with becoming a vampire, and you were already checking into my heritage, so you probably assumed that I wasn't a hundred percent vampire. Answer me this: did you know that my blood kills?"

"When Dani reported back to me that the vampire who bit you immediately dropped to the ground screaming before his flesh developed black lines running all over it, I had my concerns that you carried ghoul blood."

"You have known for some time that I had ghoul in me. You also knew that my blood kills. Oh, and you know what? Out of the courtesy of my own heart, I'm not going to even count that if you were checking into my heritage, then you knew that I was adopted. Because let's face it, that is some straight up Jerry Springer shiznit. You would have to have a big pair of cojones to broach that subject."

"Is that all you and Gallen talked about?"

"Yes, that's all—wait a minute. What do you mean, is that all? What else do you know that you should tell, but are too stupid to?"

The arrogant pig appeared relieved, and that really ticked me off. "Tandi, I'm sorry you think I should have told you, but I wanted to get more information first." I started to interrupt, and he said, "You want to know why I didn't tell you, so give me a chance to speak. Yes, I was aggravated by your lack of hunting skills because to a vampire, that means you're an easy target, but I was mostly disappointed that I didn't know how to help you. After the attack that killed Greta, I knew that it was you who had killed that vampire. Only a ghoul could cause a death like that. I called Ariana, who's only confirmation was that she thought it took me long enough to figure it out. In the same conversation, she said that you were related to an old friend of hers, Gallen. She said that it was the fae in you that would keep you alive. Alive from what, I do not know. Trust me, I had plenty of questions, but she refused to answer any of them. Sometimes, I hate that old woman."

I let out a breath, watching it fog up the window. "Why didn't you tell me any of this?"

"Right now, it's a problem that you are part vampire, ghoul, and fae because people are scared of what they can't explain. I wanted to have a solution before I gave you the problem."

"The fae in me is apparently getting stronger and sometimes overrides my vampire instincts, doesn't it?"

"Yes, but you still have the weaknesses of a young vampire. With that cuff I gave you, you won't perish in the sun, but you are not strong enough to stay awake during daylight hours."

"What about the ghoul blood I carry? I'm sure those nasty creatures are going to have some kind of negative outcome for me."

His dimple winked at me for a second. "You would be correct. As of right now, the only thing I can think of is you probably shouldn't be opening up a vein for anyone anytime soon."

"Stephan! What about Greta? I gave her my blood, and that didn't kill her."

At the mention of Greta's name, Stephan reached over and held my hand. "There are two theories that I have thought of. One is that she was human and with a slower metabolism than a vampire, your blood acted more slowly in her."

"What is the second theory?" I asked.

"That perhaps out of love, your fae blood somehow made your blood non-toxic as you were giving it to Greta."

I was a firm believer that love cured all things, but was my love for Greta powerful enough to change my blood from harming her? That sounded too good to be true.

Still holding onto his hand, I drew up my legs underneath me. "Being part ghoul and not knowing what I am capable of is not a good thing, is it?"

"No. It's not. Knowledge is important, and I'm sure that there is a balance to all three. Ariana is no longer taking my calls, so I won't be able to ask her."

"Why won't she help us?"

"She sees around corners, Tandi. If she thinks that her advice or answers to my questions will set either of us off the path of finding the key, she won't tell us anything. It's frustrating to no end, but I understand her predicament."

"How did you meet this Ariana?" I asked.

"She's as old as time, so of course I've heard of her, but it wasn't until recently that she decided to insert herself into my life. Apparently, she thinks—or excuse me knows—that I'm needed to retrieve the third key."

I stared out the window, arriving at the conclusion that I might never truly understand exactly who I was, and the one person who could tell me wouldn't. Ariana had her own agenda. I hoped she was batting for the good guys, and Stephan wasn't just blindly following her advice. Time would tell.

S tephan had pulled off the interstate about five minutes ago, and after a series of nauseating turns, was currently climbing up a windy road that had room for only one car to pass at a time.

I grabbed hold of the "oh shit" handle and peered out of the window. The higher we went, the steeper the drop got. "If we fall off this road, we're dead."

"The vamp in you won't let a small tumble down a cliff kill you, Tandi."

"Small tumble my cute behind. And what if the car combusts into a ball of fire? Then what, Sherlock? I don't want to be made into a s'more."

"I realize that the land is flatter where you come from, but I can promise you that I'm very good at navigating mountain roads."

I snorted. "You say road; I say goat trail."

"Up ahead there will be a small place where I can turn around. From there, we will exit the car and carry on by foot."

"What on God's green earth for?"

"Because the wards that were set in place by the witch who we are soon to visit will shut down the engine of the car if we try to keep driving."

"And why are we visiting a witch?"

"Because she owes me a favor."

Unfortunately, sooner rather than later, he turned the car around to point in the direction that we had just come from, and we exited the vehicle. We climbed over roots and rocks for what seemed like an hour but honestly could have been fifteen minutes. The truth was I deplored any and all kinds of exercise. Not to mention the fact that I hated the great outdoors with its mosquitos and wildlife. Louisiana had its fair share of both closer to the wooded areas and the swamps, but that's why I avoided anywhere that didn't have a controlled environment. Air-conditioning was my friend. I didn't long to get close with nature, that was what the National Geographic Chanel was for. But I refused to complain.

"Are we there yet?"

"You've asked me that question five times already."

Well, I personally didn't see asking a bloody question as complaining, and I was about to tell him that, when I saw smoke curling up from a chimney. I pushed the next branch out of my way and about had a full-blown heart attack when my face got caught in a spider web. It was amazing how just the feel of a sticky web hitting a body part could turn the least athletic of us into a stealth, black-belt wielding ninja. I dropped to the ground and snatched at that web, wrestling it like a python.

"Husband of a Disney princess whore. Get it off. Get it off!"

I must have stirred up an ant farm when I was thrashing around on the ground because they were coming out of the woodwork, literally, and the first troop had seized my leg. I was under attack, and Stephan just stood there laughing. The asshat. As I swatted at my leg, I realized that these weren't the ants like I saw on A Bugs Life; these were what my grandmother used to call Piss Ants. They got their classy name from Southerners because they could bite the piss out of you. I started rolling like I was on fire. Leaves were sticking to my hair because of the damn spider web, and I had acquired a mouth full of bark somewhere along the way. I was going to die in the middle of nowhere because of ants. How freaking embarrassing.

"Adolebitque!" a feminine voice shouted, and I watched in amazement as the ants who were conquering my body and were mere moments away from planting a flag on my ass burned to ashes. I jumped up, patting my limbs to make sure that I wasn't on fire, too.

The same voice mocked, "Stephan, really? You saw the poor child needed help, and you just stood there." I was certain she was trying to sound patronizing, but at this point I didn't care. The ants were not stealing my soul, so she could patronize away.

"I'm sorry, Athela, but you have to admit it was mildly entertaining."

"It was that." She chuckled.

Well, I was super happy that I could provide entertainment. For the first time, I got a glance at ol'

Athela to see that she wasn't old at all, but young and beautiful, with long, curly black hair and emerald green eyes. Standing tall in her gypsy-looking attire, she ran a hand lovingly up and down Stephan's arm while giving me a calculating look. That was just great. She saw me as a threat, but I didn't care what she thought of me, as long as she continued to save me from the surrounding nature.

"Why don't you bring your worn-out friend into my home, Stephan? She can... try to clean up some, while you tell me what is the reason behind this impromptu visit. Not that I am not delighted to see you."

"Of course," Stephan purred out with all the charm that I was never the recipient of. I would be jealous, but I was still picking bark from my teeth. "After you, Athela."

My shields up, I studied her as she picked up her long skirt and sashayed her way through the small trail, making it look like she was floating on air instead of stumbling every five seconds like I was doing. Was I jealous? Maybe, but we all had our talents, and so what if mine wasn't hiking Satan's mountain? I would much rather know all answers to any and all trivia questions pertaining to Pretty Little Liars, and I bet I could beat her plump butt in a game of Monopoly. I would so own the Boardwalk, and what would she have? Baltic, that's what.

When the trail widened, Stephan dropped back, so he could walk next to me. I caught a glimpse of a small cottage around the bend that reminded me of a quaint version of the witch's house in the tale of Hansel and Gretel. Hope today's little rendezvous didn't end with little miss gypsy queen trying to shove me in an oven.

"Little one, pray tell, what Disney whore were you referring to?"

He was still laughing at me. I glared at him. "Snow White, I reckon. After all, she did shack up with seven different men. Oh, and by the way, thanks for your help back there."

He put his hands in his pockets. "I assumed that you had it under control, and you are one of those today women who insists on standing on her own two feet."

"Ha! Well, you assumed wrong. Not only was I not standing, I was rolling around, and it wasn't for your amusement. There is no reason on this earth that I wouldn't accept help when my life depends on it."

"Tandi, they were ants."

"You see ants, I see an army."

He chuckled. "My apologies then. Next time, I will make sure to come to your aid."

My fist punched him in the arm. "There better not be a next time, buddy. I am officially a part of an elite group that has survived an ant attack while being engulfed in a web. Lightning better not strike twice."

The witch must have heard our exchange. "Or what? It's Tandi, correct?" she said. At my nod, she smirked before quietly walking up the steps to her front door.

"I guess if it happens next time, Athela, I will just give up on life. Honest to God, I don't want to go through that experience again."

"Then you will never be a warrior."

Were we still talking about ants? I had nothing to say. I mean, seriously. This lady, if she could be called that, didn't know me from Jack and already hated me

just because she saw me as competition. She needed to lighten up. Miserable cow. I clomped up the steps after the both of them.

Athela pointed to the back of the small house. "Why don't you go and try to make yourself presentable while I catch up with Stephan? First door on your left."

I rolled my eyes so hard I'm sure they bounced, and I knew they both had caught the look because Stephan laughed while dear, sweet Athela crossed her arms and glared. Whatever. I didn't need friends. I had the greatest of friends waiting back home for me. Man, I missed Charlie. She was currently off slaying being the Queen of Witches while I on the other hand was being defeated by mother nature.

After closing the small bathroom door behind me, I giggled for a solid minute at my appearance. My whole head looked like a batch of non-colored cotton candy. That must have been Lucifer who spun that web. If only my lip gloss was that strong. As I was picking the sticks, leaves, and—God help me—bugs out of my hair, I could hear the slow hum of conversation in the small kitchen. It sounded like Athela was making tea. Oh, yay. A tea party. Just what I wanted to have.

I was a pretty happy-go-lucky kind of girl, but I couldn't help but feel a little depressed. Today was my birthday, and not one person remembered. Greta would have remembered. I wiped a tear that had leaked out.

I heard a gypsy giggle and I started murmuring very un-ladylike things under my breath. Stephan was out there flirting. I just knew it. A pit in my stomach grew and I recognized that emotion. Hells bells I was jealous, but I'd be damned before I let either one of them know. I would take my massive crush on Stephan to the grave.

It took me at least five minutes to get everything out of my hair, and then I pulled the long mess into a bun, so hopefully I wouldn't have a repeat on the way back down the goat trail. As I walked out, I realized two things. A bargain had been made, my fae blood sensed magic in the air and Athela looked more than pleased with herself. She was clapping her hands and smiling while she promised Stephan he would have no regrets.

"And what would you like the spell placed in?" Athela purred.

Stephan took out an emerald bracelet and laid it on the small, round table. "This."

She picked up the bracelet and let it slide from one hand to the other. "I have all the ingredients here that are required for your spell, but it will take me the better part of an hour to transfer it to this. Go outside and let me work, and when you return, not only will I have your charm, but I will also have a blood contract waiting to be signed by you."

Stephan nodded, pushing back his chair from the table. "Come, Tandi. We will go see what nature awaits us."

Athela smirked and I scowled. I bet she didn't need us to wait outside, the heifer. Letting my voice tremble a little, I said, "As long as you promise to protect me, Stephan."

Her smirk dropped. Mission accomplished. He held the door open for me and gave me a knowing look, which I returned with a saucy grin. Neither one of us talked

while we walked on a different trail leading to a pond behind the house.

He sat on the bank, and I plopped down next to him, waiting for him to speak first. After all, patience was a virtue. Thirty minutes later, I had made a necklace out of grass and wildflowers, and my patience had long run out. Stephan must have picked up on my distress because he laughed.

"I think that is the longest that you have ever remained quiet." At my scowl, he said, "I love it here."

"Well, it looks like you're very familiar with the place."

"Jealous?"

"Of Athela?" I was for sure bothered by their closeness, but this was me taking it to the grave. "Um, no. I mean, obviously y'all have a history, and she's a little mean-spirited when she thinks she needs to be territorial, but the woman saved me from killer ants, so I'm good."

"Hmm. You do realize I can pick up on your emotions as well? It's not a one-way street."

Still not admitting to anything, I said, "I don't mind if you pick up on my emotions because there is nothing for me to be embarrassed about."

"I'm glad you like her because we might be getting married."

Gravy and cornbread. "Come again?"

"I needed her to make a bracelet for you. A special one that will allow you to communicate with Gallen anytime you want, but will align the time to the same time here on earth. It's heavy magic that she will be dealing with, and even if it weren't, she would still want something in return."

"But marriage?" I squealed. "I would never ask you to sacrifice yourself just so that I can visit my Pops in another realm. There has to be another way. Go tell her never mind."

Why would he do this? This made no sense whatsoever.

"I have a plan, little one."

"One that you probably won't share. What is with this contract?"

"I'm assuming that she will have me sign something similar to a vampire contract. Even though she is not a vampire and can't do the normal ritual that vampires would do, I'm sure the contract will be identical." He plucked a piece of grass and started twining it around his finger. "Most vampires go into a contract that is good for a hundred years. Anything less than a century creates chaos, especially for masters and the lines they have created. At the end of the century, they can either go their own separate ways or choose to renew their vows. The only other way out of the contract besides death is a magical exorcism if you will, and it isn't pretty."

"Well, that is freaking intense. So, this is how people in the vampire community get hitched, huh?"

"Not necessarily. There is the rare occasion that vampires find their mates. The one soul that aligns perfectly with theirs, but that is so rare—or maybe it is more accurate to say that vampires get tired of waiting for centuries for 'the proverbial one'—that they just find the one that is most compatible. Like I said, finding one's true mate is rare."

"Color me confused, but what is your plan to get out of this?"

"She's given me a month before we are to wed. By then you will know if the charm works. Sometime in the upcoming weeks, I will come back and make her forget we were ever here to begin with. If she doesn't remember anything, then she will never enforce the contract."

"You can do that? Make people forget certain memories?"

"It's something that I don't make a habit of, but yes, I can. I want to erase this whole visit from her memory, so she forgets about you, too."

"Stephan, why are we doing all of this just so that I can visit my grandfather?"

"I'm not doing it so you can have social time, Tandi. We will soon be in Akeldama's territory where she takes absolute joy in others' pain. Right now, you are a weakness with your three different counterparts, but if we knew how to make them work together, then I believe you would be unstoppable. I need you to be unstoppable. Gallen will help you. I have questions that I need you to ask him, but you cannot be gone for two months this time. If you miss Akeldama's daughter's wedding, she will consider it treason."

"You are having this charm made for me, so I can visit him and ask your questions?"

"These questions are about you, Tandi, and the answers might save your life."

"Stephan, why is my life in danger?"

"Because you are mine, and Akeldama has a way of destroying everything that belongs to me."

I was assuming that by him saying "mine" that meant he was my master vampire, and technically I did belong to him according to vampire laws. But before I could ask any more questions, he stood up and dusted his slacks off and offered me a hand up.

"Let's go back to the cottage. I'm sure the spell is complete by now."

I refused to let go of his hand, and he raised an eyebrow in question. "You won't really have to marry her, will you?"

"No." He chuckled. "Have you not realized by now that I am a scheming, manipulating, lying S.O.B.? But she doesn't need to know that I've already found a way out of her bloody contract."

"Why is she forcing you into marriage? None of this makes sense."

"Is it so hard to believe that someone wants to marry me, little one?"

I rolled my eyes. "For the love of Pete. Can you just answer the question?"

"That is a complicated question. The short version is I'm the Prince of Vampires. The first made, and if it wasn't for Akeldama, I could rule the vampire nation. I have no interest in ruling, but Athela doesn't know that. Akeldama's crown protects her by weakening other vampires' powers. As soon as I get within five feet of her, it's like I'm a newborn babe. Most everyone has heard of the crown, including the witch population—"

"I'd like a detailed explanation," I huffed.

"Don't get testy. I'm trying to explain now." I made a go-ahead motion with my free hand. "Athela believes she will eventually find a charm to nullify the power of the crown. Since I'm the only one powerful enough to take down the queen, Athela needs me to do the dirty work. I would be ruling all vampires with a wife who was a witch ruling the vampire nation beside me."

"So basically, she's not wanting to marry you for your good looks, but because she wants the fame, power, and glory."

Both dimples showed as his head tilted towards mine. "I'm sure the good looks didn't hurt the cause."

Dang he was hot. Especially when he looked at me that way. Like I was a rare jewel meant to be appraised.

I cleared my throat. "I think this is a horrible idea. Mark my words, this will come back to bite us in the butt. Not to mention the fact that it just seems wrong to erase her memories."

He raised my chin to make eye contact with me. "I can promise you that erasing her memories of us being here will not hurt her. I can also promise you that having Athela as Queen of the Vampires would almost be as bad as Akeldama."

His head started to dip towards mine, and my eyes widened at his intent. With his free hand he stroked the side of my face ever so gently. He was going to kiss me and all I could do was stare at his lips with anticipation. Right before his lips met mine, a black raven swooped over our heads, letting out a shrill sound. I stumbled back, jerking my hand from Stephan's. While I rubbed the goosebumps on my skin, Stephan studied the beady-eyed bird as if it was a person.

He mind spoke to me. "Let's head back so we can get the charm and get out of here. Then after the wedding on our way back home, I'll stop in and pay Athela a visit."

Just another reminder of how conniving Stephan could be if he wanted something. The fact that he was doing all of this to supposedly help me still didn't make me feel any better. All his secrets were going to be the death of me. There had to be something in it for him, and did that mean that he'd eventually betray me too?

chapter fourteen

After an hour of watching Athela drape herself all over Stephan while giving me the stank eye, I was more than ready to tackle the goat trail back to the car. Bring on the ants as long as I didn't have to hear one more stinking giggle, and no one batted their eyelashes that rapidly unless they had a gnat in their eye. Right before we left, she asked Stephan why his and my auras matched. I didn't know what the heck that meant, but I quickly realized Stephan did as I felt his emotions hit me. It wasn't necessarily fear but close, so I was naming this emotion dread.

He did a wonderful job of acting like he had no clue why our auras matched, but I could tell that Athela wasn't convinced. I badgered him until I was blue in the face, but he insisted our matching auras meant nothing. After that Athela had a different glint in her eye for the remainder of our visit. I was more than ready when Stephan said our goodbyes.

We had finally made it back to the car with my new charm. Supposedly as long as I was wearing it, I could visit my pops anytime without everyone putting out a missing vampire bulletin. I wasn't going to worry about Stephan and the blood contract he'd signed. He was a big boy, and if he said he could get out of it, then I had to believe him. And if he couldn't break the agreement, maybe he would let me be a part of the wedding. That would piss Athela off and possibly break my heart. I wasn't ready to deal with the whys as of yet, so I just pushed that thought to the back of my mind.

We were staying at some fancy hotel, and yet Stephan wouldn't get us separate rooms. He said since we were but a short drive to the Queen's mansion, he would feel better knowing that I was close. He gave me dibs on the first shower while he brought in our bags, and now I was currently watching Judge Judy and her condemning ways while he was showering.

At some point, I heard Stephan come out of the bathroom, and I briefly quit feeling sorry for myself when I saw him with his towel hung low on his hips. Beads of water still coated his beautiful skin. He had an eight pack that would make most MMA fighters jealous. Why he would cover that up with a shirt on a daily basis was beyond me. It should be illegal to hide that. The trance was broken as he grabbed his bag and returned to the bathroom, which was just as well. It was hard to have a pity party when you're feeling thankful that there was a man who looked like Stephan in the same room as you. Plus, it would be super embarrassing if he picked up on the emotions sliding off me.

"You going to get dressed?"

I muted the TV. "Why? Aren't we in for the night?"

He was tying his boots, and boy did he look good in a pair of jeans. The suits and slacks were hot in a powerful kind of way but the jeans… man oh, man. His brown eyes smiled at me. "If you want to spend your birthday in front of the TV with a borrowed hotel robe on and your hair wrapped in a towel, be my guest, but I thought we could go bowling and then to a movie."

He remembered my birthday! My inner child squealed with delight. He was watching me so intently that I had to play it cool.

"Bowling? Did you just ask me to wear someone else's shoes?"

"Come on, birthday girl, live a little."

I didn't consider getting athletes foot living a little, but it sure beat sitting here, wallowing in my own misery. I can't believe he remembered my birthday. I could no longer contain my grin. "Give me five minutes to get dressed."

"One more thing," he said. "I got you something." He pulled out a golden necklace from his suitcase. I was shocked.

As he handed it to me, I asked, "Is this really for me?"

"Whom else would it be for?"

I touched the engraved heart on the front before I put it on. It was so beautiful and thoughtful. Giving him a smile, I said, "First a cuff, then the charmed bracelet, and now a necklace. You better be careful, or a girl might think you like her."

His dimples winked at me. "Oh, Tandi, I thought we'd already established that." He pointed to the necklace I'd just draped over my neck. "Be careful with that. It was my mother's. My father gave it to her a long time ago."

I started to pull it off. "I can't accept this then."

His hands reached out to stop me. "Yes, you can. My mother would have wanted you to have it. You are a very special lady, just like she was." He gave me a long look before saying, "Go get ready. I'll be here waiting for you."

I couldn't help but think that was a double entendre. The hungry look in his eyes was making my heart beat so fast. It took everything I had to walk past him towards the bathroom. Before I closed the door, I asked, "Stephan, why are our auras the same color? Athela acted as if that wasn't normal."

He gave a small shrug. "I have my theories, but they might ruin the night. Let's not talk of manipulative witches and auras on your birthday. Deal?"

I felt myself nodding, but it almost killed me to not press the issue. As I shut the door, I reminded myself that tomorrow was another day, and my questions could wait until then. Right now, a handsome man was waiting on me, so he could celebrate my birthday with me.

The night was a blast, even the sucky movie we watched about astronauts. The whole night I got to see a different side to Stephan, one less stoic and more animated. He laughed and made jokes and went out of his way to make me feel special. Every time I felt the cold of the necklace on my skin, I smiled. The ruby cuff gleaming on my arm was beautiful and practical, like the bracelet, it would be handy to have. But the necklace... I didn't need it, but I sure wanted it. He gave me something of sentimental value. It was becoming harder and harder not to fall in love with this cranky vampire. After we had returned to the hotel, and I had exchanged my pair of jeans for a cute kitten pajama set that was sure to keep me a spinster for the rest of my life, Stephan sat down on his bed, facing mine.

"Tandi, will you visit Gallen for me tonight?"

I played with the bracelet on my wrist, biting my lip with worry. "What exactly is it you want me to ask him?"

"This is all just theory, but I think that maybe the poison you carry in your blood from your ghoul counterpart is overwhelming your vampire and fae counterparts. It's possible that you might need something more substantial than human or animal blood because your vampire powers aren't growing. You might need to drink vampire blood instead."

"Oh, that's just freaking great. Now, I'm a cannibal."

"Don't think of it like that. Blood is blood." He got up from his bed and crouched in front of me. "Will you ask him, Tandi?"

"Yes," I said. "Is there anything else you want me to ask?"

He started to say something but then stopped himself. "No, in fact, I don't want you to stay very long, just in case the charm doesn't work as we hoped."

He handed me a watch. "Keep this on you. I've made sure that our watches are synchronized. That way when you get back, we will know if the charm worked. Don't stay more than two minutes, okay?"

If the charm didn't work, that would still mean I would be gone for several hours, which would be problematic, since we were supposed to be in attendance for some vampire brat's wedding. "I'll keep it short." I took off my cuff and necklace and laid them both on the end table. I didn't know how this whole traveling thing worked, but I didn't want to lose them.

"Don't ask about anything other than what kind of blood you should consume."

"Got it. Pop in and ask the one question and then skedaddle." I would have added, "Easy peasy lemon squeezy," but I thought that might be overkill. I waited for him to leave the room, but when he gave me a carry-on motion with his hand, I lay back on the bed and closed my eyes. I said the magic word "Teia" out loud and then bam, I was no longer breathing in the sexy scent that Stephan always eluded, but instead I got a whiff of grease.

First thing I noticed was the gigantic margarita blender in the middle of the restaurant, and my pops sitting at a nearby table. Who would of thought Pops was a Jimmy Buffet fan?

I hugged him because it seemed the natural thing to do. I liked the man, even if he always seemed to be sporting a weird Hawaiian shirt. This one was pale blue with giant marlins all over it. Hideous, but my cute romper made up for his lack of fashion. Our family tree wasn't totally failing.

"Hey, Pops."

He pulled my chair out for me. "I assume your vamp knows you're here this time?"

I nodded. "And I can only stay for a couple of minutes, so I have to ask you my questions quickly."

He stroked his silvery beard, and in a Southern accent that was endearing, even if it was fake, he said, "Shoot."

"Is it possible that I need vampire blood to become a stronger vampire?"

He thought for a second. "Tandi, keep in mind that you have to balance all three. Your fae side, once at full potential, might be too much for your body to handle. There is a balance that you must find if you want to survive, but yes, occasionally drinking the blood of a vampire will make you stronger, but more importantly, draining some of the ghoul blood you are carrying is more imperative at this point. Once every week or so should do the trick. The ghoul blood is also limiting your fae abilities."

"My blood is poisonous, though."

"Is it?" He gave me a small smile. "Regardless, I'm saying that you should release a little blood once a week.

What. The. Heck. I only had a small window of opportunity here, and he was wasting it with his riddles. "Okay. Moving on. My friend recently died and—"

Pops interrupted me. "I know, and I am very sorry for your loss. Over the years, I've had to watch most everyone I love perish, and I know from experience that any loss leaves a void, but I cannot tell you who killed your friend."

"Why the heck not?"

"Let's just say I share a mutual friend with your vampire, and she has asked that I not indulge in sharing about that."

Ariana. I was really starting to hate this woman. "Yeah, because it will set me off on a different path and yadda, yadda, yadda. So, about this key... same thing?"

He smiled. "Afraid so."

"My allotted two minutes is up, so I have to go, but I'll check back in with you soon."

"Please do. Your charm works, but I assume your vamp wants to know that for himself."

I'd decided to not argue with him about the whole your vamp thing, but one day we were going to have a lengthy discussion where I laid it out for him plain and simple. I got up from the round table and gave him one more hug. His beard lightly scratched my cheek.

"See you soon, Pops."

Before I could say the word to take me back to the hotel, he said, "Oh, and Tandi, tell your vamp I said the sooner he drains a good portion of your ghoul blood, the better chance you have of surviving the next forty-eight hours. Ghouls are lazy creatures unless they have incentive, and you need some vampire strength for what is to come." He winked at me. "When Ariana foresaw you coming to me, she did agree I could tell you that much."

Stephan was pacing when I returned. "I thought I told you two minutes it's been ten." I rolled my eyes because I had a feeling he was exaggerating. "And where is the watch I gave you?"

"Apparently, I don't get to keep anything that I go in there with including your watch and my clothes." Shaking my wrist, I said, "The bracelet excluded, of course. Thank goodness I took off my other jewelry."

"They just dissolve?"

"Yeah, I mean, I'm sure there is some lengthy scientific explanation as to what happens, but honestly I don't care about the means just the end. And the end result is I lost my favorite kitten pajamas, but in return I got this kick-ass romper from last month's Vogue issue. I must not have been gone too long because you haven't gone off the deep end like ol' Jack from The Shining, so that's a plus."

"Thank the heavens you lost those hideous pajamas. Now, if we could discuss more important things other than your love of movies."

"Whoa, dude, chill. I love movies with insane people. It boosts my self-confidence." I was interested in seeing how much I could push his buttons before he lost it. For no other purpose than to gauge his willpower. If I were a betting woman, I would say within the next minute, he was going to blow.

Jaw clenched as if he wanted to throttle me, he said, "Tandi! I need you to focus. Now."

Yep, less than a minute. I so needed to go to the casino.

"Since you asked oh-so-politely, Pops said that you are correct in assuming that vampire blood, instead of human or animal, will give me bursts of strength, but what I really need is to drain some of my contaminated blood in order to help my fae side along with my vampire side."

Lost in thought, he resumed pacing. "Interesting."

"When I think of having my blood drawn from my body, I can think of a lot of words, but I can assure you that 'interesting' didn't make the list." I took my long hair down from a ponytail and started finger combing the mess. "Oh, and he couldn't give me any info on who was behind the death of Greta or where the key is."

That got him to stop pacing. "I told you to go and ask one question and come right back."

"Yeah, well, apparently I didn't have my listening ears on."

He was pinching the bridge of his nose as if he was in pain. "If you wouldn't mind, let's go into the bathroom before I cut one of your veins. I don't want to get blood all over the carpet. That would be hard to explain to the housekeeper."

I wanted to pitch a fit and tell him that he was out of his ever-loving mind. There would be no bloodletting going on today, but that would be me just stopping the inevitable. This might be my only chance to become more powerful. Whether it was my fae or vampire part that would shine through, I wasn't sure, but if I were going to be camping with the enemy for the next day or so, I would take what I could get.

After nodding, I went to the bathroom and held my arm over the sink. I didn't want a drop of blood to get on my romper. If Pops knew how much I loved clothes, he wouldn't have had to ask me twice to come back and visit him.

"Okay. I'm ready. Just don't get any on you."

He stood beside me holding a small knife. "It wouldn't kill me unless I ingested it."

"Let the bloodletting commence," I said.

His light brown eyes met mine. "It'll hurt just for a second."

After a sharp sting, I closed my eyes. I was getting dizzy and didn't think viewing my blood running down the drain would help the nauseated feeling I had. I was a sorry excuse for a vampire, but really there was no need for a visual. He re-opened the vein multiple times due to my fast healing. Several minutes had passed before he announced we were done. If anyone had told me a year ago that I would be in a fancy hotel bathroom letting a hot man drain some of my blood, I would have told them to lay off the moonshine. Stephan picked me up in his arms, and my head rolled onto his shoulder as he cooed something to me. I had a hard time believing that this was my life. Oh, how the mighty had fallen.

"Little one, I'm going to lay you here on the bed. Rest for a minute."

A burst of energy went through me, making me sit straight up. My arms outstretched and I smiled. "I feel amazing."

Stephan threw a couple of bags of blood towards the bed, and without opening my eyes, I caught both. "You need to refuel before daylight hits."

"I thought I needed vampire blood?"

"It would be better, but I can't give you any so human it is."

"Not that I'm asking you to open a vein for me, but I am curious as to why you can't?"

"It's complicated." His mood had changed, and he became less easy going and more stoic, but since I was ravenous, I didn't give a fig. After my belly was full, I snuggled under the covers getting more tired as I felt the sun starting to rise.

"Stephan, this has been the best birthday ever, even if I did keep rolling the bowling ball into everyone's lane but ours. Thank you."

I was too tired to be shocked when he crawled on top of the covers and lay behind me. I had never been this close to a man in my life, and instead of being excited, I just wanted to sleep.

"I'm glad you had a good birthday. You deserve it." He threw his arm over me and pulled me up against his chest, and I went to sleep with a smile on my face. Best. Birthday. Ever.

chapter fifteen

As soon as the sun fell, we were on the road headed to the queen's residence, and I was feeling better than ever. Well, that was until Stephan spoke.

"Tandi, I have a feeling I know who sent those rogue vampires and why. I'm going to trust you with this information, but you have to promise me that you won't act until the time is right. Can you do that?"

Yes. Maybe. No. "Sure."

"I can tell when you're lying. Give me your promise, or I will continue to leave you in the dark."

After weighing my options, I said, "I promise that I will wait until the time is right before staking whoever was behind Greta's death."

"I think the vampires were after you because word had traveled that I was getting you a cuff. Usually, vampires live centuries before their sire gives them one. It's to ensure that something so priceless isn't wasted on weak vampires that won't last a year in their new conditions."

I pointed to my forehead. "Do you know why I'm squinting? Because you're not making sense. Try to break it down for me."

"Akeldama has always been a very jealous ruler. She must have caught wind of me acquiring your cuff, and assumed that there were tender feelings on my part to get a newly turned vampire something so invaluable."

My blood boiled. My friend died because I was gifted with a cuff. I would kill the Queen. "So she wanted me dead. But I didn't die. Greta did because of her jealousy."

"Don't make me regret telling you this. We will get her, but you have to be patient."

I felt tears rolling down my face. "Promise me that she will pay for this."

"I swear it to you." He reached over the console and held my hand the rest of the way to my number one enemy's territory.

The first person to greet us was Dakin, with a charming smile for me and pure resentment for Stephan.

"Welcome, Gem." Dakin's smile dropped from his handsome face as he greeted the man beside me. "Stephan, wish I could say the same."

There was a history there, one that I wanted to delve into, but not while under the scrutiny of Akeldama. That woman was ostentatious. I took a great amount of pleasure that her mansion was ugly with its dark gray stonework, massive pillars, and upper balconies strategically placed along the front side. Her mansion didn't resemble any of the plantation style homes in South Georgia due to its almost gothic exterior, and since it was almost the size of a hotel, it was just plain tacky.

"I can assure you I want to be here as much as you want me to be here. Show us to our rooms like a good little servant, so we can freshen up before the big event," Stephan said.

"You really pushed it to the last second, didn't you? I thought you were going to defy her order and not show up. Not that it wouldn't have been entertaining as to what she would have done to you, but I didn't want Gem here to be tortured as well, just because of her unfortunate association with you."

Ugh. I had enough of this egotistical crap. "But we are here," I said. "And you are right about us cutting it close, so we need to stop flapping our jaws and get this show on the road. I'm assuming that we have rooms?" At his nod, I added, "Great. Mind showing them to us, so we can get changed for the big event?"

Stephan chuckled. "Blunt as always."

Dakin offered me his arm. "Forgive me, my lady. Right this way."

We followed him up five damn flights of stairs… with luggage. Wasn't I supposed to have some sort of super strength? I was too busy hating my life to be weirded out by the architecture of the house.

"Why would anyone have this many steps in their home and no elevator?" I asked Dakin on the last landing.

"Oh, there is an elevator in the south wing of the house, but this way you get to admire the many paintings and tapestries that most museums would kill for."

The. Hell. He. Says. I didn't notice one work of art because I was too busy saying my ABC's backward to try and keep my mind off the pain in my thighs. The purebred vampires didn't seem to be having any issues. Good for them. Dakin pointed out another piece of art to me. I mentally congratulated myself for not rolling my eyes. If I wanted to see paintings, I would go to a gallery, not climb five levels of hell. Now that I knew that ghouls were known for their laziness, I could blame my hate for anything athletic to my genetic make-up. It wasn't my fault I was reborn this way.

We finally came to a heavy wooden door that looked like it was made for a giant.

"This is your room, Gem, and Stephan, you will be in your old bedroom. The one on the east side down the corridor, the last one on the left."

Stephan all but growled. "Afraid not. I'll be taking the one next to Tandi."

"Sorry, old friend, but I was instructed to give you the one next to Akeldama's."

"I'll handle Akeldama."

"As you wish." Dakin turned to me and bowed his head. "If you should need anything, please let me know, for I am at your service."

Stephan followed me into my room and immediately started to check it out. I wasn't quite sure what he was looking for, but he seemed to be satisfied when he came up empty-handed.

"There are spies that we can't see all over this estate. Only state what you wish others to hear." Without notice, his voice entered my mind. "Tell absolutely no one that you carry fae or ghoul blood. It could mean your death. And try to stay away from Akeldama. As soon the wedding is over, we leave with or without answers. I will come back here later to find the key, and find a way to get Akeldama to take off her crown long enough to avenge Greta's death when I know that you won't be collateral damage."

My fingers massaged my temples, and I whispered, "I hate it when you do that. And just for the record, I do not like something that is so invasive, so keep that mumbo-jumbo to a minimum."

"Just remember that this 'mumbo jumbo' is something that most vampires can't do. Something that I have kept hidden from most, so keep a lid on that as well."

"Sure," I whispered. "As long as you quit doing it."

He eliminated the space between us in one stride and grabbed my upper arms, pulling me to him. "I need you to know how serious this is. You are on Akeldama's radar. Keep your head down and do nothing. I can fight her but not here. Let's not worry about anything other than surviving. Understand?"

He didn't want me asking about the key or Greta's murder. That I understood. Didn't mean if the opportunity should fall into my lap, I wouldn't seize it but I heard him. However, there was something that I didn't understand.

"Why am I on her radar?" I whispered.

He briefly laid his forehead on mine, something that he was prone to do, and I had to admit I was getting used to it. It made me feel like we were… connected. "You just are. Please, Tandi, don't fight me on this one. I wanted to use the last two months to prepare you but now…"

"Okay. I get it." At least he wasn't doing that mental thing anymore. That made my skin crawl.

At my agreement, he let me go and gave me a sexy smile that made me let out a little sigh and dang if he didn't hear that. In high school when you had a small crush on a guy, you could fake it and act all nonchalant, but that was when I had been dealing with humans. Dang vamps.

"I'll be next door if you should need me."

I put my luggage on the bed and nodded. This was me being nonchalant. Just because Stephan was the sexiest man I had ever laid eyes upon, it didn't give me the right to fall for him. Well, maybe it did. After hearing the door shut, I sat on my bed, taking in my surroundings. The stonework continued on the inside of the bedroom, which was in hues of blue and gold. There was no canopy, thank goodness, but the room still screamed old world.

All of a sudden, I felt like someone was knocking on my soul. I used to not believe in cosmic awareness, but that was when I didn't believe in supernaturals, either. Now, I wouldn't be surprised if the clown from It was real. I shuddered at the thought. I loathed freaking clowns.

Closing my eyes, I took in several deep breaths, and that was when I heard the sobs. Someone was crying, and she was begging for help. I had to find her. I felt the tug again. One minute I was on my bed wondering if what I packed for the wedding was fancy enough, and the next I was standing in front of a girl that was in a white beaded gown crying on the cold stones of the floor. We were currently in what looked to be a tower. There was no furniture, and she was the most pitiful thing I'd ever seen.

"Um…"

She jerked up from her crouch and hissed. Even with the smeared mascara, she was stunningly beautiful. Long, auburn hair down fell to her waist, and slightly tilted green eyes shone bright against her porcelain skin.

"Who are you?" she snarled.

"I'm Tandi. And you are?"

She gave a breathless laugh. "Oh, like you don't know. And how did you get up here?"

"Obviously, I wouldn't have asked who you are if I already knew. That kind of seems redundant and honest to God, I have no clue how I got up here in the…"

She wiped at the smudge under her eyes. "Tower. My mother has locked me in a freaking tower. She has taken every precaution known to man to make sure that I cannot escape the wedding tonight."

"Oh, so you are the Princess?"

"Tamara. And it depends on whom you ask. Considering that my mother beheaded my father, I am now actually a Queen over the Zombies and Princess of the Vampires. My father loved her and she loved power. She thought he would use his power to give her soldiers, and instead he tried to make her something she is not. Loveable."

I didn't know exactly what to say to that because I wasn't a therapist, so I went with a safer topic or so I assumed. "You were the first girl that Akeldama turned?"

"Ha! I wish I could say that. Wouldn't that be awesome? Did you know there is a three percent chance that a vampire can get pregnant after you've been turned? That is how unlucky I am. But most vampires already know that I carry her genetics, so you must be brand spanking new." Her tears had stop flowing, and I could see that there was a warrior hidden beneath the beauty. After she was through inspecting me, she asked, "If you are not here to spy on me, then why are you here?"

I had actually heard about this girl from my best friend Charlie's brother. The last time I heard Wes was out searching for her but something told me to keep that information to myself.

"I wish I knew. Would you believe me if I told you that I heard you crying and one minute I was on my bed and the next I was in front of you?"

She gave me a saucy look. "No, I wouldn't. That's fae magic, and you are clearly a vamp."

I had somehow traveled to her. I checked for my necklace under my clothes and was relieved to feel it under my fingertips.

I shrugged. "Well, then I have no explanation. Since you seem to have yourself under control, I'll just mosey on back to my room and get ready for your big moment."

She laughed. "I would like to see you try. Unless you were escorted in here with about ten guards under the authority of my mother, then you just being in here is treasonous. Even if you get past the guards in the hall, you won't get past the mass that are stationed in the hall. She will kill you before my first sip of champagne tonight."

Crap on a cracker. "What do you propose, Tamara? With that gleam in your eye, I am guessing you already have a plan of action."

"Of course, I do. I need to escape because my evil mother is going to use me as a tool to destroy the world. She is forcing me to marry that vile man, so she can appease her greed and get a second key to the portals, and my fiancé is more than happy with the trade because he believes that I'm worth more than the key. He's delusional if he thinks he can force me to raise the dead for him, so he can have his own army. Which would be just as destructive as the keys, in my opinion. I am the only one of my kind, part vampire and part zombie, and they mean to use me for their gain. No, thank you."

I studied her for a second. "You don't look like any zombie I've ever seen on T.V., or am I confused?"

One dainty shoulder lifted. "I might not be a zombie in the sense that I have risen from the grave, but in the sense that I have the authority to make the dead rise. They listen to my call, and no matter what shape they were in when they were laid in their grave, they rise to my command. Put me in a graveyard, and I could have an instant army. That's how my mother and Cecil, my fiancé, plan on using me."

"Okay, so you currently have mama issues, you might have some P.T.S.D. from witnessing mommy dearest go all black widow on your father, and you're in a loveless engagement, but I somehow missed the plan."

"Listen, Barbie, the moment you somehow magicked yourself in here without a way to magic yourself out was the moment that you signed your own death. So, we will fight our way out of here. We take down as many as we can and make sure that when they take us, they don't take us alive. We will go out with a bang. Make a statement."

"Yeah, so I love making statements but not suicidal ones. What's option B?"

"What witch did you use to get you in here, and was she trying to spy on me? Maybe you could call upon her and she could—"

"I can't call upon someone that doesn't exist."

She tossed her long red hair behind her. "You and I both know you didn't just abracadabra yourself in here."

"I have an idea."

"Do tell."

"What would you give me if I could 'abracadabra' you out of here?"

Suspicion was written all over her face. "What do you want?"

"My friend recently died. Her name was Greta. Your mother was responsible for her death."

"Oh, and you want retaliation?" I waited to see if she mentioned the crown. If she did, I knew that I could trust her and if not, then I was up the creek without a stake. "My mother feared that someone with enough power would try to dethrone her, so she had a supreme witch make her the crown that sits upon her head. Every single one of us grows weak when we are near her. I'm sorry, but you can't harm her unless you can figure out a way to get her out of that crown, and it's rumored that she showers and pleases her lovers with it on."

What Tamara didn't know was that I wasn't all vampire, and it was possible that being around Akeldama wouldn't weaken me—or at least not all of me.

"Thank you for the scoop. You said earlier 'second key.' What about the first key? Do you know where it's located?"

"Of course, I do. My mother lords it over my fiancé. Please tell me you have been listening. As soon as I marry that creepy Cecil, they are going to band together to make an unstoppable army. I would rather die."

"Yeah, I'm not really digging how quickly you are willing to throw your life down the toilet. I think I have a way to get you out of here, just tell me where she keeps the key. Is it in a safe? And if so, I'm going to need the number."

"Oh, you're funny. You think my mother needs a safe? She keeps it out in the open. Who is strong enough to take it from her? You want to see the key? I'm sure that she'll have it where everyone can view it tonight, but you won't be leaving here with it."

We would just have to see about that.

"Once Mother opens the portal, she can't pick and choose which degenerates she allows to come over here to earth. Whoever happens to be waiting next to the door is the one or ones who are allowed over. My mother is confident enough that if a reckless degenerate came over, she believes she could control or annihilate them before they do too much damage. Cecil doesn't have as much faith in his abilities. Another way he will use me. He will have me call up an army if the degenerates get out of line."

"Well, we can't have that now can we? Come hold my hands, and let me see if I can hocus pocus you to somewhere else."

She looked at me with skepticism. "Why would you help me? I haven't given you anything that you have asked for, and if they find out that you tried to help me, they will skin you alive."

I shrugged. "Sometimes us girls just have to stick together. You are obviously in need of a friend but not only that. If you do get married, your mother would have her hands on two keys, and that means she could open more portals and do more damage. That doesn't seem great for us here on earth, so why wouldn't I help you escape?"

Tamara still wasn't sure of me. The expression on her face told me she thought I was either on crack or was somehow going to betray her, but nonetheless she came over to me begrudgingly and extended her hands. "This better not be a waste of time, Barbie."

"Hmm. Remember if this works, you will owe me a huge ass kissing."

Holding on tightly to her hands, I said the magic word in my head to take me to Pops. I felt her trying to jerk away, but I refused to let her go. Within seconds we were at my destination. Tamara was beside me, whimpering.

"Are you all right?" I asked.

At her nod, I took a moment to orient myself before I dragged her behind me as we crossed the bustling street towards my grandfather.

He shook his head at me in the way of greeting. "New York? Really? I hate this place with its smelly sidewalks and rude people." He tilted his head in acknowledgment to Tamara. "And who is this?"

"Pops, this is—"

"I'm just a friend. A friend who will be forever grateful. I must go—"

160

"Wait for a second, child," Pops said. He laid a hand on her forehead, and her body immediately stopped trembling. "One that doesn't carry fae blood in their body should not travel the fae lines. It contorts the bones. I will heal you this time, but think twice before jumping into lines that are meant for fae."

She was in too much pain to fully register what he was saying, which made me feel like the backside of a donkey.

I watched while he healed her, and then I apologized profusely. "I didn't know that—"

She gave me a bright smile. "Please don't regret taking me. What other choice did we have? We would both be dead by now if you hadn't risked it. Besides, your grandfather here has fixed me good as new. My fae friend."

My eyes widened. "You can't tell anyone about that."

"Not a soul. You have my word." She glanced around. "I want to get off these streets for a while and then lay low for a bit. Maybe you can tell me how it is a vampire as yourself has fae blood as well."

I shook my head. "I can't and even if I wanted to, I have to get back."

"Get back?" she screeched, causing several tourists to give us a wide berth.

"If I don't go back, Stephan will be the one that takes the fall for it, and I can't let that happen. I can poof myself back to my room. Or at least, I'm hoping I can."

"But… but—"

"Listen, any girl that refuses to be part of an evil plan is fantastic in my book. Me and you will have plenty of time, Lord willing, to gossip on a beach in the future, but right now I have to get back. My other friend needs me."

Pops, who was leaning on the side of a building, straightened up. "How about I call you Roxane? With all that red hair, you look like a Roxane." Without waiting for Tamara's permission, he said, "Tandi will be fine. If she finds herself in trouble, she can always escape using the fae line. How about you say goodbye, and this old man will buy us a hotdog. I know you can't eat it, but you can still smell it and pretend. I might not like this place, but they do have great hotdogs. And maybe while I'm eating, you can tell me what it is that you are running from and in return, I can think of a way to help you stay hidden."

"That would be great, sir." Her eyes welled up with unshed tears, and then she shocked me by giving me a soul-crushing hug. "Thank you so much. You have just changed the future."

That was what I was afraid of but instead of commenting, I hugged her back. I took a step away from her and walked into an alley smelling faintly of urine. Closing my eyes, I pictured myself in a form-fitting black lace gown. The same exact one that a famous actress had worn on the red carpet. At least there was an upside of kidnapping the princess. When I returned, I would be donning the best-looking gown in that place. Oh, crap, my necklace. I glanced down and realized I still had the cuff and the necklace. That made no sense.

"It's because they mean something to you." Pops smiled. "You can control what you lose in the fae lines."

Tamara and Pops had followed me into the alley, and she gave me a once-over. "Now, that is a trick I would love to have."

Pops grinned. "You think that she came here to save your life, but really the girl loves fashion."

"So true." I laughed. "See ya later, um...Roxane."

"Wait!" She grabbed my hand, and her beautiful face scrunched up. "Tandi, Akeldama wants to open up the portals, so she can let the most evil of beings come through. With her wielding the power, she can rule all of earth. She is not going to let some teenager stop her by taking the key. You must be smart and please be careful."

I gave her hand a squeeze. "I'll do my best."

"See you soon, friend."

"Pops, take good care of her, and I'll come back to visit soon." I gave him a quick hug and said my magic word, concentrating on the room that I prayed I returned to.

I laughed when I opened my eyes to see that not only was I in my appointed room, but no one was ringing the alarm bells. If the estate wasn't in a panic yet, then no one knew the princess was missing, which meant that I was going to be fine. I would put on my make-up and my dancing shoes and be absolutely surprised as everyone else when the wedding was canceled. Maybe with everyone running around, I would have a chance to take that key. I just stole a princess, who was to say that I couldn't steal a key?

*A*n hour later, Stephan had come to escort me to the ballroom. He had made a couple of inquiries on my attire. He couldn't figure out where I got something so exquisite without visiting my grandfather. Since Stephan had this uncanny ability to know when I was lying, I just shrugged and said, "I really can't remember." And that was the God's honest truth. I couldn't remember which alley it was, or what street I had poofed us to. I know it was somewhere near Macy's, because someone had passed us on the street talking loudly on their phone about the excellent deals they just bought at the store, but the exact location was a mystery even to me, and because my prevarication was wrapped in truth, he seemed to buy that I didn't remember where I picked up the beautiful dress.

"Well, you look stunningly beautiful."

His eyes traveled the length of me and there was such a hunger in his gaze. Finally he cleared his throat as he stepped up beside me to escort me. He was still staring at me as I hooked my arm through his and dipped my head shyly as I walked beside him. On the way to the throne room, Stephan commanded me again to lay my revengeful plot of killing the Queen to the side.

His words sternly entered my mind. "Remember that we have to wait until the time is right. If you lose your temper or act hastily, then everything we've done this far will be for naught."

I gave him a curt nod, as we finally reached the throne room.

Akeldama's estate was probably the second or third largest in America. It had to be a hundred thousand square feet, with at least thirty of that being different rooms for hosting, the rest was living space. Her throne room was made for entertaining and was easily big enough to fit every vampire in the States. Looking up to the wraparound balcony, I saw Dani for the first time, unabashedly flirting with two vampires. Her eyes met mine, and she gave me a small finger wave.

It wasn't until Akeldama came in and sat on her throne in a flourish of burnt orange silk that somehow didn't clash with her bright red hair that I was secretly glad he had commanded me to chill. I wasn't on a kamikaze mission. When she motioned Dakin over to her throne, I knew all hell was about to break loose. I knew the moment Dakin leaned over to whisper something in her ear that the princess's disappearance wasn't going to be as cut and dry as I had initially hoped for.

Dakin walked over to us. "Stephan, our Majesty wishes a word with you."

Giving me a light squeeze on my elbow, Stephan said, "Stay here and don't talk to anyone. I'll be right back."

I tried not to show any worry on my face as Akeldama whispered into Stephan's ear. He gave a curt nod and then remained by her side. I knew he felt my emotions as his eyes met mine.

"May I have your attention please," Akeldama said, tapping her long nails on the arm of her chair. "There has been a change of plans…"

She was slowly looking around the room.

"Each one of you will be brought before me," Akeldama said. "My former right-hand man, Stephan, will ask you each a question. If you lie, you will be tortured before I drain you dry. Try and leave this room, and I will kill not only you, but everyone in your vampire line. Until then, dance, drink, and be merry."

I was up the creek without a paddle. Dani found me a couple of hours later, sitting alone on the bottom stair. The crowd had thinned out, and there were only a few vampires left. She plopped down next to me, looking stunning in her blue dress, making her look like a fairy princess.

"Anything exciting happen earlier?" she asked.

I lifted a shoulder nonchalantly. "Nope. Just stayed in my room relaxing. And you?"

She gave me a small smile. "Flirting with everything that moves. It's nice to see that I haven't lost my touch."

A nervous laugh escaped me.

"I wonder what this is all about?" she asked. "The last time Akeldama was this ornery was when she found out that her late husband was conspiring behind her back. The poor guy literally lost his head."

My stomach rolled. No one knew that I'd helped the princess escape. It was going to be okay; I just needed to show no fear. "Why does she need Stephan and why is he standing off to the side of the throne?"

"Most vampires are just reborn with strength, but there are a few that have more powers than most. My brother is part of that few. One of his powers is knowing when someone is lying. It's as if he can smell the untruth in their words. If he chooses, he can actually fish around someone's head like he is looking for a file on a computer, but very few know that, so keep that tidbit to yourself and he can't stand close to her because of her crown. It will cancel out his powers."

"He can also feel others' emotions and let his emotions be shown?"

Dani gave me a deer-in-the-headlights look. "Um. I'm not sure how much I'm supposed to say, so maybe you should ask him that question."

"Like he will answer my questions."

Dani jumped up. "The line is starting to thin. Let's go answer whatever questions they have for us, so we can get it over with. I'm assuming it has something to do with the missing princess. I've been trying to overhear what the others are saying, but it's hard with all the chatter. Stephan can listen to just one person out of thousands but not me. It's so unfair that he got all the cool stuff."

Crap on a stick. I was dead. Before she tried to execute me, I would just grab Stephan and Dani and travel the fae lines. My grandfather would help me. I know he told me not to bring anyone else through the lines but under the circumstances, I didn't have a whole lot of other options. My body started to relax at my half-ass plan. I'd always lived by the seat of my pants, and it had worked for me. It would work this time. They didn't know I was part fae, and I could escape their clutches. I was five seconds away from practicing an evil laugh. I was losing it.

I released a small laugh that came out more like a nervous chuckle.

"Hey, are you okay?" she asked.

Standing up beside her, I made eye contact with Stephan over the crowd. He was looking intently at me. "Yeah. I think your brother is doing that weird Jedi thing right now."

Looping her arm with mine, she skipped us over to a line that had almost fizzled out in front of the throne. She didn't have a care in the world, meanwhile anxiety was pouring out from my pores.

When it was our turn, Akeldama gave us a feline smile. She silenced the thinning crowd so her voice could be heard. "Look, Stephan, your sister and your pet. Hello, Dani. It has been so long. Have you missed me?"

Dani's eyes turned to slits. "The feelings I have for you couldn't possibly compare with anyone else I know."

Stephan intervened before Akeldama could say anything. "Shall we start?"

Akeldama returned Dani's glare. "Begin the questioning."

"Do either of you have any knowledge of the whereabouts of the Princess?"

Dani and I both said, "No."

Akeldama was watching Stephan with as much scrutiny as he was watching me. His face betrayed nothing as he said, "Truth." Then he asked, "Do either of you have any knowledge of anyone conspiring to kidnap the Princess?"

Again, we both answered, "No."

"Truth your Majesty."

"Have either of you seen the Princess while you have been here?"

For the final time, we answered, "No."

"Truth, Dama."

Akeldama made a shooing motion, already focusing on the vampires behind us.

"Apparently, someone has taken the Princess," Dani said loud enough that the guard who was escorting us from the room heard her. He was to ensure that no one who hadn't been questioned yet left with us. "This should get interesting."

As we were walking up the stairs, I heard Stephan's voice in my head. "Go straight to my rooms, and talk to no one. You and I have a lengthy discussion ahead of us, little one."

I told Dani I wanted to wait for Stephan, and after she walked me to his room, she began searching his quarters in the same manner that he had done my room earlier. After she was done, she grabbed me and whispered into my ear, "I could feel your arm trembling on mine when we were questioned. I don't know what you know, but if she knows he just lied for you, she'll kill you both. Take it to your grave."

When she released me, I took a step back and gave her a curt nod.

There were guards on every hall now and making sure the closest one heard her, she said, "They have the whole place on lockdown, but as soon as they find the princess, we can witness the wedding and go home."

With a shaky smile, I said, "Sounds like a plan."

As soon as the door shut, I crawled into Stephan's massive bed and rested my eyes. The sun was coming up soon, and I couldn't party all day like these old timers. The last thought before sleep came over me was Stephan was going to be so pissed.

chapter seventeen

A weight shifted on the bed. My head roared with the question, "What have you done?"

Rolling over, I grabbed a pillow and slammed it over my head. "That is a total violation of privacy."

Stephan grabbed the pillow and threw it to the floor. "I'll show you violation." Without another word, he grabbed both sides of my head and applied a slight pressure. My body arched from the bed in discomfort as his hands heated. It felt like he was plucking things from my brain at an unbearable speed. Just when I was about to beg for him to stop, he released me.

"Why would you do something so stupid?"

Sitting up in bed, I glared at him. "As you saw, I didn't entirely have a choice."

He put his fists on either side of my legs and leaned in so close to me I could see my reflection in his eyes. "Why go in the first place? Couldn't you just mind your own business for once?"

"I'm sure you saw that I didn't intentionally go to—" Mindful that there could be ears listening through the walls, I said, "It was like I was pulled there. Maybe this thing… well, that one of three that I have going on makes me empathize with others more. It's like my soul knew there was a need to help, and then there was this tug, and my mind relaxed, and then there I was… helping."

He growled. "Don't. Help. Anymore."

"Well, by me helping, I found out that you know who has the you know what."

"Of course, Akeldama has the key. Again, you're not helping by telling me something I already knew."

Before I could retort, there was a knock on the door. Stephan straightened. "Come in."

Dakin stood at the door with an additional ten guards. He looked remorseful, which gave me a sick feeling. "Her Majesty is requesting both of your presence in her private library. For Gem's sake, I wouldn't let her stay in your bed again while you're here."

"Oh, but," I sputtered, "it wasn't like that. I had questions, and I wanted to wait up for him, but the sun came up and… for Pete's sake. I'm still in my gown from last night!"

Dakin gave me a pitying look. "I believe you, but it won't matter to her and Stephan knows that."

I looked over at Stephan.

"It's my fault I told you to meet me here, but unfortunately, he's right."

"I won't say anything," Dakin said. "But that doesn't mean that she won't find out."

"Yeah," Stephan scoffed. "Because you are so honorable."

Dakin gave him a level look before turning on his heel. Stephan walked beside me, as we headed to the private library. He grabbed me by my elbow and didn't let go of me as we walked through the halls and down the steps.

Interesting. Akeldama in a private library. What could she possibly be reading from her collection? How to make someone bleed internally in three seconds flat?

I gave him a questioning look, and he replied in my head. "Being summoned by Akeldama is very seldom a good thing. If it comes to it, use your fae magic and leave and go to your grandfather."

It was sweet to think he was willing to take the heat for me, but there was no way I was going to leave him.

I was mainly a big ball of sweat by the time we reached the queen's library. My confidence was at an all-time low; I didn't feel like I was in control, and I had a sudden suspicion that everyone in this room was out to get me. I was literally a self-help author's dream reader.

Akeldama sat on a chaise lounge in front of a roaring fire with her servants and her guards scattered around the room, waiting to be at her beck and call. When she smiled first at Stephan and then at me like the cat that had not only ate the canary, but played with it first, I knew she had somehow figured out the mystery of the missing princess.

Dani was soon shuffled in, and my heart sank a little at the sight of her as she came to stand next to us. I could barely hold onto the princess; how was I going to carry both Stephan and Dani through the fae line?

Akeldama's gaze covered every inch of Stephan before she met my eyes. "There is someone demanding entry onto my estate, and do you want to know why she is on her way up here right now?"

Stephan seemed bored. "I'm sure I have no clue, Dama."

She slowly stood and did that eerie walk thing where she appeared to be floating across the floor. She circled the three of us like a hawk above its prey. "This woman gained entry because she says she has some golden information about your pet here."

At the knock on the library door, Akeldama said, "Do enter."

Dang that gypsy to heck. I knew I shouldn't have overlooked her evil ways just because she killed some murderous ants. The witch, Athela, came bustling in the room wearing vibrant colors and lots of jewelry that made a clanging sound as she strolled.

I wondered if Stephan had ever pondered that maybe his taste in women was so atrocious that he should just swear them off entirely. Honestly, they might be the death of him. And me.

Akeldama went back over to the chaise lounge to sit while Athela stood proudly flanked in the middle by two guards. "What is your name, witch?"

"Athela and I have information that you might find useful about the young vampire, Stephan's friend, and all I ask for is a place in your court, and of course, some monetary gain."

"Of course." Akeldama gave her a searing look. "Perhaps. If the information is worth it, we will find you a spot amongst us."

"Not just a spot. I want to have a trusted spot in your inner circle. I want Stephan to be made to go through with his end of the bargain by making me his wife with your blessings, and more importantly, your protection."

Well, that conniving, back-stabbing traitor. What was her plan? She couldn't possibly think that she could get close enough to the queen to kill her, and even if she did, then what? The man she forced to marry her would be content with ruling vampires with her? One word—delusional.

"That's a lot of demands." Akeldama studied her with something very close to disgust. "A bargain, you say? What has our dear Stephan got himself into I wonder? I'm assuming all of this has to do with the princesses disappearing?"

Athela's beautiful face scrunched up in confusion. "No, I know nothing about that. However, I do know that... that—"

Athela grabbed two fistfuls of her dark, curly hair and pulled, groaning. Then she let out a scream that seemed to go on forever, and the only thing keeping her on her feet were the two guards on either side of her. She started convulsing and slobbering more than a St. Bernard. I began to move towards her, but Stephan put a hand on my arm, holding me in place. I was the only one in the room who appeared genuinely shocked or seemed to care that she was dying right in front of us.

What shocked me even more was when her body succumbed to the pain and she passed out, Akeldama started clapping.

"Bravo, Stephan. Bravo. I haven't seen that trick successfully pulled off since the last time you did it. Do tell, what was the witch about to reveal that you didn't want anyone knowing?" Stephan didn't say a word, which made Akeldama smile even more. "Pet, what do you think she was about to say?"

Dani and Stephan had not moved an inch. "Um. That Stephan was a bad lay?"

My mind was reeling. Did Stephan just short-circuit this woman's brain?

Akeldama's head dropped back with laughter. "No, that couldn't be it. I've been there, done that, and wouldn't mind a repeat. Try again, pet."

"I don't know if I should say…"

"Come, pet, sit next to me." Akeldama slid her feet off the chase lounge and patted the seat next to her, but I couldn't move because Stephan still held me by my arm. "I won't hurt her, Stephan. Come, pet."

Obediently, I went and sat beside her. "Now, tell me, pet, what was it that she was about to say before Stephan here fried her memories?"

Fried her memories? As in all of them? I would worry about that later. Right now, I had to sink or swim, and I was a helluva swimmer. "Well, you see, I'm not really supposed to tell anyone," I said in my sweetest southern accent.

She started playing with my hair. "Oh, but you can tell me anything."

She tried to use some kind of glamour on me, but my fae magic fought through it. I nodded like I believed her, and was entranced by her. There was such a strong power radiating from her I was certain if I were a hundred percent vampire, I would have been groveling at her feet by now. Submissively, I said, "I'm not a good vampire. What I mean to say is, things aren't coming as natural to me as they should. Stephan thought the witch could make a spell to bring out the vampire in me." I let a tremble color my voice. "He said that being weak meant death to a vampire."

"Hmm. Yes, this is true. Witches are worse than the Valkyries when it comes to shiny things. And we all know that witches trade their charms and curses for monetary gain, so what did he promise her?"

"Power. She wanted the power of being married to him."

"Hmm. Does he care about you so much, pet, that he would promise his hand in marriage just to make sure no one knew that you were weak?"

Still pretending that I was in a daze, I said, "He made a promise to my family that he would take care of me."

Akeldama's hand tugged on the strip of my hair that she had between her fingers as her head whipped toward Stephan. "I guess frying her memories was easier than a future wedding and divorce?"

Stephan just shrugged.

"Well, this is all very interesting. I was hoping the witch was coming to me with information with my daughter, but I do find this entertaining." Akeldama trailed her hand down my arm, leaving red marks where her long nails scraped the skin. "And you are right; we do hate weaknesses so much so we flush them out. This will be a good lesson for Stephan for he should have never interfered. So, pet, it would seem we have time on our hands until my beloved daughter is returned to us, and with the estate on lockdown, I fear the vampires will grow bored. No one has ever said I was an ungracious host. Tandi, you will provide them entertainment."

"I'm sorry?"

Ignoring me, she said to Dakin, "Put the bind on her. After all, we don't know what magic the witch bestowed upon her."

Dakin retrieved something gold and shimmery from a box. He placed the cold metal around my upper arm like a cuff, and it magically tightened almost to the point of pain. The metal seemed to have liquid gold in it that continuously moved in a clockwise motion.

"What is the meaning of this?" Stephan demanded.

"This, my dear, is to nullify whatever charm your witch invoked on your pet here. We wouldn't want her to have an unfair advantage over the other vampires who don't need magic to have strength. Tandi, I do hope you make it through the first contender."

"First contender? What are you talking about?"

"Oh, I'm sorry. I thought it was clear. Dakin will be going around asking the vampires if they would like the chance to eliminate you one on one. You each will get a weapon, of course. Honestly, once the word is out about how weak you are, there will be a mob of vampires lined up to torture and kill you for sport. Plus, this way is more entertaining for the rest of us."

Dani came over to us and sat next to me and reaching over, she squeezed my hand.

"Akeldama you cannot do this," Stephan roared.

"Hmm. I think I can and I will. While I have been out building an army, what have you been doing, Stephan? Living quietly at home baking cookies? Your power might rival mine, which infuriates me to no end because I made you! However, you having the same strength as I proves that we were made for one another. Until the day that you admit you belong by my side ruling, you will obey me because I have many backing me. Not you."

I could feel his emotions boiling off of him. I jumped up from the couch and blocked his path. This time it was me who grabbed Stephan's arm as he took a step forward. I could still vanish through the fae lines. The cuff around my arm cancelled out the charm that was in the bracelet, so the time here would be different for me than wherever I traveled to, but I couldn't do that. Even if I successfully brought Dani and Stephan with us, Akeldama would eventually find us. And I would have to give up on my quest of discovering who was behind Greta's death and the key that could destroy earth. No, I would stay and fight. And I would win.

"When will the first match be?" I asked, shocking Akeldama.

"Tonight. Dakin will instruct some of my servants to make the courtyard ready. The upper outside balcony is truly the best place to watch the spectacle. Everyone will have a good view."

"Whatever pleases the crowd," I murmured.

Akeldama made a shooing motion with her hands. "Leave me now. Go and love on your pet, Stephan, like this is her last night."

She was still laughing as we walked out of the room. The good news was she didn't know that I was part fae and ghoul. The bad news was I was probably going to die. This sucked.

chapter eighteen

"I can't believe you fried Athela's memories. And I remember you saying that it wouldn't hurt her. What the heck, Stephan?"

"Usually, I can sneak into a mind without them ever knowing I was there and it doesn't hurt. If time is of essence, then unfortunately they feel it, and as you witnessed, I didn't have time," Stephan said.

"You should be glad that he fried her memories," Dani said. "At least this way she is in too much pain to be any fun for Akeldama to play with, and she will kill her quickly."

"She's going to kill her?" I screeched.

Stephan made a motion for me to lower my voice. "Of course, Akeldama is going to kill her. Athela was dead the moment she came in here, trying to bribe the Queen of Vampires. There is nothing we can do for her."

"And why would you want to?" Dani asked. "She was about to sell you up the creek."

It seemed that everyone who we came into contact with was malicious. We needed to get out of this place.

"We could go. I could travel the fae lines with each of you," I said to a pacing Stephan and a quiet Dani once we were back in my room.

Dani flopped back on my bed. "Sooner rather than later, she would just find us. I'm surprised she hasn't found her daughter yet. By the way, where is she?"

"Somewhere safe," I replied.

"You literally jumped straight from the frying pan into the fire," Dani said, staring at the ceiling.

"Thank you for that. I didn't realize what dire circumstances I'm in. Thank goodness I have you to point it out for me," I snarled.

Dani laughed. "I don't know why everyone is panicking. She will put the lesser vampires on the roster first."

"Unless I'm fighting a preschooler, I'm pretty sure I'm screwed."

Stephan stopped pacing. "No, you're not. Tandi, if I am correct about you, then your power hasn't even begun to surface."

I flopped down on the bed next to Dani. "That's the problem, though, isn't it? My powers, whatever they may be, haven't surfaced, and even if they did, would they be enough to help me out within the next few hours?"

"Do you think you can travel the fae lines even with the manacle on?"

"I'm not a hundred percent sure, but my gut is telling me yes. If this manacle is nulling any powers that are lent to me by magic, my bracelet won't work, causing a huge time difference, but I can still travel the lines because I'm part fae. I don't need a charm to travel."

"Then you should go. Your grandfather can keep you safe."

"He's right, Tandi," Dani added.

"Are y'all crazy? If I leave you guys, she will take her anger out on the both of you. I refuse to run."

Stephan let out a string of curses. "At least go visit your grandfather. He might be able to give you some kind of insight on what to do tonight. Just make sure you don't dally too much, or we are, as you put it, screwed."

"You want me to go right now?"

"Yes."

"All right. I promise I won't stay too long." I closed my eyes, but before I said my magic word to take me to Pops, I asked, "Hey, why didn't Akeldama suspect you when it came to the whereabouts of the missing princess?"

His face showed no emotion as he said, "Because I was with her."

Like with her with her? My pride wouldn't let me ask for details. I escaped before he could see the hurt on my face. I shouldn't care if he was with that horrible woman, but the image of him and her together caused a weird kind of pain in my chest.

I sat in a cabin with snow pressed up against the windows. The wind howled as I held my hands up to the roaring fire. The hardwood flooring creaked behind me, and I turned to see Pops in a ski suit.

Chuckling, I said, "That's fitting."

"When in Aspen… why are we in Aspen?"

I shrugged. "It fit my mood."

"Speaking of outfits, why are you dressed like that? A grandfather never wants to see his offspring in tight, black leather."

I looked down at my outfit that was a replica of one I had seen in a movie. The black leather corset I was wearing tied in the back. My leather pants were so tight I almost couldn't breathe, and I had on motorcycle boots. Somehow, I was still wearing the cuff Dakin had placed on me, which was confusing because I really wanted to lose that thing. It must be very powerful magic. "I'm trying to create a visual effect. There is a couple of sayings that come to mind like, 'When you look good you feel good' or 'Fake it 'till you make it.' But I don't have time to talk to you about that."

He went and sat in a leather chair in front of the fire. "Let me guess, you can't stay long?"

I felt remorse for always having to keep our talks so short. Especially since we just found each other, and I made a silent vow to remedy that once I wasn't in a life or death situation. Please, Lord, let that be soon.

"I'm sorry, Pops, but I do have to keep this short. You see, I might have got myself in a pickle, and I need your help."

"Well, of course, you're in a bind. You are exactly like your great-grandmother after all. My wife was beautiful, smart, sassy, and trouble with a capital T."

"Well, this trouble with a capital T that I have walked right into is with Akeldama." He winced when I said that name. "As you probably know, she is vile and has forced me into… Um, have you ever seen Fight Club starring Brad Pitt?"

"No, can't say I have."

"No worries. I'm kind of a movie guru. It's a talent of mine. So, basically, I have to fight other vampires because Akeldama thinks I'm weak, and she wants me off the face of the planet, but at least this way I'll provide her some kind of entertainment."

He leaned back in the chair and stroked his beautiful silvery beard. "You could just go with me into my land. You don't need to fight anyone."

"If I am as much like my great something or other grandmother as you say, then you know that I can't do that. I need you to help unleash what little powers I do have."

He gave me a dazzling smile. "You are my granddaughter. Your powers are vast. Of course, once we unlock all that you can do, you will still have to be very careful how you use your fae abilities. We don't want Akeldama knowing your strengths. It's better that she thinks you're weak. The vampire in you is lying dormant under the other counterparts, to bring it out you need to—"

I gasped as my head began to throb. A very familiar voice said, "Tandi?"

I touched my temple. "Stephan?"

Pops eyes widened. "Ha! He can reach you in another plane. I knew it, but this just confirmed it. Truly amazing."

I was about to ask, "confirmed what?" but Stephan's voice rang loud and clear in my head. "You need to get back now! Return through your bathroom."

I stood quickly. "I have to go, Pops."

"But… I haven't helped you." He stood with me, looking anxious. "Tell your vampire that I will send you a gift. He can find it at the front gates of Akeldama's property. It will help you."

I nodded said the magic word and then closed my eyes to find myself back in my guest bathroom. There was a shouting match going on. Some voices I recognized and some I didn't. Wrapping a towel around my head to cover my dry hair, I slowly opened up the door, and every eye turned to me.

"Is there a problem?" I asked the guards who stood toe to toe with Stephan while Dani sat on a chair painting her toenails. "Can a girl not wash her hair without being bothered?"

Stephan smirked. "As I previously said, 'she is in the bathroom.'"

The guards studied me as I walked out. "We assumed you made a run for it."

One of my shoulders lifted up. "Well, you know what they say about assuming."

The tallest of the two guards said, "The next time we come back, it will be to escort you to the ring. Make sure you're ready."

After they shut the door none too gently, Dani gave up the façade of painting her toenails, and none of us moved for several minutes.

"I'm going to go guard the hallway, so you two can chat," Dani said. "I'll let you know if anyone is coming."

As soon as she left the room, Stephan asked, "What happened?"

"I didn't have enough time—"

His voice shook in my head. "You were gone for nearly half an hour."

I had told him to stop that. "I think we've already established that one can lose track of time in the fae world, so get over yourself."

His eyes narrowed. "Well, now that is interesting."

I was shocked. I had just communicated with him through his mind. "But how… I thought you said that it was rare."

He studied me the way a scientist studies a bug through a microscope. "That's why I said that was interesting."

Concentrating, I tried again to send him a message. "Now, it's not working."

"That's because you are a weakling."

"Asshat."

He laughed. "Ha. I got that one. It seems that you need to be riled, little one, in order to use some of your powers. Perhaps you don't think so much when you're angered."

He was so dang handsome when he smiled; then I remembered his last parting words to me before I went to visit my Pops. He had been with Akeldama, his former lover, when I was helping the princess escape.

He must have noticed the change in me because his smile dropped. "Why are you mad at me?"

"I'm not mad. I'm indifferent."

"I can tell you're mad, Tandi. What have I done?"

"I don't want to talk about it, but since you are willing to discuss emotions, why don't you tell me how we can sense each other's?"

He gave me a long look and then took a step closer to me. I was still pissed. What did he mean, he was with her? Had they been playing checkers or naked twister because there was a huge ass difference. I took a step back from him, and he let out a tired sigh.

"So, I'm assuming the talk you had with your grandfather was a total waste?"

"No, not really. He said he was sending me a gift, and it would be at the front gates of the estate."

Stephan gave me a quizzical look. "Hopefully, it will be something great because we need a miracle. I'll go retrieve it; you are not allowed to leave this room by Akeldama's orders."

I wanted to say something snide like, "oh, and we would hate to upset your girlfriend," but this one time I kept my mouth shut. I had bigger things to worry about than my irrational jealousy.

I gave him a fake smile. "I will be waiting here with bated breath."

"By the way, you looked beautiful in the gown but this… this is every man's fantasy."

Then almost quicker than the eye could track, he was gone. I refused to let his words get me all hot and bothered, so I forced myself to wonder what gift my Pops was going to give me. Maybe it was a magic sword that had a mind of its own and could find its enemy all by itself. Maybe it was a potion I could drink, and it would wake up these stupid powers that everyone thought I had. Now, that would be handy. I came up with several different guesses all equally absurd before Stephan came back in. I looked at his empty arms and threw my hands up in the air. "Well, what the heck is it?"

His handsome face was full of disbelief. "It looks like I'll have to intervene tonight and save you."

At that moment, a small cat came strutting in behind him. Its coat mimicked a leopard, spots and all. "What the hell is that?" I asked.

The cat stopped in front of me. "Rude much?"

Stephan glared at the cat. "Your grandfather got you a talking ferret. Congratulations."

The cat hissed. "Aww, is the little vampire still mad that I called him a hyped-up, over-confident fang banger? Did I hurt your whittle feelings?"

Stephan gave me a mild look. "Do I have permission to kill Garfield? He annoys me."

The cat jumped onto the bed. "Those loafers annoy me. I can practically smell the dead cow from here, but you don't see me pissing on them, do you?"

Stephan snarled, and I put up a hand to stop him from advancing on the cat. I sat down on the bed, watching the cat groom himself. This was unbelievable. There had to be a mistake. "Um, excuse me, but do you know why my grandfather would send you to me?"

"The name is Tracker, doll face, and I'm assuming he sent me to protect you," he said in between grooming his hind leg. I could see enough to know that he wasn't neutered. Oh, boy.

"How is a cat going to help me?" He stopped his licking to glare at me, if a cat could glare. I started to apologize, but in my defense, that was a legit question.

"This is just the form that I feel most comfortable wearing, thanks to my ancestors. Would you prefer me in my human form?"

Before I could say anything, a swirl of bright colors and wind wrapped around the cat like a tunnel. Before I could count to three, a man stood in front of me. He had shaggy, golden hair, slightly tilted eyes, a pointy chin, and a smattering of freckles across his face. He was naked as the day he was born. I had never seen that appendage before, so I couldn't help but stare. Stephan put his body in between me and the very naked man.

"If you value your life, shapeshifter, you will change immediately back into an alley cat."

Another wind tunnel swarmed the man and once again, I was staring at a golden cat.

The cat stretched. "Did you see that, doll face? The vampire was jealous because I am hung like a horse."

Stephan clenched his jaw. "Keep making jokes, and I will send you to the vet to be neutered."

Trying to diffuse the situation before it escalated any further, I stood up and placed a hand on Stephan's arm. "There has to be a reason Pops sent him here. Could you give us a moment? Maybe if I talk to him, I can figure a way out of the fight tonight."

Stephan started to say something but stopped. "I will not leave you alone with this creature, but I will sit over there," he said, pointing to an armchair in the corner of the room, "and give you a moment to question him."

I rolled my eyes, but I guess that was the best I was going to get out of the prince. Sitting back down on the bed, I thought about the best way to approach the subject of the cat's usefulness.

"So, Tracker, do you have any ideas on how to help me out of this tricky situation I find myself in?"

The cat picked at a thread on the comforter. "You mean the one where the Queen of Vampires has it out for you and has forced you into fighting members of her line, so she can inadvertently kill you?"

I felt a little relief. "Yes, that about sums it up."

"Okay, good, we're on the same page then. So, the answer to your question is no. I don't know how to solve your problem, but honestly, I'm more of a fly-by-the-seat-of-my-pants kind of guy. Procrastination is my friend, and late is the only way I play the game."

Stephan snorted, and I cut my eyes to him, vowing him to be silent. "So, really you are of no use to me?"

"Doll face, have you not listened to a word that I have said? I'm so helping. Wake me five minutes before you leave to go play vampire slayer."

The cat rolled onto his back and fell asleep spread eagle. I had no words. None. What the hell just happened?

"Am I to still remain silent, little one?"

I answered back in the same manner. "How do you like someone in your head? Get. Out. Of. Mine."

Stephan leaned back in the chair. "One more thing. I won't let you die. I vow that to you."

His words rang strong and true. It hit me that Stephan really cares about me. I just didn't know if he knew it or not. My tender feelings towards him didn't last long. I studied Stephan as he closed his eyes and rested his head on the back of the chair, and whether Tracker feigned sleep or was really sleeping, it didn't matter. I was pissed. My life was at stake, and the man who was supposed to be my charge acted like I wasn't going to be fighting for my life, and let's not forget my sweet, precious Pops. What did he send to bring me victory over my horrifying enemies? A freakin' seven-pound cat. Men! Couldn't live with them, and you sure as hell could do a lot better without them. Maybe.

chapter nineteen

The huge courtyard had been turned into a WWE main event, and I was the live attraction. At first, I thought there were mats lying in the middle of the room, but on closer inspection, I noticed they were large, black plastic tarps of some sort, probably to help with the loss of blood I was about to endure. The Queen didn't want me to get blood on the grass. Just when you think life couldn't possibly get any worse, some evil bitch was there to show you how little you really mean to her world. I woke the cat, Tracker, up as soon as Stephan sensed the guards approaching, hoping he would have some last-minute advice. But the cat just stretched before turning himself into a praying mantis, and then he climbed into my hair and was currently hiding. Stephan reached down and gave my hand a little squeeze. "I won't let you die, little one."

Before I could ask for more reassurance, or at least get an idea of a solid plan that he might have, the Queen of Vampires herself had climbed to her gaudy throne that one of her minions must've carried out for her, demanding everyone's attention with her obnoxious clapping.

"Silence!" Her green eyes cut through the room. "Now that I have your attention, most of you know that someone has made the grave mistake of kidnapping my daughter and when I find the perpetrator, they will suffer unmeasurable pain."

Tracker piped up and whispered into my ear. "Wow. Sadistic much?"

"Anyway, since we were all gathered here for the wedding of the Princess, I—being the great Queen that I am—didn't want you all to be bored waiting on her return. So, we will have a match tonight with Stephan's pet—a new vampire that lacks the basic skills needed to survive in our harsh, unforgiving community. There was a sign-up list that was passed around, and it looks as if we have twenty-one vamps that would like to challenge the weakling. Are there any questions?"

Before I could stop myself, I said in a testy voice, "Yeah. Only like a thousand. How about—are there any rules?"

The crowd broke off into two groups: the mumblers and the laughers. Glad to see I could still shock and amuse people at the same time.

Akeldama's eyes narrowed. "Our kind doesn't believe in rules when it comes to fighting. Really, anything goes."

I crossed my arms over my chest. "You want me to provide the entertainment, correct? Then I want rules, or I will not even try to fight whoever meets me in that ring."

"Then you would be a fool."

"I've been called worse by my own mother, so can we agree upon establishing some rules?"

Akeldama almost looked like she admired me for a split second. "Sure, pet. Let's talk about the rules. What is it that you had in mind?"

"Let's not fight until the death, at least not this first week. Let us instead fight until first blood." She looked like she was about to object, so I hurried on, "I mean if I am as lame as everyone seems to think, your entertainment will be over before it begins. And what if the princess isn't found right away? Who will provide the entertainment then? Would anyone on the list be willing to still fight if their opponent was actually worthy?"

There were lots of murmurs amongst the vampires. Akeldama's voiced boomed, "Quiet." After everyone settled down, she said, "Okay, Stephan's pet. You have a point. We will say the first seven challenges are to be stopped after drawing first blood."

Stephan spoke up. "If an opponent by accident kills the other opponent, then they have signed their own death warrant. I would like to gladly volunteer to be the one to deliver justice to the fallen vampire."

Akeldama rolled her eyes better than anyone I had ever seen. They literally looked like they bounced around in her head before settling back down. "Did you hear that, dears? Accidentally kill his pet and he will kill you. All right, I will grant that… for now."

The praying mantis in my hair whispered, "Say something to stop outside forces from interfering with the challenge but somehow exclude me."

"Um, and no one outside of the makeshift ring can lend a hand to either opponent. Basically, no interference of any kind from outside of the designated fighting area."

Akeldama's eyebrow arched. "Or?"

"Or Stephan gets to whack them, too."

The praying mantis laughed. "Is your vamp in the mafia? It is so whack that you just said whack. I don't know if we can be friends."

"It was cute at first that you thought you actually have a choice in any of this, but let's not forget, pet, that as soon as I tire of you, your usefulness will have expired."

"Then I'll try to remain useful."

She gave me a calculated look before addressing the crowd. "All right then, dears, you heard Stephan's pet. There are two rules: during the first seven challenges, there will be no death blows, and no outside interference or the rule breaker will be killed by my former right-hand man. Now, we can begin. The first person to sign the list was Andre, who is a highly skilled swordsman. Hopefully, he will at least play with her for a few minutes, so this won't be a total waste of time."

The crowd laughed because apparently the queen was a riot. A handsome vampire stepped forward and took a bow. "I will try my hardest to accommodate you, my beautiful Queen."

Tracker whispered, "Oh, great. I just threw up a little bit in my mouth but don't worry. I didn't get any in your hair. Just F.Y.I., you might want to start using a better conditioner. Now, tell the old hag to get this show on the road; I don't want to ring in the New Year as a bug. Do you know how hard it is to find other praying mantises in the winter? And don't get me started on what those trifling hoes do to their mates after they're finished."

I couldn't afford to tell Tracker to shut up. Honestly, I didn't know what he was going to be able to bring to the table at this point, but at least I felt like I wasn't going in alone. I met the man she called Andre in the middle of the swarm of black plastic.

"Hi."

He gave me a brief, condescending look that scanned from my toes to my head. "I'm only here to win favor with the Queen; introductions and small talk are not necessary nor welcomed."

"Aww, I'm not welcomed to Doucheville, population of one. Too bad. I so wanted to see the sights."

Andre glared at me while Tracker tugged on my ear. "Yeah, baby, drop the mic and walk away. Maybe I was too hasty in declaring you non-suitable as friend material."

Akeldama clapped her hands again. "All right, dearies, I believe that everyone has had the chance to place their bets. Donavon, if you don't mind being the unofficial referee, I think we can begin."

A man with beautiful caramel skin, who looked to be in his late forties, dressed in a dapper plum-colored suit with a matching fedora hat, stepped closer to the makeshift arena. The lights dimmed, and he gave me a little wink. "Good luck, kid. You're going to need it."

Tracker tugged my ear. "Get to the far corner, doll face."

As I walked to the corner, I wondered how long it would take before Andre the friendly vamp drew first blood. It could be worse; I could be wearing white.

"All right, listen up, doll face, we can't let anyone know that you are part fae. Yeah, your grandfather briefed me.

So, we need to use your fae powers that some very rare vampires have also. You know how you can visualize this sweet body that you're rocking into any outfit of your choosing? Well, we're going to do the same thing as soon as the Will Smith look-alike over there tells us to begin."

I glanced to where the unofficial referee Donavon was listening to whatever Akeldama was saying. I muttered, "Okay."

"When Donavon brings over the weapons selection, I want you to choose the fingernail blades. We're going to go in close on this one."

Going in close sounded like the worst freaking idea ever. I needed like a boomerang or lawn darts. I would settle for a laser beam, but fingernail blades? I refused to have a panic attack.

"You with me?" he asked. I nodded, not caring if I looked like a total lunatic. "So, he is going to taunt you for a bit. He is skilled with the sword but extremely narcissistic. Let his arrogance be his demise."

I had no clue what the hell this cat/praying mantis/man was saying. Minutes before I had to be in my first fight and this joker was talking in riddles.

"Oh, good, they are wrapping it up. Finally. So just a recap, I want you to imagine yourself in different disadvantageous positions, creating the illusion that maybe you have fallen or tripped, then when he goes after you, appear behind him and make him bleed, doll face. Some vampires can do this; it's called flashing, but not like the flashing that creepy Uncle Tommy does. When fae use this power, it's called glamour. But these pricks won't know the difference. Bada bing, bada boom, fight over."

Recap, my perky behind. I didn't get any of that info the first time around, and I wasn't totally positive that I understood what he wanted me to do this time. But none-the-less, if that asshat Andre killed me for good, at least I knew Stephan would bring him to his doom as well.

Donavon came toward us with a box full of weapons. Andre, of course, grabbed up a long, shiny sword that looked like it belonged to Sir Lancelot. He took a few professional swings with it, and the crowd oohed and awed. I dug around the box until I found some gloves that had pointy razors on the tips. I started putting on the gloves when I heard laughter from the same crowd that thought Andre was so cool. Whatever. I used to be the last kid picked when we had to be on teams during PE. They couldn't break me.

Donavon leaned in as close as he could to me while still holding the box. "Are you sure about that?"

I wiggled my fingers in the gloves. "Honestly, I'm not sure about anything anymore."

He gave me a half smile. "It was very ingenious of you to suggest a first blood rule. I'm pulling for you, kid."

I looked around at all the vampires crowding the courtyard. Some were still in the mansion, hanging over the upstairs balconies as well. "Then you are about the only one."

"I wouldn't say that." His eyes found Stephan standing at the edge of the crowd. Stephan gave him a small nod, and Donavon returned the notion. He closed the lid and then announced in a loud voice, "As soon as I leave this ring, the fight will begin."

I watched with trepidation as he carried his box out of the ring. This couldn't possibly end well for me. It was too late for cold feet. I needed to focus. Tracker said… well, honestly, I didn't know what the heck Tracker had rambled about.

Donavon shook me from my thoughts. "Please, begin."

Andre smirked as he glided towards me, swinging his sword in a figure eight. He danced around me, and every once in a while, he would thrust his sword at me, making the crowd jeer. I'd dealt with a thousand jocks just like this bozo at my old high school: they didn't impress me then, and I wasn't amused now. I moved with a grace I didn't know I possessed and concentrated on dodging each of his strikes. Truth be known, he wasn't trying to draw first blood. Yet.

I dodged to the left and immediately did the foot sweep technique that Stephan had taught me. Andre landed on his backside and looked as surprised as I was. He got to his feet with a small glare. The blade of his sword came at me fast and hard then. I barely had time to dodge. Every swoosh of the blade made my stomach clench. He was getting faster and closer to drawing blood.

He looked up adoringly at Akeldama on her golden throne, and when I saw her give him the nod, I knew that meant he could draw blood anytime now. I got motivated. I moved fast to the right, and when he looked at the empty spot, his jaw dropped open in confusion. I just flashed! Holy Swedish meatballs! I didn't have time to do a proper celebratory dance because Andre had a murderous look on his face. I once again flashed, but this time I came up behind him. My hands encircled his neck, and when he moved from my grasp, it was too late. The damage was done; he had cut himself on my nails. He touched his neck. When he pulled his hand away, it was covered with his own blood. No one moved. Not a sound was made.

"But how… how did you…" Andre glanced from me to Akeldama and back again. "This makes no sense. She is weak; how could she possibly possess the skills to flash?"

Akeldama tilted her head to the side, studying me while we all waited with bated breath. "It seems if you have been holding back on us, Stephan, when it comes to your pet's talents."

Stephan made his way to me slowly, almost as if he was on a stroll to nowhere particularly exciting. "Dama, what can I say? Tandi never ceases to amaze me."

"Is that what keeps your attention so riveted, your pet's hidden talents? Honestly, Stephan, she will have to do more than flash to amuse me."

"I'm sure whatever talents she has, Dama, they won't amount to half of what you've obtained," Stephan said.

She gave him a calculated look. "Meet me in my chambers, Stephan, and bring your pet if you have to."

I held my head up high as I strolled from the courtyard behind Stephan. Whispers and quizzical looks were cast my way, and I ignored them all. I would love a few moments to sit down and think about what had just happened, but there was no time for that. Not when I was on to the next catastrophic event. Any meeting with the evil queen would be nothing less than disastrous.

chapter twenty

Akeldama was stretched out on an antique couch, her flaming red hair hanging in perfect waves over her porcelain shoulders. She looked like someone staged her that way. Gag. The moment we walked into the room, she gave Stephan a seductive smile and purred, "Darling, come sit next to me."

How the heck was he supposed to do that, considering Akeldama took up all the space on the couch? Stephan walked the distance to the couch, and when she lifted her legs, he slid underneath. I swear if he started massaging her feet, I was leaving the room.

"I wanted to talk with you, love."

Stephan's brows rose in question. "Of course. When it comes to you, Dama, you know that I am an open book."

"I would like to know why her?" Her head tilted towards me, but her eyes never left Stephan's face. "After all of these years of refusing to change a human into a vampire and now all of a sudden, you have this pet trailing behind you… it's rather confusing."

"You wouldn't believe that I did it out of the kindness of my heart?"

Her head fell back in laughter. "Oh, Stephan. That was funny. Remember the battle we had with that group of rogue vamps somewhere in Virginia? Don't forget, love, I know how ruthless you can be. In fact that is what made me fall in love with you." She gave him a scandalizing gaze, and then she licked her red lips. "Well, that along with other things."

I felt my stomach clench. Stephan wasn't mine, and I had no claim on him, but the familiarity in which she spoke to him really chapped my hide.

"Um, excuse me, your Highness, but was there a reason that you asked us to come here? Not that I mind standing here while y'all reminisce over the blood and glory days, but I'm a little tired."

Her nose flared as she looked at me. "Your pet is quite cheeky, isn't she? I was wrong to include her. The next time I request your presence, don't bring her." Ignoring me completely, she trailed her hand down Stephan's muscular chest. "Darling, I really wish you would think about joining my ranks again. Not merely as a soldier, but as my King. We were always so good together. Things here on earth are about to get far more fascinating and—"

"What do you mean, Dama?"

Curling her body closer to his, she said, "I'm sure you are aware of the seven keys that has everyone in such an uproar? I have one in my possession, and when I marry my daughter off to that deplorable Cecil, then I will have two. He is willing to exchange one key for her hand in marriage. Of course, I told him the wedding was to be delayed. Anyways, as soon as the princess is returned, I will have two keys, Stephan. Do you know what this means? With those keys, we will be able to control who comes and goes to earth. We could banish anyone that gets in our way to another plane. We would be unstoppable. Who in their right mind would go up against the two most powerful vampires in the world? Think about it, love."

Stephan laced his fingers with hers, and it took everything I had not to clench my fist. He feigned innocence as he asked, "You already have one key now?"

She gave him a little smile then slithered to her feet. She crossed the tacky gold room and leaned over the wooden desk, purposely pushing her butt in the air while she twisted this way and that way as she rifled through the top drawer. She straightened back and faced Stephan, holding out a black ball the size of a moon pie. Gawd, how I missed my moon pies and little Debbie snacks.

He took the key from her and studied it. It was the size of a plum. He flipped it a couple of times in the air before giving it a small twist. He now held two parts of the ball in his hands. Seeing the key for the first time cemented my thoughts as to who killed my friend. That was if Ariana was to be trusted because she did say whomever was responsible for Greta's fate also had possession of the key. Anger boiled up inside of me. I plotted her death, and she didn't have a clue as she leaned closer into Stephan.

"Amazing, isn't it?" she asked.

"You just have the key out here in the open?"

She let out a laugh. "Stephan, darling, no one is stupid enough to take anything that belongs to me. You know that. The only person that is strong enough to guard the key other than me is you, and that's another good reason for us to pick things up where they left off."

My voice shook with rage. "It was you that sent those vampires to attack us that night, wasn't it? May I ask you why?"

Stephan's voice sounded in my head. "Not now, little one. We will strike when the time is right."

"If I must admit, I was a little flabbergasted that Stephan not only made a vampire after all of these years, but he sought out a cuff for his new charge. We all know a vampire has to offer a favor in order to get the charmed jewelry. Stephan hates owing people, so I thought maybe you mattered to him."

My temper got the best of me. "So you tried to kill me? Did you know an innocent woman died because of you?"

At her indifferent shrug, I took a step forward. An invisible force stopped me in my tracks, and I knew Stephan held me in place with his mind. He probably just saved my life with that rare talent of his, but I wasn't very appreciative at the moment. The queen with her stupid infatuation wasn't aware of our exchange.

Akeldama sat down next to him and threw one leg over his lap. Her long fingers gently took the key from his hands. She put the key back together and then stuffed it into the cushions behind her. "Tell your pet to leave us."

Stephan never took his eyes from hers as he said, "You heard her. Wait outside."

My blood boiled, but Stephan was right—now wasn't the time. There were so many things going through my head, and none of them were very ladylike. Being Southern bred, there was one thing I did have in abundance: pride. Akeldama was observing my face to see how I handled the order my sire just gave me. I put my hands on my hips, a grin stretching across my face. "Sure, thing, boss. According to the witch, this endeavor shouldn't take too long. But if it's all the same to you, I'm going to call it a night."

Akeldama gasped at my audacity and Stephan's lip twitched. I didn't know why in the world he thought me belittling his stamina was funny, but I was not in the mood to humor him. It wasn't until I flipped my hair over my shoulder and headed out of the queen's chambers that I remembered Tracker.

"Jeez, watch it, will you," he hissed. "I might have fallen asleep sometime during that snooze fest. The queen is hot but boring as hell."

Damn bug. If I didn't think I might need him in the future, I would've squished him.

There was a knock on my door, and I ignored it, but it didn't stop Dani from coming in anyway. I would pull the covers over my head, but I knew that wouldn't deter her either.

"Why, hello, chicka. You totally slayed it out there today." She plopped down on my bed next to me.

"Oh, hey Dani, come on in, make yourself comfortable."

"Hmm, you're acting a little bit bitchy. What's got you in a foul mood?"

My voice dropped to a whisper. "Um, oh, I don't know. Where shall I start? There is a woman who hates me—an evil, gaudy, crown-wearing queen to be exact. In fact the gaudy queen hates me so bad that she is now making me fight other vampires until her precious daughter returns. The whole reason of coming here was to find who was behind Greta's death and to find the key. The former we can't do anything about because I've been ordered by Stephan to wait until the time is right, but the key we can get it just as soon as... as..."

Tracker leapt from my hair, transforming back in his cat form. He jumped on Dani's lap. "As soon as the vampire that our doll face here is crushing on quits banging the queen, who, if we are all being honest, is pretty hot."

Dani threw the cat off of her. "When the hell did you have time to get a talking cat? And did he just say that my brother is humping Akeldama?"

My life officially sucked. "How did you know he was talking about your brother?"

Dani laughed as she dusted the cat hair off of her pants. Her brown eyes swung to me. "Oh, you're being serious?"

Tracker strolled over to her and sat at her feet. "Listen, beautiful, I feel as if we got off on the wrong paw."

I rolled my eyes. "Dani, this is Tracker. He is a shapeshifter sent to me in secret by my grandfather. I don't know why my Pops thought I needed such an annoying gift but whatever."

"Annoying? I sure helped you out in the ring tonight, didn't I, doll face?"

"He was in the ring with you?" Dani asked.

I nodded. "As a praying mantis, believe it or not."

Dani looked from the cat to me. "Sure, why the hell not. So anyways, back to this key, where is it?"

"It's in the royal high-n-ass-es chambers. She and Stephan were about to start their make-out session, and so to free his hands, she took it from him and put it in the cushions."

"Tandi, I know my brother doesn't care for her, and I also know that if he is acting interested in her, it's for a reason like getting his hands on the key."

I knew that, too, but it didn't hurt any less.

"I wish there was a way to sneak in and get the key while she was being occupied."

Tracker was busy licking his balls, but he stopped long enough to give me a disgusted look. "It is truly hard to believe that you are the girl that all the fae world is talking about nonstop. Supposedly, you are a rarity with a bevy of powers, and yet you sit here moping when you could be going and confiscating the key."

Dani looked over at the cat with mild interest. "Yeah? You know something that we don't know, furball?"

"I was going to give you the best shag of your life tonight but because of that, you missed out on something epic."

"More like an epic failure," I said.

"All right, fine. You twits obviously would rather insult me instead of stealing the key, so I'll take my very valuable information and go somewhere else." He started strolling towards the door, and no one stopped him, so he added, "Because Tandi here is not just fae but a powerful fae. She could turn herself invisible, steal the key, replace it with glamour, and be back in this room in five minutes flat. But no, you geniuses would rather insult the one cat that could help you. Brilliant ladies."

"Wait," I said. "Are you serious?"

"Baby, this puss don't lie. Besides, the sooner I help you, the faster I can get back to the fae world. Too much of earth makes me sick."

Dani shrugged her slender shoulders. I could tell that she didn't believe our furry friend, but she was going to let me make the call.

"All right, tell me what I need to do to get that key."

"Same thing you did today, doll face. What you imagine is what you get, so imagine yourself invisible. In your heart and in your mind, have a constant mantra going that no one can see you. When you truly believe that you can do something, then you will do it. Just a little warning, though, vampires can't will themselves invisible, so be careful who you tell." He gave Dani a scathing look.

She tossed her short hair. "Look, cat, if you can help Tandi, then you're a friend to me, too. I'm sorry for my offensive comments earlier, okay?"

"So, you do want to shag?"

"That's a solid no from me," she said without blinking.

"You want to just take a moment and think about it?" Tracker asked.

"I'm good," Dani said.

While they were talking, I was willing myself to be unseen, and when Dani started looking around the room, Tracker laughed. "Way to go, doll face. Now, make yourself want to be seen."

With nothing but a thought, I did as he asked and was giddy with excitement as I reappeared with little difficulty right in front of Dani. "How freaking cool is this? I might not be able to slay a deer, but I can become invisible."

Tracker gave me a disgusted look. "I wouldn't mention that to too many people. A vampire that can't even kill a deer screams pathetic with a capital P."

"Oh, hush," I said. "Now, let's come up with a plan on how I'm to steal this key."

"Doll face, what have I been telling you? We don't need a plan. You're going to think of the key you saw and recreate it just like you do with the clothes that you magic yourself. It's the same thing. Then you're going to go invisible with your fake key and replace it with the other key."

"You don't think Akeldama will notice that it's not the right key?"

"Not if you do a good enough job of replicating it."

"Oh, boy," Dani said. "Do you think we should wait for Stephan to see if he thinks this is a good idea?"

"No, I don't. You see, Dani, if he really is using the Queen to get to the key like you said, well, then there were other ways to go about it. He should have consulted with us first, so we could make a plan, but no, he wanted to lie down on the grenade. So, no, we don't need to talk it over with him first."

Tracker jumped up on the bed. "Ladies, just so we're all on the same page, when you say that he jumped on the grenade, are you referring to him having sex with an extremely beautiful woman with a banging body? Because if so, sign me up for combat."

"You're disgusting," I said. "I'll be back with the original key in twenty minutes. Dani, go find yourself someone to talk to, so that if something should happen and we're found out, at least you will have an alibi."

"What if you're caught?" she asked.

"Then I'll flee to the fae world where I'll marry a fae prince and have lots of fae babies."

We both knew that was a lie, but it was the best that I had. After she left and Tracker wished me luck, I concentrated on making the key I'd seen earlier. When I was satisfied with the results, I turned myself invisible and headed out to meet my fate. Whether it be success or failure, I didn't have a clue.

chapter twenty one

C crept through the corridors and snuck past the guards outside of the queen's chambers. After going through a narrow hallway, I paused outside of the door leading to the main sitting room where I had departed earlier. I could hear Stephan and Akeldama laughing, but there was no way to know exactly where they were positioned. I quietly opened the door, just barely enough for me to squeeze through. I closed it behind me and then turned around to assess the situation. Akeldama sat on the corner of her desk; her dress was hiked up to show her long, white legs that were crossed at the knee. She was laughing and reminiscing with a Stephan who appeared utterly captivated. I almost stumbled when she spoke of the first time they'd made love. I made my way over to the couch and quickly exchanged the real key for the fake key. If I could make it out of here alive, I could say that I literally lent a hand in saving the world from fake bitches. Akeldama hopped off the desk, stopping me in my tracks. I was too scared to move.

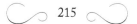

"Stephan, darling, would you like some blood?"

"Sure, Dama."

"You know, you could drink from the tap if you wanted." She rubbed her neck as she arched her back. "That is something I haven't let anyone do other than you."

"You're very tempting, Dama, but I think I'll take it from the bag… this time."

She pouted a little but sashayed her way to a wet bar on the other side of the room. Now was the time to escape while her back was to me. Stephan whirled around and made eye contact with me. But there was no way he could see me. I was still invisible! His eyes narrowed and then he jerked his head towards the door. He moved up behind Akeldama and peered over her shoulder. He was blocking me from her view. But there was nothing to view. I tiptoed as quickly as I could, and with one last look at their backs, I opened the door and retreated to my room. There was no way in hell he knew I was in there. Right?

Twenty minutes later, I was back in my room, pacing. I had taken an extremely quick trip to see my Pops to give him half of the key to hide. Apparently, he was the most powerful man in the fae world, so I had little doubt he could keep it safe. A smile touched my lips as I thought of Pops. A man who favored Hawaiian shirts was feared by the whole fae community. I didn't want to make the same mistake as Akeldama and keep the key together. She might not learn from her mistakes, but I could learn from them. I had cast some glamour on the other half of the key to make it resemble a hairbrush. Under the circumstances, it was the best I could do.

There was a quick knock on my door before Stephan entered. I really wished these doors had locks on them. "What have you done, little one?"

As he closed the door and stepped into my room, I hissed, "What do you mean, what have I done? Our goals coming here were to find out who was behind Greta's death and to find the key. It looks like I'm two for two. While you were off playing kissy face, I was actually doing something beneficial. You know, like saving the world."

He grabbed my upper arms. "You truly have no clue what you've just done, have you? You have helped the princess to escape, and as long as she is gone, you will have to entertain the Queen. You got lucky today, but what about tomorrow? We are all trapped here until the princess returns, so you either tell me what you've done with her so I can drag her back here, or you will be fighting every day until someone kills you. And let me assure you, little one, eventually Akeldama will realize the key she holds is a fake. We were the only two in that room when she brought it out. What will we do then?"

I pushed on his chest, but he wouldn't let go. "Then I'll take full blame, Stephan. Okay? Is that what you want to hear? You can go back to your Georgia estate and forget all of this ever happened." I felt tears welling up, but I pushed them down. Out of all the things I could cry over, I'd be danged if I let the thought of Stephan forgetting about me be my breaking point.

He tilted my chin up, forcing me to look at him. "I wish it were that simple, Tandi, but you are unforgettable. And for the record, I wasn't playing kissy face with anyone. I was trying to portray someone that Akeldama expects me to be, so that I could steal the key when the time was right. You've really worked us into a corner."

"So, you are banging her while patiently waiting for the time to be right?"

"Is that what has been bothering you?" he asked with a devilish smile.

"Absolutely not."

"For the record, I have been flirting enough to keep her distracted, but I haven't been 'banging' anyone, and the timing will be right when I find a way to remove the crown from her head."

"Whatever. You don't owe me an explanation."

"It sounds like I did." He leaned in and gave me the most soul-searing kiss I'd ever had. He started out gently, as if he was afraid he would hurt me, but as soon as my body melted into his and I let out a small moan, the kiss quickly turned feverish. His tongue met mine as he wrapped his arms around my waist, pulling me closer to him. My body thrummed with energy as he kissed me harder, deeper. I threaded my fingers into his hair and held onto him, as my body grew limp in his arms. The sensations rocking my body were foreign—I had never felt like this before. He didn't just want to kiss me: he wanted to own me, and in that moment I would have given him anything to make me melt into the floor with his searing kiss. That was until he pushed me away from him, and the room no longer spun.

Everything was still dizzy and without his warmth, I felt cold. I was still coming out of the passionate daze when his next words froze me in place. "That should have never happened."

I touched my fingertips to my swollen lips. "What? Why?"

"Tandi, there are things that you don't understand and—"

"Then you should explain them to me."

"I don't have time for this right now. I need to be mingling with everyone downstairs to see who is on the roster to fight you tomorrow night. I have to focus until I can figure out a way to find the princess or take Akeldama's crown. Unless you have a better plan to get us out of this mess you landed us in?"

My eyes narrowed at his pissy tone. He regretted what just happened between us? Fine. He wanted to blame me for our current situation? Sure, why not? But he was not bringing the princess back here to be used as a pawn. Not even to save me. I might not have liked my parents, but they did raise me better than that.

"We are not going to find the princess, Stephan."

His jaw clenched as his voice was quiet in my head. "If it comes down to her life or yours, I would gladly sacrifice hers."

"I'm sure that I should be flattered but I'm not. She is a girl just like me and—"

He gave a curt laugh. "Really? She is a Vampire Princess and a Zombie Queen; she can hold her own, I assure you."

"I am not betraying her after helping her to get away from here. I'm not doing it and neither are you."

Stephan took two steps closer to me, bringing his lips about an inch from mine, but whatever he was about to say died as my door swung open. We quickly broke apart, even though Stephan looked like he was about to strangle me instead of kiss me. Dakin and four guards stood in the doorway.

A short, chubby guard laughed. "Hmm, what do we have here? It looks as if things are about to get very interesting. Akeldama has been looking for her favorite lover. Apparently, you told her you had to go check on something and would be right back. Our Queen had a feeling that you were checking on your pet."

"Howard, was it? It has been a long time since I've rearranged someone's face. Open that door again without knocking and I will make up for lost time."

The guard scowled at Stephan before quickly leaving the room the room.

The other guards stood behind Dakin as he shot me a look of pity before he addressed Stephan. "You do realize that your non-relationship with Gem here is the only thing saving her from Akeldama's clutches."

"It really wasn't what you think," I said. "Honestly, if you would have waited a couple more seconds, you probably would have witnessed a murder because the look in his eyes wasn't pretty."

Dakin gave me a half smile. "Gem, any man who is around you for more than five seconds and doesn't fall head over heels is stupid, and Stephan isn't stupid."

Stephan growled as he positioned his body in front of mine. I felt my eyebrows reach my hairline. What in the world was he doing?

Dakin snickered. "I think I made my point."

I had a sneaking suspicion Dakin might have thought I was hot, but he was nowhere close to voicing his undying love for me. It was more like he wanted to bait an old friend who had somewhere along the way become an enemy. There was something about Dakin that was pure and honest. It was hard for me to believe that he was Akeldama's right-hand man.

I took a step around Stephan just for him to grab me by my arm and pull me into his side. For someone that regretted kissing me five seconds ago, he sure had no problem peeing a circle around me.

"Dakin, what does Akeldama have over you?" I asked.

Stephan and Dakin both said, "What?"

"I know that she holds something over you because… I can't explain it, really. But I can sense the good in you, and it's just hard for me to believe that someone like you would be in league with someone like her."

"She speaks of treason," Dakin said to Stephan.

"And if you think to tell anyone, I will fry your brain," Stephan said.

"I wouldn't do that. Not because I like you, but because I like her. You say that you can sense something in me, Gem? I've long forgotten what it felt like to be good but know this. I sense something in you, too. You are going to change our society. Call it a hunch." He started to walk out of the room but stopped in the doorway. "I am rooting for you, Gem, but the moment this door opened that weasel

Howard ran to Akeldama to tell her what we witnessed and to gain favor." He held up a hand. "Regardless of what you say was really happening, one would be a fool to not see where this vamp's loyalty lies." His head tilted to Stephan. "And when that loyalty is not with Akeldama... She is very jealous, so you better prepare yourselves."

The door closed and I huffed. "What does that mean?"

"It means that nothing with you is ever easy."

"Well, maybe I don't do easy, Stephan. I've come to realize that's all you do."

"What are you talking about?"

"You are literally the only vamp here without a legion following you. Why is that?"

"Maybe it's because I don't want the responsibility of taking care of others, Tandi. Any and all problems that they have amongst each other I would have to listen to and judge accordingly. Maybe I want more out of life than being a babysitter."

"I know when you first turned me I was a bit of a disappointment to you, Stephan. But at this moment, you are a disappointment to me, as well. I helped a stranger and landed myself in a heap of a mess, but what kind of coward would I have been to ignore her cries for help? If you were proactive and had the courage to be the master vampire that you are, then we could avenge Greta and walk out the front door with the key."

"Are you that sure of who I am? You seem to always have everything all figured out. And just like everything thus far, nothing is as it seems. Put this in that all-knowing, judgmental book of yours. I have never been disappointed in you." For a moment, he looked as if he was going to throttle me. After a couple of intense seconds went by, he stormed out the door. I was glad to see him go. I needed some space.

Something buzzed by my ear, and I swatted at it. "I'm sure that would have been awkward for most, but honestly I enjoyed the hell out of that little debacle."

I looked at the fly that had landed on my shoulder. "Gross. What is it with you and bugs?"

The fly flew down to my bed, and as bright colors swirled around it, I waited patiently for Tracker to turn back into a cat.

"Look, doll face, I'm sure even your hick butt has heard of the term 'to be a fly on the wall.' I can literally go anywhere and listen in on any conversation without anyone paying me any notice. By the way, the accountant has a little thing going on with the groundskeeper and one of the guards. She's a hoe."

"Um, thanks for sharing."

"Even though you're really hot, I think I'm going to have to side with the smoldering vampire on this one."

"What? Why? And exactly how long have you been here spying?"

"You call it spying; I call it finding entertainment in this small, cruel world. A bug's life is not long; surely, you don't begrudge me for finding pleasure in the small things in life."

This creature was probably centuries old, but I wasn't going to point that out. I was more interested in his first comment. "What do you agree with Stephan about?"

"Since it's past time that we took the gloves off, I'll be honest with you. You are a newborn babe; you know nothing of this world. If a master vampire wishes to have his own army, he first has to get permission from his sire, the one who made him. Akeldama doesn't allow anyone to have an army. She thinks it's a conflict of interest."

"What's an army consist of?"

"Anything more than fifty vampires constitutes as an army. Akeldama has more than five hundred vampires underneath her, and none of the masters are allowed to make fifty vampires. The only way that will ever change is if someone kills the queen; then her line will automatically become theirs to rule. The point is the only way to create an army is to destroy the queen, and that is impossible to do as long as she has the crown on her head. So, yeah, you are kind of judgmental."

Tracker was right, and there were things that I had no clue about when it came to this new life I belonged to. Sometimes, things were so black and white to me, but I needed to realize that there were lots of shades of gray. I owed Stephan an apology. Another thing I wasn't great at.

"I can tell you feel bad, so here is some more salt in the wound. Stephan almost had a line before. He wanted to be his own master and Akeldama permitted it. He was the only one that she has ever given permission to. Of course, they were close back then, and she had hoped with his newfound freedom he would realize how much he wanted to rule by her side. Some say that him creating his own line actually had the opposite effect on him. Long story short, she kidnapped a very young Dani to lord over his head. You would have to ask him the details, but he ended up giving over the vampires that he had created to Akeldama in order to save one human."

There was a lump in my throat. "His sister?"

"Ding. Ding. Ding. We have a winner."

"Was Dakin one of the ones he handed over in order to save his sister?"

"You are on a roll tonight."

The cat jumped to the floor and wound itself through my legs, making a figure eight. "Look, I like your young blood approach of seize the day, but there are things on a larger scale that you just don't understand."

"You're right. There is a lot that I don't understand, but Stephan hasn't been very forthcoming in answers. Maybe we're both at fault." I scooped the cat up and sat on the bed. He curled in my lap and closed his eyes. "Could I challenge Akeldama?"

"Only if you wanted to die."

I lay back on the bed and closed my eyes, as I petted the cat. I didn't have a death wish, but I also had to do something and returning the princess wasn't one of them. I could feel the sun coming up as I slipped into exhaustion. "One more thing. If I wake up snuggling a human in nothing but his birthday suit instead of a cat, I swear I'll skin you alive."

"Maybe you could take on Akeldama," he purred.

I fell asleep with a smile on my face. Too bad I wouldn't wake up with one.

chapter twenty two

Dani woke me up as soon as night fell, telling me I had unknowingly pissed off her royal highness. And in pure Akeldama fashion, she was demanding an audience with me. At some point, Tracker had turned back into a fly. I guessed it was more convenient for him to do his snooping. The moment I stepped out of my room, Stephan and Dani flanked either side of me as we approached the throne room on the first floor. Technically, I wasn't sure what the room with an ugly ass throne in the back was called, but that's what I had labeled it. We stood there with a patience I didn't know I possessed as Akeldama whispered something to one of her guards. I tried to act like I wasn't bitter just because I was at her disposal when I could literally think of a thousand other things I would rather be doing right now, like shaving my legs or watching Tracker lick himself. Obviously, I wasn't doing a good enough job because Stephan did the Jedi thing I hated.

"Don't let her get under your skin. It'll just make her happy."

I was happy to know we were still talking to each other, but I was about to tell him what I thought of his intrusion when Akeldama cleared her throat. Her gaze swept over me with calculation and something else. Something that even though I couldn't put my finger on, I knew I didn't like.

The Queen of Vampires said, "It has occurred to me that we agreed to desist after the first sight of blood for the first seven fights, which honestly is weakness in itself. This no longer works for me."

"What are you suggesting, Dama?" Stephan asked.

"Your pet will fight six contenders tonight, and tomorrow's fight will be to the death."

Dani squeezed my arm. "Can we ask why the sudden change of heart?"

She gave me a seething look before turning a longing gaze on Stephan. "Things have changed so it seems. Besides, this way it will be more entertaining."

"For whom?" I asked.

"Why me, dearie." She tapped her long, red nails on the armchair of her throne. "Of course, the fights will stop the moment my daughter is returned. Maybe Lady Luck will be on your side, and you won't have to fight tomorrow."

And that wasn't going to happen. I refused to betray that poor girl who had had a lifetime of this pure evilness now smirking at me. I could tell that she wanted me to grovel or throw myself down on her mercy and beg to not fight tomorrow. Boy, was she about to be disappointed.

"Cool, so if we're done here, I'm going to go back to my room," I said.

Her eyes narrowed. "Yes, pet, go rest."

"Wait, Dama," Stephan said. "How many men do you have out looking for the princess?"

"Only my best. About twenty-five or so."

"Wouldn't you say that I am better than the whole lot?" he asked.

"What is your point, Stephan? I grow weary of this whole conversation."

"My point is we are all here waiting on her return. What if I helped you speed up the process by finding her and bringing her back."

She seemed to think about this for a second. "You are the best hunter. You would volunteer to do this for me?"

Stephan nodded, and I premeditated murder again. I was going to break that perfect nose on that perfect face. I was going to bury him under a Georgia pine. That way every time I passed one on the interstate, I would recall his ghastly death.

"I'll find her, Dama." The hell he would. "All I ask is that Tandi only fights one fight a night, and the fighting stops at first blood. Give me a week, and I will find your daughter and bring her home. We can stop this challenge, see the princess wed, and all be on our merry way."

Her emerald eyes glittered with jealousy. "Do you love her that much?"

Stephan appeared baffled. "Love? Absolutely not. She isn't much of a vampire, as I'm sure you're fully aware of by now, but she is someone I have turned. And because of that, I feel a connection. As her sire, I owe her a duty to protect her. We all know she will not likely be the victor. This is a means to an end."

Akeldama looked suspicious but slightly appeased by his words. Dani's fingers dug into my arm as a warning to remain silent, but I was having an extremely hard time.

"This display, as intriguing as it is, wouldn't be because you hold affection for her?"

"No, Dama. She is nothing but a young, inadequate vampire who I feel the need to protect."

Her gaze bounced between Stephan and me. Finally, her ruby red lips tilted up in the corners. "Come kiss me, Stephan. Just once for old time's sake."

He started walking to her, his steps slow. "She is testing us, little one. Control your expression and don't say a word."

"Stephan, don't you dare do this. Let me fight these contenders. Please have faith in me. I bested the first one. Who's to say I can't do it again? And my powers… maybe they are different than the conventional vampire, but they are just as great if I use them right."

He climbed up the steps to the throne and my gut clenched. He couldn't do this. Dani squeezed my arm harder, if that was possible.

"This will save your life."

"I will save my life. Trust me! Please."

He made it to the top of the stairs and moved toward Akeldama with intent. He placed his hands on either side of her armchair and leaned forward. From where I stood, there was no passion in the kiss; it was more robotic, but it was still a kiss. The deed was done. As he straightened up, I schooled my features. My expression reflected total boredom, even though I was seething on the inside. I knew he could feel my emotions just as I could feel his. At this moment, his guilt did nothing for me. I had feelings for him, strong feelings, and he just kissed his ex-lover in front of me. I knew he was doing what had to be done, but it didn't mean that I had to like it.

Akeldama immediately tried to read my body language as Stephan walked back down the steps. "Do you have anything you would like to say, pet?"

"Yes, actually, I would," I said. "You wouldn't happen to have the Bravo station, would you? None of us expected to stay this long, and my show comes on tonight at nine Eastern time."

She gave me a disgusted look and shooed me with her hand. "Be gone."

I turned to Dani. "I'm guessing that's a no?"

Dani's brown eyes twinkled. "At least you won't be fighting the whole night thanks to Stephan."

Oh, yes, thanks to Stephan. I would praise him for not letting all of this play out and taking a bullet for me, or in this case, swapping spit with the devil. Yes, praise him. Not. I didn't know if I was more upset about the kiss, the jealousy that was currently humming through me, or his lack of faith in me. So I'd just pick one and go with it.

"Oh, I'm sorry," Akeldama piped up. "I can see how confusing this must have all been. I didn't agree to your pet not fighting six contenders tonight, Stephan. But I do appreciate the offer of finding my daughter, so here is what I will do. She will fight two tonight."

Stephan's guilt was quickly gone, and now anger rolled off of him in waves. "But I thought—"

"Stephan, darling, there is nothing I can do about it. The contender tonight is very excited, so I mustn't break his heart, plus there is the ogre."

"What ogre?" Stephan roared.

"I opened the portal two weeks ago to see what I could bring over, and this horrible ogre awaited me, so now I have him charmed so he can't escape the dungeons." Akeldama shrugged her dainty shoulders and waved her hands in distress. "I've already promised everyone that he would fight tonight. And I'm not entirely sure that we can keep him in the dungeons much longer. He is so strong he is fighting the charm."

Dani's voice shook. "She won't survive a fight against an ogre."

A wicked smile came across her beautiful face and for a moment, Akeldama let her act drop before becoming distressed again. "Then Stephan would have to try and kill the ogre, and those things are nasty creatures. I don't want to lose you, Stephan. Oh. I have got myself in a pickle, haven't I?"

"Cancel the challenge and have the ogre killed while he is under the charm and in the dungeon," Stephan said through clenched teeth.

"Oh, I wish I could, but everyone is already talking about the fight. I'm sorry, Stephan, but there is nothing that I can do."

"Like I said, Dama, you know that I have a better chance of finding your daughter than anyone else, and I will do it. But in exchange, I ask that I fight the ogre."

Her green eyes turned to slits. "As you wish, Stephan. As you wish."

I jerked out of Dani's grasp and fled the throne room. I assumed we were done, and I couldn't stand another second of looking at her smirking face. Both siblings flanked me once again. Dani, reading the tension between Stephan and I, told me she would see me after the fight and veered off into a different direction.

We reached my room. After I opened my door, Stephan started to follow me in. I stopped him with my arm on the doorframe, barring him entry. "Listen, no offense, but my inadequate self is super tired. I think being so incapable of even the smallest task has just worn me out, so if you don't mind, I'm going to take a quick power nap."

He put his hands in his pockets and rocked back on his heels. "Tandi, please—"

"Uh, nope. Terms like please don't work for either one of us apparently. Whatever you're about to say is going to fall on deaf ears, so you might as well move it along."

Forcing the words into his mind, I said, "And you will not find the princess because I won't help, you jackass."

"You've already told me that. I don't expect you to, but I needed to buy some time… I had to save you."

"Oh, yes, ever the martyr." I spoke the next words directly to his mind. "Are you telling me that you will leave the princess be? That you will not hunt her down?"

He didn't answer, and he didn't need to. His look of contrition said it all. "Tandi, let me in so we can talk."

"Two words, buddy. Georgia. Pines."

I slammed the door in his baffled face, and when I was sure he had walked away, I threw myself on the bed face first where I bawled like a baby. I knew I obviously had flaws; maturity was not really my forte along with patience, manual labor, and my utter distaste for anything tie-dyed. But I had my strengths, too, and if he couldn't see them, well, then the hell with him. I could've saved myself if he would have just trusted me, but to him I would always be the little weak vampire incapable of fighting. I let out several hiccups as I wiped the tears from my face I thought if I was being honest with myself I didn't even know what the hell an ogre was so the chances of me beating one was slim to none, so why was I really this upset? That kiss. I couldn't stop picturing it in my head. I was head over heels for Stephan and my emotions were all over the place. With that admission I started crying all over again. It was going to be a long night.

chapter twenty three

I was dressing for my next fight when Tracker strolled in my room in cat form. "Does no one think it's suspicious that there is a cat roaming the hallways?"

"Are you serious, doll face? Only the people I want to see me can actually see me. So, about tonight's fight."

"You have a suggestion?"

"Um, yeah, no. I just wanted to know what time it started. I kind of have a date and need to bounce."

I didn't ask him what form his date would be in because I really didn't care.

"I got this hot little number, and she's a beaut. She's a purebred Egyptian Mau, and she really knows how to purr, if you know what I'm saying."

"No, I actually don't, and I can honestly say that I don't want to understand." Here I was putting on my shoes to go battle God only knew, and this was the conversation I had to endure. "Truth be known, I'm actually a dog person. They seem to be more friendly and loyal, less self-centered."

Tracker flicked his tail in agitation. "Humph. I could have sworn you had a crazy cat lady look to you, but I must have been mistaken."

I just shrugged and pretended I didn't know an insult when it was flung my way. "I need blood. Want to donate?"

That shut him up. I couldn't possibly understand why my Pops thought it had been a good idea to send Tracker to me. He really was useless. One might say he got me through the first fight, but I was thinking it was purely coincidental on his part. I gave myself a quick look in the mirror, and not for the first time today, thought maybe yoga pants and a black thermal shirt was too underdressed.

"I wonder if I should take a quick trip to see Pops, so I can get a banging outfit."

Tracker pawed at the laces on my shoes. "You do realize that you can glamour yourself something to wear without traveling through the fae lines, right? The only difference is that the clothes you glamour here on this plane will eventually turn back to whatever you were originally wearing, but the magic in the fae lines allows whatever you create to become tangible."

I actually hadn't thought about it, but I wasn't about to tell him that. If I had to fight, I might as well be cozy. Besides, my new butt looked bootylicious in yoga pants. And why in the world was he going into detail about such frivolous things when he should be coaching me about the imminent fight?

"Tracker, do you have any advice for me at all?"

The cat rolled over onto his back and stretched out all of his legs like a starfish. "I'm not much of a motivational speaker, and I'm not really good at pep talks, which your grandfather knows. But in his defense, I don't think he realized how needy you are. Since I'm not prepared, I'll just say this: Do…or do not. There is no try."

"Really? You're quoting Yoda? You can't even come up with your own encouraging speech, so you have to steal something off of Star Wars?"

"Is that what you think? Perhaps this Yoda stole that line from me, doll face."

I shook my head as I walked to the door. "Come on, turn into a bug, and let's get to the courtyard."

"We're not waiting for the vampire to come and escort you?"

"We are absolutely not."

I waited impatiently as Tracker turned into a flying ant that most of the South loathed because when they stung, it hurt almost as bad as a bee.

He flew circles around my head and in an almost non-audible voice said, "I might have witnessed that little exchange between your vampire and Akeldama. That kiss was so boring I've decided not to lust after the queen's body anymore. From here on out, Dani is the only girl for me."

"Spying again?" I asked as I opened my door.

"Call it what you like, but when your grandfather put me in charge of watching over you, well, I take my job very seriously. Of course, I can't help it if I also witness something boring yet highly entertaining and will be great gossip fodder for years. I mean, only if I was to gossip when I get back to the fae world, and rest assured, I have very loose lips."

I let out an aggravated sigh as I marched to the ballroom early just because I didn't want Stephan to walk me there. Somewhere along the way, I caught myself wondering how important Tracker truly was to the fae society. Like, if he accidentally got squished while in bug form, or if I decided to finally sink my teeth into him on pure accident, would my Pops be totally livid? Would he spend my lifetime without ever speaking to me again, or would it be a month? Because a month I could totally work with.

I waited silently on the edge of the mat, wondering if I should stretch or something. The truth was I had never stretched a day in my life. It just seemed like way too much effort.

I put my hands on my hips and looked at the room now piling up with pale people, waving their money to a vamp going around the room with a clipboard.

"Oh, great, they are placing bets again." Tracker landed on my ear, making me flinch.

"Stop, that tickles."

"Maybe more than one person will bet on you today."

I was completely shocked that someone had bet on me last time. Trying to keep my lips still, I asked, "Who do you think bet on me?"

"I don't think, doll face, I know because that's my job. It was Stephan, and don't look now, but he just walked in and doesn't look pleased that you got here before he did. Oh, the saga continues. I love it!"

I absolutely hated it when someone said, "don't look now." Didn't they know that was the first thing you were going to do? I made eye contact with a pissed off Stephan. He motioned for me to come to him, and I just shook my head before averting my gaze.

"Oh, that's not going to help the situation. I would say whatever happens fill me in because inquiring minds want to know. But there is a high chance I'll witness it."

I bent down as if to retie my shoe, so no one could see my lips moving. "I will buy a bug zapper if you listen in on any of my private conversations."

"Wow, touchy, touchy. Your hormones must be raging."

Akeldama came through the courtyard with an ostentatious red ball gown swirling around her. Someone should have really told her that wasn't her color. She made a big fanfare of gazing around the yard and the upper balconies of the mansion, which allowed the vampires to get the best view. Sickos.

"Welcome to the second challenge. Tonight, we have none other than Ian from central Georgia coming to fight the lovely, but slightly pathetic, pet of Stephan. And speaking of my former right-hand man, he will be fighting an ogre in two hours' time right here in this courtyard, so make sure that you all come back here to cheer on our Stephan." The crowd roared and I glared. "Calm down, dearies, so we may begin."

Tracker buzzed from my ear. "This vampire has power, but he is not reeking of it. He seems to have a lot to prove so be wary of him."

The vampire was literally out for my blood, so of course I was going to be wary of him. I could feel the presence of Stephan on the outside of the makeshift ring, but I didn't dare take my eyes off of the guy making his way to me. He had a slight build and almost orange hair with a smattering of freckles all over his young face. He had a baby face that never lost all of its fat before he was turned. His eyes revealed his soul was a lot older, though.

Unlike the first fight, there was no count down this time. No referee. No weapons for us to choose from. How were we supposed to make each other bleed? Ian stepped onto the mat, and it was game on. He started coming at me like a banshee from hell. I dodged his first couple of blows, but the third hit sent me flying. The crowd cheered, and Akeldama clapped like a schoolgirl. I scrambled to my feet quick enough to dodge his foot flying at my face. His motions were almost a blur. I couldn't be on the offense because I was too busy being on the defense. It wasn't as if he would make me bleed with a punch, but when I picked myself off of the ground for a third time Tracker piped up, almost sounding bored.

"Did you know that Stephan can make eye contact with a vampire of lesser power and make them do his will? With your mix, I bet you are just as powerful. Think you can with all your soul and mind, and you will be able to do it as well."

I was trying to compute what he'd said when Ian threw me on the ground again, but this time he didn't let go of my neck as he body slammed me. The pain was almost unbearable as he squeezed my throat.

He purred, "Darlin', I'm hoping you taste as good as you look."

I watched in horror as his fangs elongated right in front of me.

Tracker whispered, "You better do something because he is about to tap a vein."

Concentrating while being strangled was no easy feat, but once I made eye contact with him, I told him what I wanted him to do with all of my will.

I forced my voice into his head. "Ian, you don't want to bite me. You really don't."

I felt his hand loosen around my neck, and hope surged through me.

"Ian, you don't want to hurt me. But you are hungry. So very, very hungry. Bite the vein in your wrist."

He released my neck but didn't get off of me. Still straddling me, he put his arm up to his mouth.

"That's it. Take a bite. You want to feel your own blood. You need to feel it."

The crowd went silent as Ian bit into his flesh. Blood ran down his mouth, and his eyes closed for a split second, breaking the connection I held over him.

He glanced around in confusion. "What? What just happened?" His blue eyes met mine again in fury. "You did this to me." His hands were back around my neck but before he had the chance of tearing into my neck the way he had originally planned, Stephan flashed to my side and flung him off of me.

"I believe the rules were until first blood. You were the one to bleed first. Come at her again, and I will kill you," Stephan snarled.

Ian glared at me for several more seconds before he hung his head down in shame and slithered off into the gaping crowd. I refused to wait around to hear what her Majesty had to say, so I scrambled up and held my head high as I left the courtyard and its stunned crowd.

Tracker tickled my ear. "I would love to hang with you, doll face, and celebrate, but I really want to be a fly on the wall right now. Oh, the things that will be said about you—juicy stuff. It's so boring in the fae world, but when I get back, you will be bringing joy to everyone with these tales. I will be a legend, and you will be my amusing, trusty sidekick."

"Glad I could amuse someone," I muttered as I entered the mansion and started walking aimlessly.

"Who are you amusing, Gem?"

I glanced down the wide corridor to see Dakin headed my way. "Apparently everyone. Weren't in the courtyard?"

He gave me a small smile. "Yeah, I might have seen that. It seems like you have some pretty cool tricks up your sleeve."

I didn't know how much to say or not to say. I just shrugged. "Tell me, is there a library in this place other than the Queen's private one?"

"Bored, Gem?"

"Since I'm stuck here with all of the world's friendliest vampires until either the princess comes back or someone kills me, I might as well find something to do with my time."

"Not having an easy go of it, huh?"

I followed him through a series of turns and down a flight of steps, hoping he was leading me to the library and not the dungeon. "I don't know, let's see. I'm at a place that I don't want to be, with a queen I didn't even know existed a couple of months ago but now wants me dead."

Dakin stopped in front of a wide set of doors. He swung them open and ushered me in. Begrudgingly, I had to admit that the library was super nice with its bookshelves, floor to ceiling windows, and staircase leading to the upper level, giving access to the higher books.

"Wow," I said.

"It is pretty amazing. Listen, try not to get too down and out. I really believe the princess will be found. Especially, since Stephan has agreed to track her."

He was carefully studying my profile as I glanced at the books. My instincts told me that Dakin knew something that he shouldn't. "That will be a lovely day when she returns. Not that I'm ungrateful for the Queen's hospitality."

"She doesn't plan on allowing you to leave here alive. Well, unless Stephan comes back into her fold. Just be wary of everything and everyone."

"Why does she hate me so much?"

"Because you matter to him."

He was staring off in the distance, and not for the first time, I sensed something so inherently good about this man. Now that I understood a little more about how he got under Cruella de Ville's reign, I wanted to help him.

"Dakin, I know that Stephan handed his line, including you, over to her, but can't you branch off the way Stephan did?"

"Stephan actually tricked Akeldama into a blood vow. One that gave him his freedom. He is still a part of her line, but she can't force him to do anything he doesn't want to. She realized her mistake, but it was too late; the contract couldn't be broken. Blood vows hold serious magic that she didn't want to come back on her tenfold for breaking." He pulled another book down and inspected the inside cover. "He didn't just hand us over. There is some bad blood between us, but it's not because of that. He was forced to hand over his line. Akeldama had his baby sister. It's a sad story and not one for me to share. Once Stephan had Dani in his possession, he would have come back and fought for us and Akeldama knew it. That is why she eliminated them."

"What? Everyone he created?"

"Stephan had been very selective of who he'd turned. He only turned those that really wanted this life. He had twenty-three in his line, and I'm the only one that she didn't kill."

"What does she hold over you? I know that she is wielding something over you. If you tell me, maybe I can help."

His blue eyes smiled down at me. "You are truly a Gem, but you can't help me. I made a vow a long time ago—one that cannot be broken—just as Akeldama can't break the vow between her and Stephan." His eyes never left mine as he said, "He has come for you. Don't you think it is amazing in a house full of vampires he can zone in on you? It's as if…" His eyes got round as saucers, and pure disbelief washed over his face. Whatever he was about to say died on his lips as Stephan entered the room.

"What the hell are you doing in here with her?"

I had to seriously remind myself of how mad I was at him for signing up to be the leader of the search party for the princess because he was the picture of perfection. He hesitated for a moment, and a slow smile crept on his face.

"Your walls, little one."

Dang it all to heck and back. I crossed my arms over my chest and glared.

Dakin laughed. "Yes, Stephan does have the talent to listen on thoughts that should be private. Too bad we can't return the favor. Of course, with the ease that he found you, one doesn't have to eavesdrop to put the puzzle pieces together."

In a flash, Stephan appeared directly in front of Dakin. They were now nose to nose. "I can take over from here. Would you mind shutting the library doors on your way out?"

Dakin gave me a wink, like he just accomplished his mission by riling Stephan. "Sure thing. I think I'll go try to calm down Akeldama. I am absolutely positive that she is irate by now."

As soon as he left, the smirk reappeared on Stephan's face. "So, you think I'm perfect?"

"They say Lucifer was handsome, so don't go getting all excited. I have a ton of questions for you, starting with how did you know where to find me? And why did Dakin think that tidbit of info was amusing?"

"How about we start with an easier question?" At my deadpan look, he sighed. "No one is guarding the library, so feel free to ask your questions without worrying someone will eavesdrop."

"Even when I was invisible, you knew that I was there, unlike the Queen of Vampires. Why is that?"

Stephan performed his signature move of putting his hands in his pockets and rocking back on his heels. "I've given you blood twice within a small amount of time."

I sighed dramatically. "Stephan, this is like pulling teeth. We both know that's not all there is to it, or you wouldn't be wigging out. Spill the beans this century, please."

"It takes several months before my blood will be completely out of your system. If we share blood four times within those months, it creates a… contract between us. One that is hell to get out of."

"What kind of contract are we talking about? Like what you were talking about at the witch's house? Like I'm fixing to be your trophy wife because if we're being real, what other kind of wife would I be?" At his non-amused look, I said, "Kidding. I'm just kidding."

"I'm glad you still have your sense of humor. Hold onto that wit and remember it for after what I'm about to tell you. If vampires share blood four times during a short time frame, then yes, a vampire marriage contract happens."

I was stunned. "Define a short time? Because if I recall, I was visiting with Pops for a couple of months, so surely any of your blood is out of my system."

He rubbed the back of his neck and my anxiety rose. "The time frame is generally around six months.

"What? Did you plan on telling me?"

"No, because I wasn't going to give you any more of my blood."

"Stephan, I've had your blood in me three times already. The night you brought me back as a vamp, the night I accidentally attacked you after I awoke, and then the last time was when you healed me after the attack. And if you forgot about all of that, what if I had accidentally devoured someone else's blood four times in a short amount of time? I would be married to them just because you didn't tell me."

"That's ridiculous but let's say that you did trade blood with some poor soul and a marriage contract took place, it wouldn't last long because I'd kill him. And even though I should have told you, keep in mind that it would have been impossible for you to share blood with anyone. The contract is only good if both vampires share blood. If you have someone's blood in your system from three different occasions, they would have to take some of your ghoul blood to create a marriage contract. There is a good chance that if they did that, they would die from your poisonous blood."

I sighed as I realized he had a point.

"Maybe I have been wrong in keeping things from you and I apologize. I just have this need to protect you. I'm not making excuses. I'm just letting you know why I have been holding back some things. I was looking for you because I wanted to tell you something before you heard it from someone else."

My heart sank. If he said he was now sleeping with Akeldama in order to save me, I would kill him right where he stood. Or if he had somehow found the princess… my heart dropped and I felt nauseated. Forget burying him under a Georgia Pine. I would scatter his ashes from coast to coast.

I realized my stupid walls were down when he burst out laughing. "So that is what you meant when you said Georgia Pines before slamming the door in my face. Who knew that you were so violent?" At my scowl, he said, "Seeing how loyal you are to this princess made me understand that I can't hunt her down. Not without losing you." He placed a strand of my hair behind my ear and seemed to be weighing his next words. "No, what I was going to tell you is that whoever you defeat in the courtyard, Akeldama kills later that night."

"What? Can she do that?"

"I'm afraid so. She views you as weak, and if they can't kill you, then that means they are the weakest vampire in her army. She has no use for them."

I really hated this woman. Even though every vamp I had fought was out for blood, it still made me sick to think they had lost their lives because they lost to me. It made me feel guilty. Tears trickled down my face. I couldn't kill a bunny, and yet I was inadvertently killing vampires. She made my skin crawl, and somehow, someway I would make her pay.

chapter twenty four

There were two chairs facing one another in the far corner of the library. Stephan dried my tears, scooped me up, and carried me like I was light as a feather over to one of the wing-backed chairs in the small sitting area. He sat in the opposite chair and scooted it closer to me.

"Good news is she hasn't tried to open up a portal recently, so she doesn't know that anything is amiss with the key just yet."

"That is good news but no more keeping things from me. I know that you are working on a plan. I want to know exactly what that is. If we take the key and run, she will come for us. My Pops has hinted that I could go and live with him, but I wouldn't just desert you and Dani. I'm not sure how a full vamp would survive on a fae plane. I refuse to bring the princess back, so it looks like we are on a hamster wheel. I don't like that feeling. I don't want to wake up another night in this tacky place. I need to know what your plan is."

He leaned forward in his chair and rested his elbows on his knees. "Let me give you a history lesson first." I tried my hardest not to groan. "When I was twenty-one years old, I fell madly in lust with the butcher's daughter of all people. She was stunningly beautiful and after our first encounter, we started seeing each other. Once I got to know her, I realized that nothing was ever enough for her. Not my time, her beauty, or her lifestyle. She didn't want a simple life, and her father couldn't afford to give her the things she craved. Never satisfied, this young girl tracked down an ancient witch she had heard tales of. The girl stole every ounce of coin that her parents owned to entice the witch, who in return gave her what she wanted the most: beauty that wouldn't fade, unfathomable power, and the means to be wealthy for all eternity. The witch had created a monster, but the girl didn't see it this way. Later, I found out that the first thing this girl did was kill that very powerful witch because she wanted to be the only one that the witch made. She left her destruction for miles and miles, but she didn't turn anyone. Not until me."

Stephan was looking blindly into the distance, staring at nothing at all. I got up from my chair and kneeled in front of him. I gently laid one of my hands on his leg. That got his attention. He grabbed my hand and gave it a gentle squeeze, and he didn't let go when he continued with his story. "She didn't give me an option, Tandi. All except for one that I have turned, I made sure they knew what they were getting into. I even tried to convince them not to make the change. She made me because she wanted me for an eternity. When she found out I was just as powerful as her, the only thing that kept her from staking me in my sleep was her twisted love for me. I bided my time, and when the moment was right, I asked her to take a vow to allow me some freedom. She agreed because she didn't really think that I would leave her side but I did. That's when she kidnapped my sister."

"How old was Dani?"

"She was twelve at the time. For six years, she kept her a prisoner. She was a well-treated prisoner but still a prisoner. The worst part was she wouldn't tell me where she held Dani. I would have killed Akeldama where she stood, but she was the only one who knew where Dani was hidden. I tried to quietly go into her mind, but she sensed me, and after that Akeldama grew nervous of how desperate I was. She immediately made a witch charm her crown that she wears. She loved me, but she didn't trust me. As long as it sat upon her head, I couldn't access her memories, or better yet, swipe her memory. We all become weak when we get close to the crown. It drains us of our power."

"How did you find Dani?"

"I didn't. Akeldama had demanded an audience with all of her vampires, much like she did for the princess's wedding. My line showed up to find Dani in the middle of some vampires who were bleeding her dry on the Queen's command. Then came the ultimatum. I could either rule by her side or watch her turn my baby sister into something that I didn't even want to be. A vampire."

He got very quiet and just stared at our clasped hands. "What happened next, Stephan?"

"Dakin, who was like a brother to me who I've known all my life, had somehow kept hidden from me that he had fallen in love with Akeldama. He was angry and jealous that she would go to such extremes to have me by her side when I didn't even want to rule with her. There was a wedge between us that I didn't notice until too late. As the crowd waited to see what I would decide to do, Dakin strolled forward and knelt before her throne with a proposition. He told her that someone as beautiful as her should never have to beg for anyone's hand in marriage, and I should be taught a lesson. He claimed that when I was alone, I would realize the mistake I had made and would grovel my way back to her. He convinced her to demand that I turn over my line in exchange for my sister."

I was dismayed. "Why would he do that to you?"

"After the years passed, I realized that he thought he was giving everyone what they wanted. He knew I didn't want to rule with Akeldama. He also knew that I had been crazed looking for my sister, and I would do anything to have her back. I assume he thought with me out of the way, he could have a future with Akeldama. But he didn't know her like I knew her. She wants what she can't have."

"If you and Dakin were as close as brothers, I imagined that hurt you very bad."

One shoulder lifted in a shrug. "I was stunned by what I thought of as his betrayal. But as my sister lay motionless on the floor, I had bigger concerns than his love for Akeldama. In the back of Akeldama's mind, she thought no one could ever just walk away from her, or from a line that I had created with people I considered friends. She thought I would be back beside her in no time. So, she agreed to let Dani go with me if I gave my line to her. To her astonishment, I grabbed my sister's body off of the floor and left that night. Dani wasn't healing. I panicked and gave her enough blood to make sure that she survived. The one person that I didn't make understand the circumstances, and she was forever changed that night."

"You did everything you could to save her and—"

"I did everything I could to make sure that she didn't have this life. But in the end, I failed her."

I thought back to Greta, and tears flooded my eyes. "Was Dani upset with you?"

A half smile came across his face. "No, she was too excited to be away from Akeldama. She said that she didn't care if she came back as a demon as long as she had some strength and power to never be taken as a prisoner again. She has never once begrudged me for making her into a vampire."

I was ashamed that I'd ever blamed Stephan so harshly. Greta didn't want this life, and he'd had the strength to grant her wishes.

Dakin had already told me, but I wanted to hear it from Stephan's mouth. "What happened to your friends?"

"Akeldama recognized the look I gave her when I scooped my dying sister off the floor. She also realized the loyalty that my line had was for me only, so she had them eliminated while I was getting Dani acclimated."

"I'm very sorry, Stephan." I squeezed his hand in comfort.

"I had every intention of hunting down the princess because sometimes it's just easier to play her games than see someone that I care about get hurt. You have no clue what she is capable of."

My emotions were all over the place.

"If you have your freedom and no longer have to take orders from her, then why are we here now?"

"Because that privilege doesn't extend to my line. I could have denied her, but she would have sent someone after you."

"It seems as if you are always protecting me." My heart swelled with pride.

His dimples showed. "I like the reading I'm getting off of you now. What's that scent? Lust?" I glared and he laughed. In one tug, he pulled me into his lap. "Admit it. Admit that you feel something for me."

"If I did feel something for you, I would have to be crazy because you are the biggest pain in the butt ever."

"Every time your walls are down, you let me know how big of a pain that I am. Well, that along with how hot I am."

I went to punch his arm, but he caught my fist and pulled me close to him. My head tilted slightly back, and that was when he leaned in to give me a deep kiss that was demanding. I knotted my fist into his shirt for fear that he would stop doing that magical thing with his tongue. He deepened the kiss and I moaned softly. He kissed me for what seemed like ages before he pulled away slightly. We were both staring into each other's eyes with so much lust it was a wonder we didn't combust into flames.

To break the long silence after that soul-scorching kiss, I asked, "Are you going to say this one was a mistake, too?"

His hand rubbed along my thigh. "Yes, actually it was, but I just couldn't help myself."

I started to hop off of his lap, but he held me in place. "It's not the kiss that is a mistake, little one. It's kissing you here that is the mistake. Remember what happened the last time? She almost had you fighting to the death."

"If it comes down to you swapping spit with her and me fighting, I would rather me fight." He didn't say anything, but I had a feeling that he disagreed with me. "I've done good so far," I pointed out.

"Yes, you have, but I would prefer not risking you."

"Because you made me and feel responsible for me?"

He grabbed my chin and forced me to meet his eyes. "No, because I have deep feelings for you."

He was about to say something else, but it was almost as if he chickened out, so I decided to have mercy on him. "Tell me you have a plan."

"I do. I told Akeldama that I would find the princess and bring her back." I started to tell him what he could do with his plan when he said, "Here me out. I believe this will work."

I listened while he laid out his plan, which was well thought out. I expected no less from him. After he was done speaking, I agreed that it did sound like our best option. Maybe the three of us would escape this place alive and with the key after all, and if we met our doom instead, at least we would give all the gossipers in the fae world something to talk about. Tracker would be happy at least.

I tapped my foot while standing next to Dani, waiting impatiently to see my very first ogre. Stephan stood in the middle of the courtyard appearing bored with the whole situation. He was the only person I knew that would fight an ogre wearing slacks and a buttoned-down shirt. He looked like he was fixing to make a commercial for some over-priced cologne instead of fighting some beast. Vampires milled around, talking about how long it had been since any of them had seen an ogre.

"Why haven't we begun yet?" I asked.

Dani shrugged one dainty shoulder. "Maybe she is trying to build the anticipation up."

"He will be able to defeat the ogre, right?"

"Ogres are known to be man-eating savages, but most of them prefer children. They are sick creatures. If it were any other vampire, I would say they don't have a chance, but we're talking about my brother. He will defeat it." She eyed the crowd until her gaze fell upon the throne. "As long as she keeps that crown at a distance, so it can't nullify his powers then we're good. This will be over before it begins."

Chills rippled over me as a roaring sound came from the distance. That did not sound good. Twenty vampires escorted the ogre into the courtyard. He was still wearing his magical chains, and he did not look happy. The ogre stood at least nine feet tall and wore nothing but brown

leather pants. He was completely bald, which brought more attention to his pointy ears that had several piercings. He wasn't as pale as Akeldama, but he came in a close second. His shoulders were wide and muscular, and every inch of his body radiated strength from his gigantic hands to his massive thighs. Stephan couldn't fight this creature. He would die.

Akeldama spoke from her throne. "Ogre, I will take your chains off, but you are to only fight the man in front of you. If you follow the rules and you survive, then I will allow safe passage back through the portal to where you came from. This fight will be to the death, of course."

Sugar honey iced tea. If the ogre survived, the queen would find out that she couldn't open up a portal because her key was a fake, but I guess it didn't matter at that point. Because if the ogre lived, that meant that Stephan would be dead. This night couldn't possibly get any worse.

A box full of weapons was placed in between Stephan and the ogre. As soon as the ogre's chains were released, he immediately cracked his neck and rolled his enormous shoulders. He roared, "Kill you," as he picked up a spiked club from the box.

My mouth dropped open as Stephan found me in the audience and gave me a wink.

Dani stood aloof beside me. "Now, you see why he about lost it when you were to be the one fighting that thing."

I didn't say a word, so she leaned in close and whispered into my ear, "I know that you and Stephan have this unspoken thing between you that neither of you is really willing to talk about, but he cares for you, Tandi. He would gladly fight twenty of these beasts if that meant you didn't have to. I know witnessing that kiss hurt you, but it meant nothing to him. You know that, right?"

I had already forgiven Stephan, and we had broached the topic of his feelings, but I appreciated Dani trying to bridge the gap between us.

I was about to answer her when the ogre walked forward and swung a meaty fist towards Stephan's face only for it to stop within an inch of hitting the vampire's nose. In the next instant, the ogre went flying in the air and smashed into the ground.

"My brother can move things with his mind," Dani said. I didn't tell her that I had already witnessed that when he slammed a door in my face.

The ogre, who wasn't very bright, kept climbing to his feet just to have Stephan knock him right back to the ground with just a thought. When Stephan used his mind to jerk one of the ogre's arms back until it cracked, Akeldama stood from her throne and started making her way down the concrete stairs.

I grabbed Dani's arm. "What does she think she is doing?"

"That sneaky bitch!" Dani snarled.

"If she gets any closer with that crown, what will happen?"

"It only nullifies vampire powers, so the ogre will still be strong while Stephan will become weak." Dani glanced around at the shocked vampires. "She is trying to kill him."

Akeldama stopped on the outside of the ring. "Stephan, darling, he doesn't seem to be much of a match for you."

"What are you doing, Dama?"

She studied her blood red nails while the ogre held his broken arm close to his body, stalking towards Stephan. "Kill you," he boomed.

"You know, the vow you made me take? It states that I can't hurt you, but I fear that this ogre has no such restrictions. Make a vow that you will destroy that contract between us, and I will go watch the rest of the show from my throne."

The ogre took a swing at Stephan with his good arm, sending Stephan careening to the ground.

"Oops, it looks like your powers have been eliminated. Take the vow to break the contract, and I can go watch… from a distance."

Stephan gave her a malicious smile while he wiped the blood from his mouth. "I won't ever let you control me again."

"Perhaps not. We shall see."

The ogre reached out and swung at Stephan again, sending him flying wildly through the air where he landed with a sickening thud. I started to move forward when a bee landed on my arm. "You will just get in his way," Tracker buzzed.

The bee took off and headed for the ogre, swarming his head and making the ogre swat at the insect. It bought Stephan enough time to pick up a small knife from the box. He balanced the weight of it in his hand for an instant before throwing it towards the ogre, hitting him right in the eye. The ogre thrashed and screamed in pain before grabbing the handle and plucking it out of his eye.

Stephan was already throwing another knife. The blade found its mark, leaving the ogre blind and in pain.

"Just trying to even the odds, big man," Stephan said.

The ogre grew very still. His nose started twitching, and I realized he was now using a different sense to find his prey. He ran towards Stephan, causing the ground to shake underneath our feet. At the last moment, Stephan dodged left and threw out a leg, causing the monster to stumble and fall to the ground. Stephan produced one last knife, and as he knelt with one knee on the ogre's back, he lifted ogre's head up to slit his throat.

The crowd cheered and applauded, while Dani and I jumped up and down like schoolgirls. Everyone clapped except for Akeldama. She looked like someone just peed in her oatmeal. She flicked her long gown behind her and vanished through the crowd, no doubt to come up with some other nefarious plan. Until then, we would celebrate.

chapter twenty five

*A*fter Stephan took a shower, he came over to my room to tell a waiting Dani and Tracker about his plan, explaining in detail what was going to take place tomorrow. Tracker wasn't happy, but I convinced him that the storytelling back in his homeland would make him a legend. He seemed mollified after that.

Stephan had to go and take care of a couple of things, and Dani wanted to party until the sun came up, so she insisted we grab a bottle of wine and head out to the rose garden. She was so excited that I didn't remind her that we were in the middle of winter. The rose garden would be nothing more than bare bushes. Maybe she had a wonderful imagination.

The guards had slackened up on me here recently, but just to make sure they didn't follow us, Dani asked me to turn myself invisible until we reached our destination. Tracker insisted he tag along, so there he lay on the cement bench as a woolly worm getting drunk from the small drops Dani had poured out for him. Apparently, shapeshifters could feel the effects of alcohol.

The rose garden was the only thing belonging to Akeldama that was truly beautiful. Big, magnificent trees stood proudly along the border of her property that was several hundred acres. She had a garden that I could imagine was outstanding during the summer months, but even in the dead of winter, the well-placed shrubs and bushes made a trail or a maze of sorts leading to a quiet bench in the middle of it all.

After a few sips of wine, I told them both about kissing Stephan.

Dani's short hair blew in the wind. She tilted her head back to gaze at the night sky. "Well, it's about dang time."

"What do you mean?" I asked.

"She means, doll face," Tracker said, "that the both of you have been dancing around each other long enough. It's clear that you are meant to be together, and now can we move on to more important topics like am I black and brown or brown and black? And why is the bench moving?"

I snorted as he hiccuped. Tracker might be powerful, but he was drunk as a boiled fish. I wanted to circle the conversation back to Stephan and the way I felt but we were interrupted.

Tracker said, "Incoming. Quick, pick my lard ass up and put me on your shoulder. I don't want anyone trying to stick me in the bottom of a Tequila bottle."

I scooped him up and stood next to Dani to study the trio heading our way. They had just made it down the steps and were starting through the maze.

"What the hell do they want?" she asked.

"I guess we will find out soon enough. Should I go invisible again?"

"No." Tracker hiccupped. "You'll be fine. I know who that short one is. You have to fight him tomorrow, so I've been spying on him. Checking out his weakness. It's women, so this time in the ring, we're going to use your seductive powers that all fae have."

"I have seductive powers?"

"You sure as hell do," Tracker hiccupped. "Now, when he comes up, I want you to practice. Stick out your chest and lick your lips. Really sell it, girl. Maybe tomorrow in the ring, he will still be flustered by what happens here tonight."

Dani was trying hard not to laugh. Whether it was because she was trying to imagine me being seductive or because of something else, I didn't know.

The three male vamps walking toward us were all average in the looks department. They wore tight leather pants and equally tight mesh shirts. The leader of the group appeared to be of Asian descent, and had spiky, jet black hair with enough mousse in it that if it started raining, he wouldn't be able to see for a week. His comrades were both pale skinned and looked almost bored.

When they were directly in front of us, the leader said, "Hello, Tandi."

I looked at Dani for direction, and she intervened for me. "What do you want?"

He gave her a small smile. "I'm actually the one who will be fighting Tandi tomorrow, and I just wanted to introduce myself. I'm Zen."

"Um. Okay?" I said. My deep Southern roots had me quickly adding, "It's very nice to meet you."

He gave me a small smile. "Even under the circumstances?"

I was hoping I wasn't blushing as Tracker tickled my shoulder to let me know he wanted to see my performance.

I batted my eyelashes rapidly, sticking out my chest. With my hands clasped behind my back to draw attention to the girls, I started twisting my torso. When his mouth dropped open, I decided to gnaw on my bottom lip in hopes that it was attractive and seemingly naughty. One of his friends openly glared at me while the other one stifled a laugh.

Zen took a step away from me. "Okay, yeah. I just wanted to introduce myself before our battle. See you tomorrow."

I gave him a little finger wave and stood there rocking until all three had disappeared from our view.

Dani fell onto the bench laughing. "Oh, that was... that was. I don't know what that was, but it was nothing short of great. Thank the stars I'm not human because I would have wet my pants." She wiped tears from her face. "Oh, Tracker, you silly bug, come here and let me high five you."

A swirl of wind hit my shoulder before I felt the weight of Tracker jumping from me to the bench in his cat form. "Admit it, love of my life, that was brilliant, impressive, magnificent. I have a slew of words to describe how awesome that just was."

Dani guffawed all over again. "Yes. Wait until I tell Stephan." Then they both started snickering.

"Um, guys. I'm starting to feel like the butt of the joke. Somebody want to share?"

Dani pointed in the direction the vampires just went. "Zen is gay."

"Come again?"

Tracker was rolling on his back, chuckling. "She said he's gay, doll face. As in he is into people that have a different package than you do. He bats for the other team. His door don't swing that way. Did you see the way Zen's boyfriend was glaring at her?"

"Why the hell did you tell me to use my seductive powers?" I screeched, which only made them laugh more.

"First of all, seeing you try to be sexy was like watching a slow-motion train wreck. You don't know if you should jump up and try to help or video it, for insurance purposes only of course. Secondly, I lied. The fae don't have seductive powers. I just needed a good laugh. And I was hoping our laughter over your epic fail would create a bond between me and Dani. You know, like a drop-her-panties kind of bond." His whiskers twitched as he asked Dani, "Did it work?

"Afraid not," Dani said. "But I did appreciate the laugh."

"Y'all are jerks. Just in case anyone was wondering."

The sun would set soon, so we all made our way back inside. They were still making jokes.

Tracker had turned into a fly and was off to check the status quo between the gardener and the accountant. Dani bid me goodnight. I ignored her because I was still pissy over their joke. As soon as I had shut my door behind me, I heard Stephan in my mind. He must've sensed me in that way he does.

"You're back. Can we talk?"

I didn't reply because I wasn't in the mood. Honestly, I was glad about Stephan's plan because that meant I wouldn't have to face Zen in the ring. How embarrassing. I quickly changed into pajamas that completely covered me with cute zebras whose eyes seemed to follow you everywhere you went. I could be seductive if I wanted to. Just maybe not in these pajamas.

Two minutes later, Stephan stood in front of my bed with his hands on his hips.

"You know that I can tell you're awake."

I threw back the covers. "Okay, fine, you want to talk. Let's talk."

He covered his eyes with a hand. "Tandi, I think the image of you in those hideous zebra pajamas has damaged my retinas." He dropped his hand and grinned.

"I'm so confused right now. Are you trying to make a joke? Where is the real Stephan?"

He sat on my bed. "This thing called humor. I thought I would try it out."

"Well, maybe not tonight. I'm a little sensitive about my seductive powers."

One brow rose. "Care to elaborate?"

"Nope. I just want to go to bed in my zebra pajamas and pretend that this night never happened."

"There is something that I wanted to tell you." He rubbed a hand on the back of his neck, and I got a sick feeling. "I've been doing some research on marriage contracts, and it seems that after vampires marry, they can find each other by one another's scent but not before. Also, a marriage contract doesn't make the male vampire overprotective of the female, and Tandi since I've met you, I have wanted to do nothing but protect you. I had a feeling, but I ignored it because the chances are so rare and—"

"Stephan, what are you trying to tell me?"

"I think that…no I know that you're my mate."

I was stunned. So many emotions ran through me, and I was positive Stephan was reading them all.

Stephan put a hand on my leg. "I have wanted you from the moment that I first saw you, and maybe you don't feel the same way, or maybe you need more time. I didn't know how else to tell you, but I just knew that I needed to."

"I'm a little pissed that you would tell me something so humongous while I'm in zebra pajamas, but other than that, I might need a little time to digest what you've said. Being someone's mate is a big deal?"

"Definitely a big deal."

"What exactly does being someone's mate mean?"

"It's when two souls have aligned perfectly. Most dream of finding their mate but never do. It's the reason you can read my emotions and vice versa. You're not just a part of me—you're in me. Now that I know you exist, I have this need, this desire to protect you with everything that I have. For me, it's only you."

I put my hand in his and watched him study how little my hand was in comparison. I sat there quietly digesting his words. What he said made sense. This bond that I felt towards him grew stronger every day. I couldn't imagine not being a part of his life. In fact the thought of not being around him made me feel sick to my stomach. So I answered him from the heart. "I can't think of anyone else that I would rather be mated to."

His smile was infectious. "Come here and kiss me. I'll close my eyes so I don't see the zebras."

I was smiling as his lips met mine. Another thing I wasn't sure that I could live without was his kisses. I was becoming very needy when it came to Stephan's lips. He gave me one last soft kiss before he gently ran the pad of his thumb across my bottom lip. "Get some sleep. We have a big day tomorrow."

I held onto his hand. "Do you have to go?"

"I can lie with you for a while." He climbed on top of the bed behind me. The sun was coming up, and I was trying so hard to fight a losing battle, but sleep was claiming me.

Stephan's chest rumbled behind me. "This is just the beginning for us. Go to sleep, little one."

For the first time in a long time, I fell asleep optimistic of the future.

chapter twenty six

The next night everything happened so fast it was hard to keep up. As agreed, Stephan went out hunting the princess as soon as dawn broke. When he brought her back, every single vampire in the house was busy getting ready for the big day. The most excited was Akeldama, of course. She just knew her precious Stephan would come back into her fold and deliver.

No one, including the queen herself, spoke to the princess. Why would they? She was just a tool to get what she wanted. Stephan told Akeldama that he'd contacted the princess's fiancé, and he was currently on his way with the key. The wedding would take place in a couple of hours, and then all of us would be dismissed. But of course, there was hope that Stephan would stay. Multiple guards escorted the princess to her tower where they put her in magical steel to ensure there was no chance of escape. Or at least everyone thought the princess was trapped in magical steel cuffs.

I tugged on the cuffs and sat down on the cold ground just as Tracker squeezed under the door in rat form. I got the giggles as I thought of the movie, "Charlotte's Web."

"What's up Templeton? Talked to Charlotte recently?"

"What is up with you and movies? In your former life, you were either a homebody or the biggest loser ever. I'm thinking it was a little bit of both. And just a little trivia for you, I hate spiders. Homie don't play that," Tracker said. "So, everyone is abuzz with the princess's return, but I've got some bad news."

"No. Not today. I'm not coping well, and I don't think I want to hear whatever negative energy is about to spew from that tiny mouth you have. Just take your beady eyes somewhere else."

"Cute. But seriously, we have a problem.

"No, Houston, we don't."

"Jeez, there it is again. Pathetic. Here is to hoping after this, you actually get a life and stop watching so much television."

"Then that wouldn't be a life worth living. Just sayin'." I gave another tug on the chains. "Well, since you have a captivated audience, you might as well go ahead and tell me the dilemma."

"So apparently, the fiancé—Cecil something another—was livid that the queen lost the princess. According to the grapevine, he has been looking nonstop for her. It seems that Akeldama is a little confused about how quickly Stephan found him and the princess. But Cecil is doing a great job of convincing her that he was basically in the same spot as the princess, considering he had almost tracked her down before Stephan found her."

"Cecil better do a good job." I was casting a glamour over him, and it was draining me. It was one thing to make half a key look like a hairbrush, but another thing entirely to make Stephan look like Cecil. Thank goodness for technology. Dani had several pictures on her phone for me to study before I'd finally felt confident that I could glamour Stephan to look like Cecil.

"You did a remarkable job, by the way. The likeliness is outstanding. To be honest when you said that you were going to glamour yourself to look like the Princess, and at the same time glamour Stephan to look like Cecil, I thought there was no way you were powerful enough to hold that much magic into place. But it's working, and you're not even sweating."

"You thought I couldn't do it, and yet I believe it was you who said, 'This is going to be awesome.'"

"Yeah, if you notice, I never said it was a great plan, though. I just meant it would be awesome to retell."

"Tracker, I really dislike you sometimes." I didn't mention that I was feeling a little tired. "Has anyone missed Stephan yet?"

"No, everyone is so busy running around to prepare for the wedding."

Well, that was good news. Hopefully, no one would notice that he, along with myself, wouldn't be in attendance for the wedding either. I couldn't glamour us to be two different people and still show up to the wedding. Fae magic, yes? A magician, no.

"Are we on for the wedding or not?"

"Oh, I forgot to mention that some vamps are on their way right now to get you all dolled up for the ceremony."

As soon as the words left his mouth, I heard the locks on the door turning. Tracker scurried off, and I was escorted into a dressing room. I did what duty called and acted resentful as I tugged on my chains the entire time. Some female vampires took over and bathed me, which was extremely embarrassing. Then they clothed me. They draped my body with an almost see-through white lace material that I assumed was supposed to be my wedding dress. I could feel the strain of the magic bearing down on me, causing me to care less about modesty.

Finally, I asked one of the vampires, "How much longer will I wait here?"

She snickered. "Eager to begin?" They both laughed over that. "There was some minor issue with making sure that there were enough blood bags for the ceremony, but now that they have that worked out, the wedding should take place soon."

Sweat beaded down my spine when the guards showed up to escort me to the throne room, where they then shoved me towards the man who was supposed to be Cecil. I was trembling from using all of my strength to glamour myself, along with Stephan, and the new key Cecil was supposed to bring with him.

My legs knocked together as Stephan's voice sounded in my head. "Are you okay, little one?"

"Yeah, just tired. She is so busy lusting over the key that she is about to receive she hasn't noticed we're missing. The sooner we can skedaddle, the better. Hurry it up."

I heard him laughing in my head before he turned to the throne and addressed Akeldama.

"I see that you have indeed found her, and she will be mine." Cecil's image pulled a key from his pocket, which was really an apple that I used glamour on, and handed it to the nearest guard. "In exchange, you have the key."

Akeldama's eyes narrowed in on the key being carried her way. I was using so much glamour I was surprised I wasn't having a brain aneurysm. Stephan better hurry the hell up.

"Yes, you have stood by your word, and now I will stand by mine. Go ahead and make my daughter your bride."

My fingers were crossed in hopes that our plan worked.

"Your majesty, my people would like to witness the blood exchange. Now that you have your key, we will be on our way."

Her hand slapped the throne. "Nonsense. You will begin the exchange here and now. I want to see that the contract takes place. Who knows how powerful this child will grow to be? I need to make sure you will have complete control over her, and if she escapes again, with her being your wife, you will be able to track her down no matter where she goes."

"Your majesty, my people expect me back tonight. Surely, you can allow us to leave?"

Akeldama tilted her head to the side as she studied Cecil. I started second guessing my abilities when she said, "You will exchange blood now, and then you can leave. I will know that this marriage is completed before you leave."

I looked through the crowd and found Dani, whose eyes were big as saucers. Tracker, now a fly, was hiding somewhere on her person, but I could only imagine the language coming out of his mouth right now. Game over. I would kill Stephan if he ingested my blood.

Stephan, who was doing a great job of acting like how he thought Cecil would, started arguing with the Queen. Tracker buzzed around my head once before landing on my earlobe. "Here's a fun fact, just like the one you get off of a Snapple lid but significantly more important. Your blood won't kill anyone who you don't want dead. When your body feels threatened, you release the poison into your bloodstream. But if you goof up and kill him, I never really liked the dead lard anyway."

Hope swelled inside of me. "Stephan, I don't think my blood will kill you."

His head swiveled to mine. "What?"

"Tracker just said I can control the toxins."

"Tandi, let's say that your blood doesn't kill me. If we exchange blood, one more time we will be officially mated. We don't have to do this—"

"Yes, we do. I don't see another way. Would it be so bad being officially mated to me?"

"I can't think of anything that would make me happier."

I had to force myself not to smile. "The Princess wouldn't just bite you. You will have to be forceful and make her bite you."

His eyes that were no longer brown but blue met mine. He told two guards standing behind me, "Hold her arms." He looked at someone else and said, "Come, pry her mouth open."

I tried to act like I was putting up a good fight the way I know the princess would have, but I wasn't Tamara.

I was Tandi, and I felt drained of energy. I watched as Stephan cut into his own wrist, and once the blood started flowing, he let it drip in my mouth.

He said loud enough to make me flinch, "Spit it out, and I promise you that our honeymoon will be very painful."

Akeldama laughed, and I got pissed all over again at the thought of what the real princess must have endured her whole life.

After I swallowed his blood, he gave Akeldama a questioning look, which she responded with a nod.

The guards still held me when the man I loved gave me one last chance to back out as he stalled. Once he took my blood we will be mated. My answer was to tilt my chin up. With enough gentleness to make only the nearest vampires question his motives, he lightly turned my head and made a cut mark right above my collarbone. The thought crossed my mind that Tracker could be wrong, and panic swelled inside of me just briefly. Then I felt his emotions like never before. Lust, love, and pure joy washed over me in waves. I couldn't separate his thoughts—they were coming at me so fast. He thought I was the most precious thing in the world, and if he died in the next few seconds, at least he would die a happy man.

His lips touched my skin and I had to make myself not moan or show any kind of pleasure. At last he pulled back from me, his tongue licking the blood from his lips. Something was happening. Perhaps it was the marriage contract taking place but I was betting it was us sealing the mating bond. I felt as if I was one with him. Our souls were combined. Despite all this emotional happiness, one thing was for sure—my energy was depleted. I closed my eyes, praying that everyone would mistake my grimace for disgust. In reality, I was in pain. My body felt like I had been ran over by a train. I wobbled on my feet.

Stephan reached out to steady me while he gave a menacing look to both guards. "I'll take it from here."

He put a strong hand underneath my elbow and I was grateful. All for show he forced his blood into me two more times.

Our plan was to leave with the crowd. When Akeldama tried to use one or both keys and found out that they were fake, she would blame Cecil. We hoped since he had handed the key to her guard, she would believe that not only did he plant a fake, but he stole the first key. Stephan said it would start a war between Akeldama and Cecil's people.

Akeldama looked at the gathered vampires. "You all may leave." She turned to Dakin. "I haven't seen Stephan. Find him and bring him to me. He might want to leave, but it won't be with his pet."

Dakin was right: that heifer did plan on killing me. Man, I hated her.

chapter twenty seven

The vampires who had been stuck at the estate for days were in a hurry to leave. Now was the chance to make our great escape, and we would have if Akeldama didn't stop us with her next words.

"Do not leave yet. You must stay and enjoy the festivities."

Well, wasn't that just fan-flipping-tastic? And when Dakin showed up with no Stephan, then what? Life was so much simpler when all I had to worry about was if my jeans made my butt look big and if they did, was it in a Kardashian kind of way? I realized that I was well past the fatigue stage and going into the delirium stage when my brain started thinking about my ass.

"Stephan. I can't hold on much longer. We need to go."

"I know, love. Just hold on."

Dakin came back in the room that was now empty except for a few guards and a terrified-looking Dani, who was hopefully being ignored by Akeldama.

"Well, where is he?" the queen demanded.

Dakin said, "Some very important business came up, and he is on the phone right now trying to work it out. He told me to tell you that he would be down momentarily."

"Good. I think I have found a way to make him stay this time. We won't let him leave us again."

"Yes, Queen." Dakin nodded his head towards us. "Shall I escort them to the feast hall now?"

I didn't know what Twilight Zone I was in, nor did I care. I could tell by the emotions coming off of Stephan that he was just as confused as to why Dakin had covered for us.

Already lost in thought over what plans she had for Stephan, Akeldama shooed us with a hand. "Yes, yes, be gone."

The guards came over to unchain me, and Akeldama piped up, "No, leave them on her to make sure she is not able to escape. After they leave here, she will be his burden. He will have to watch her closely if he aims for her to do his dirty work." Her eyes glanced over me and then widened. She pointed a finger at my neck. "What is that?" she squealed.

I looked down at the golden necklace Stephan had given me. Of all the things that the glamour could have faded on, why the heck was it that? My chained hands tried to cover the necklace, but it was too late.

"I recognize that necklace. It was one that Stephan's mother used to wear and when she died, it became his most prized possession. He would have never let anyone steal it. Why is my daughter wearing it? How did you come by this?" she demanded from me.

I started to shake. I couldn't hold on to the magic any longer.

"Let it go before it kills you. You need to release it now. To hell with the consequences."

As my knees hit the ground, the magic disappeared.

Akeldama floated towards me, her hair flowing behind her with a murderous expression on her face.

"You have tricked me!" She stopped a foot in front of me, and I somehow found my way back to my feet. "You used glamour. Who are you really? Answer me now."

Stephan shifted his body in front of mine, trying to get her to redirect her anger. "She is my wife, Dama."

"You." She pointed one long fingernail at him. "How could you do this?"

One of the guards thought that it was terrific timing to show her the key. "Your Majesty, the key is no longer here. In its place is an… apple."

Her head whipped around to study the apple, and when her gaze came back around, I knew we were all dead. With one hand, she backhanded Stephan so hard he hit the wall and slid down with a sickening thud. Dani ran to him to help him back up. Before Akeldama could tear my head from my shoulders, Dakin appeared in front of me.

Her hatred turned towards him. "And you. When did you know of all of this?"

"If you weren't so blind, Akeldama, you would have noticed that they are not just married, but mated."

"Mated," she screamed. "Is this why you covered for him? What have I told you about that heart of yours?" She shoved her hand into Dakin's stomach. For the second time within minutes, my knees hit the ground as she held one of Dakin's organs in her hands. His body collapsed to the ground.

"No. No!" I cried. He couldn't be dead. I crawled over to him, my chains dragging on the ground.

"Oh, rest assured, pet, he's not dead." She squeezed the organ in her hand. "This is like a body part. Vampires can regenerate, but once I decapitate him, well, let's just say that he won't be bouncing back."

"Don't you touch her." Stephan was on his feet and running towards me. "I will kill you."

"No. No, I don't think you will." She pointed to her crown. "How quickly you forget."

Akeldama flung out a hand and froze Stephan and Dani in their tracks. Stephan's neck muscles were bulging as he fought whatever hold she had on him. It looked as if this fight would be just between the two of us. Oh, goody.

She pulled me up to my feet by my chains. "If I can't have Stephan, neither can you. They say if you kill a true mate, the other one dies, too. Let's test the theory, shall we?"

"Oh, bite me!"

Her eyes narrowed with malice. "I think I will."

Her teeth tore into my neck with none of the gentleness Stephan had shown. A spotted beast flew at her face, digging its claws and releasing a fierce howl. She let go of me in order to throw Tracker to the floor, where he now lay, whimpering.

"What has been going on under my roof?" Giving no more thought to the animal, she took a step closer to me. "Now, where were we?"

She reached out to grab me by the shoulders, but seemed to confused by the smile on my face. I couldn't help the laughter that bubbled out. She stared at her hands that were gripping my shoulders. There were black lines traveling down her arms to her palms. "What is the meaning of this?"

I knocked her hands off of me and took several steps back. "If you think that's bad, you should see your face."

"What?" She patted her face. "No, what is happening?"

"I think you are dying, at least I'm hoping." She fell onto the floor and started crawling to her throne. Guards that had been quietly standing in the corners started to run towards me with their swords drawn. I said in a lethal voice, "Leave this room now or suffer the same fate."

They looked at each other and then slowly backed out of the room. They didn't know exactly what I was, and it looked as if they didn't want to find out. Good. I went over and knelt by Akeldama.

Her hold broke on Stephan and Dani. Within seconds, I could hear both of them standing behind me.

"You know, it's always so funny to me how the mighty fall. You should have never killed my friend Greta. I hope you rot in hell for your misdeeds."

"I will kill you for this," she croaked.

I shrugged. "I don't think so, but I like how optimistic you are. Would you like for me to tell you what is happening? You now have ghoul blood in you, and soon you will be dead because of it. You really shouldn't ingest that stuff—it's not good for you."

"But… but, Stephan, he—"

"Yeah, I know it all gets a little confusing to me, too. But apparently, the fae in me likes him enough to control the poison in my blood. Cool, huh? I mean, obviously not for you, but you can't please everyone."

Stephan looked murderous as he knelt down beside her.

"Stephan, please help me," she gasped as she clawed the floor.

"There is no help for you, Dama. When you die, I will melt that crown you have so lovingly worn, so no leftover power affects me or anyone else. With your death, we will truly be free from you. When people remember you, it will not be because of your power, wealth, or beauty, but because of your tyranny."

With his last word, her lips parted in her final death. We all stood and said nothing until Tracker came strolling up, looking none-the-worse for wear. "I totally knew this was going to be a horrible plan, but one hell of a tell. Let's pretend that there is a suggestions box. My first suggestion would be to behead her, and then after that gruesome task is done, I would light her on fire. This is totally based on personal preference. But if it were me, I would scatter her ashes in every continent just to make sure that she didn't come back looking all Freddy Krueger."

Dani flipped her short hair. "He does have a point."

Tracker wound his way through her legs. "Gurl, me and you, we are like peanut butter and jelly. Cornbread and chicken. The feathers to my down comforter."

"What?" she asked.

"I was running out of things. Just go with it, baby."

Yeah, she was rolling with it all right. She was rolling her eyes.

I looked over at Dakin, who was still unconscious on the floor. "Will he be all right?"

"He will wake up some time tomorrow, starving and in extreme pain, as his spleen starts to regenerate, but other than that, yes, he will be fine," Stephan said. "I'll take care of Akeldama's body and the crown as soon as I get these cuffs off of you."

"I don't want to stay here a minute longer," Dani said. "Whoever kills the queen becomes the queen. Tandi just got herself a whole line of vampires that I have a feeling she doesn't even want, but that doesn't mean that she has to rule them from here."

There was no way I was signing up for all of this. "Nope. Not going to happen," I said. There were things I wanted in life, but overseeing Akeldama's group of malicious vampires was not one of them.

"You know, you could weed out the bad. They would either follow your rules or you would force them to go rogue, and then they probably wouldn't last long," Stephan said. "Plus, I have a hard time believing you would turn down the chance to wear a crown."

He retrieved a key and unlocked my chains. He did have a point. I loved crowns. But there was no way that I would take on this crazy role without someone who knew how the vampire community worked. All of the ins and outs. I wasn't stupid. I would need qualified people around me. Stephan, Dani, and Tracker—if I could convince him—would be a good start. Maybe I would be a good queen. The last queen didn't set the bar too high, so at least I would be better than her.

My chains hit the ground. "Would you rule beside me?"

He pulled me into his arms and gave me a hard, swift kiss. "Of course. We make a good team."

"Jeez. Not in front of the kiddies," Tracker gagged. "Gross."

Stephan rested his forehead on mine. "Now that we have the key and have defeated Akeldama, tell me that Garfield will be packing his catnip up and going back to whatever cesspool he came from."

Tracker jumped into Dani's arms. "Actually, I'm thinking of commuting back and forth. I feel like your wife was born to amuse me and in return, I shall share her stories for a small price to any fae who would like to listen."

Dani put the cat back onto all fours. "Capitalism at its finest. Let's all meet at the car in fifteen. Anything you can't pack up by then, just leave it here. I'm so ready to get the stink of anything Akeldama out of my nostrils."

I glanced over at Dakin's still form. "Could we carry him up to a bed? He just looks so vulnerable. I don't want to leave him like that."

Stephan let out a sigh. "Sure, why not? I'll come back down and do that as well. First, let me walk you to your room."

I needed to go collect my things along with the other half of the key that probably didn't resemble a hairbrush anymore. Stephan held my hand as we walked up the stairs. All these steps was another thing that I wouldn't miss.

"I have to go destroy the crown," he said, as I stopped in front of my guest bedroom door, "and take care of your friend."

"With the way Dakin helped us out, I'm thinking he might be redeemable. Would it kill you to call him your friend again?"

"You ask too much of me, little one." He snaked an arm around my waist and gave me a quick kiss. "I'll meet you downstairs."

Before he could leave, I asked, "What will we do with the other half of the key?"

"Whatever you want, my queen."

"You know, that does have a nice ring to it. The key… we can't just destroy it, can we?"

"Afraid not," he said. "But breaking up the key and giving part of it to your grandfather was brilliant. We will guard the other half together."

I started to collect my belongings, but he stopped me with one hand on my arm. "Tandi, I want you to know that… that I love you."

"Stephan, I think somewhere along the way I figured that out. Maybe it was in between my disappearance into the fae world and you fighting the ogre because you didn't want me to. Our story hasn't been easy, and if I'm being honest, there were times that I wanted to strangle you. But I can't imagine not loving you." I placed a hand over his heart. "And I do love you. Promise me from here on out, we won't hold anything back from one another, and we will be a team."

"We are going to be an unstoppable team, and now that you're mine, and I know that I won't scare you off, I promise to tell you right away everything that I learn. No matter how boring or insignificant I think it is. We are going to change the way things have been done in the past. The Vampire Nation will never be the same. We are going to rule in a way that is very different than the way Akeldama ruled."

"Well, duh. That woman was cray-cray. Plus, she wore too many ball gowns. I will be ruling our vampire community with yoga pants and a tiara, and Lord have mercy, there will never be so much gold in one room that we look like a discount pawn shop. We will rule with less gaudy knick-knacks and more sophistication. Well, as sophisticated as someone can be in yoga pants." I tried to keep a straight face as I added, "Oh, and of course, the policies will be different, too. No more opening portals to let bad guys in."

He was laughing as he went downstairs to take care of business. I had a feeling that I would never get used to that sound. Every time that man smiled at me or laughed would be like magic all over again. If this is what love felt like, I was game. We would rule the hell out of some vampires.

His voice sounded in my head just as I was gathering my bags to go down those hellacious steps one last time. "Little one, will you hurry?"

"Jeez, what's the rush?"

"Our honeymoon awaits us. I know we don't have a lot of time with us having to hold court and reassure everyone that—"

"Speak no more; you had me at honeymoon."

"That's my girl. Does a quick trip to Paris sound good?"

"Will you take me shopping?"

"After we make love multiple times in many different ways, then yes, I will."

I felt a blush creeping up my face, but I was so going to be nonchalant about all of this. I was now a queen. Queens didn't get giddy. They were super cool. Just because the thought of me and Stephan making love made me want to have heart palpitations didn't mean that I would. The pesky memory of when we had stayed in that hotel, and I'd seen him in his towel popped back into my head. I squeaked out, "Deal. It will be like I'm Pretty Woman and you're Richard Gere."

He chuckled in my head. "Please, tell me that you haven't forgotten that I can feel your emotions."

I shoved my luggage down the stairs and watched it tumble to a stop. There was no way in hell I was carrying that crap all the way down.

"Can we just pretend that you can't? We can just be a normal boy and girl."

"That sounds absolutely boring, but as you wish. I don't know how you feel, but I am very anxious to get you alone, so please hurry."

I smiled all the way down the steps, which was a miracle in itself.

It wasn't until we were back in Stephan's home, which was now our home, I realized that this was who I was meant to be. Maybe I wasn't conventional, and maybe I was an anomaly, but what made me different was also going to be what made me a great ruler.

about the author

Brandi Elledge lives in the South, where even the simplest words are at least four syllables.

She has a husband that she refuses to upgrade... because let's face it he is pretty awesome, and two beautiful children that are the light of her life.

https://brandielledge.com

the wheel of crowns

The Werewolf Queen
The Queen of Witches
The Vampire Queen

plus

Four more books to come

Printed in Great Britain
by Amazon